FOR BETTER, FOR WORSE

FOR BETTER, FOR WORSE

Margaret Bacon

Severn House Large Print
London & New York

This first large print edition published in Great Britain 2005 by
SEVERN HOUSE LARGE PRINT BOOKS LTD of
9-15 High Street, Sutton, Surrey, SM1 1DF.
First world regular print edition published 2005 by
Severn House Publishers, London and New York.
This first large print edition published in the USA 2006 by
SEVERN HOUSE PUBLISHERS INC., of
595 Madison Avenue, New York, NY 10022.

British Library Cataloguing in Publication Data

Bacon, Margaret
  For better, for worse - Large print ed.
  1. Upper class families - England - Fiction
  2. Domestic fiction
  3. Large type books
  I. Title
  823.9'14 [F]

  ISBN-10: 0-7278-7482-9

Printed and bound in Great Britain by
MPG Books Ltd, Bodmin, Cornwall.

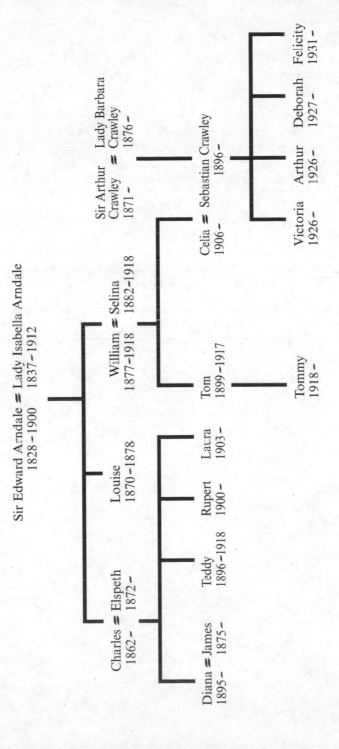

THE ARNDALE FAMILY

Sir Edward Arndale = Lady Isabella Arndale
1828–1900   1837–1912

Charles = Elspeth
1862–   1872–

Louise
1870–1878

William = Selina
1877–1918   1882–1918

Sir Arthur   Lady Barbara
Crawley   = Crawley
1871–   1876–

Diana = James
1895–   1875–

Teddy
1896–1918

Rupert
1900–

Laura
1903–

Tom
1899–1917

Celia = Sebastian Crawley
1906–   1896–

Tommy
1918–

Victoria
1926–

Arthur
1926–

Deborah
1927–

Felicity
1931–

One

The train was packed before it even left King's Cross. Sebastian Crawley, squeezing himself on board, found a space in the corridor and sat on his case hemmed in by soldiers and their kitbags. There was the usual delay before the train crawled away from the blacked-out station to make its unlit way north. He tried at first to read by the pinpoint of light from a tiny torch, but it was hopeless, so, hunched up on his case in the hot and smoke-filled corridor, he gave himself up to the luxury of thinking about Diana.

He had so many images of her: of the girl he had danced with before the last war, of the woman he had loved and hoped to find again after it was over. He remembered his despair when he found she was already married to the good Dr Bramley, whom everyone admired, himself included, for his work on behalf of ex-soldiers. He remembered her later, the dutiful widow, forgetful of herself, tending to the needs of all the

7

wounded and maimed men at the doctor's funeral, the blind and crippled whom he had helped back to life and hope. But most of all he remembered finding her again a year ago.

He recalled it vividly now as he sat on his case in the corridor of this crowded train. He remembered coming down the stairs of his parents' deserted house, opening the kitchen door only to be hit on the head by someone he took to be an enemy soldier but, even as he turned to strike back, saw it was Diana wielding a frying pan. He smiled, almost laughed aloud as he remembered the ridiculous scene. What crazy situations war can create! They had looked at each other, amazed, and she had fallen against him, laughing hysterically with relief.

He remembered how they had sat together in the kitchen, a candle burning low on a saucer on the floor. He could see her face again in the flickering candlelight, as they sat there talking. And how they had talked! They had talked of the past, of their separate lives. They had talked of the future; he had told her his plans and she had agreed to marry him after the war – if he was divorced and free to remarry. And surely he would be. Then they had gone upstairs, parted reluctantly on the landing, he to go to his room, she to hers, because that was how things were done then.

Alone in his bed, he had lain awake at first,

then dozed intermittently until a sound startled him. He'd recognized the whine of the air-raid siren and almost simultaneously heard a rumbling like thunder and the crashing of bombs.

Wide-awake now, he had rushed, panic-stricken, into Diana's bedroom, found her deep in sleep and almost dragged her downstairs, out into the garden and across the lawn towards the air-raid shelter. Bombs crashed down, machine guns rattled and the very ground seemed to reverberate beneath their feet as they ran. The moon conspired with the searchlights to turn night into day. Vulnerable as animals caught in the head-lights of a car, they raced towards safety. Then there was a tremendous crash behind them as bombs smashed on to the house just as he pulled her down into the underground shelter, where everything was dark and quiet. They had stood, gasping for breath, knowing that if they'd stayed in the house just a few minutes longer they would cer-tainly have been buried under its rubble.

Death had been so close, so real. The only possible response was to claim the other reality: love. And so at last, safe under the earth in that little dug-out, he had taken her in his arms and made love to her with all the pent-up longing of so many lost years. It had seemed right, yes, even to him, who had always been so scrupulous in doing nothing that might compromise her.

These images of the past became blurred as he fell into a restless sleep, often jolted awake by the swaying of the train or by being hit by a kitbag as a soldier struggled to squeeze past. As the train made its slow and grinding way up north, the route was so familiar that, even though the names of stations had been painted out and would have been invisible through the blackout anyway, he sensed where they were on each stage of the journey, was aware when they were approaching Gradby.

It would be nearly midnight before he got to Mrs Jordan's, he realized, stirring himself and looking at his watch. He had a key, but she would probably stay up for him. People came and went from her lodgings nowadays, moved about by war service, but she had promised that she would always find a bed for him, even if he had to share a room. It would be good to be back; Gradby had been surprisingly untouched by the bombs that had been expected to fall on the industrial cities of the north. But they had to be prepared for all that to change; tomorrow he would be discussing those preparations.

And the day after that he would catch the train to Lowsham, making the same journey as he had made with Celia after their wedding fourteen years ago. How naive he had been, how full of hope as he set off on that disastrous honeymoon! He remembered his mother's warnings, reservations loyally never repeated after his marriage. He should have listened, but then what young man who thinks he's in love pays any heed to his mother? He tried not to remember it, the awful realization of the mistake he had made. Forget it, Sebastian; think instead how good it will be to walk that mile into Lowsham and catch the bus to Netherby, where your four lovely children will be waiting.

He thought of them each in turn: Arthur, an open, intelligent lad, interested in geology and nature study, doing well at school. Perhaps he would make a career for himself in the natural sciences. Victoria was intelligent too, but far more adult; sometimes she seemed more like Arthur's older sister than his twin. Of course, girls tended to mature earlier, but she was exceptionally poised for her thirteen years. Whatever she chose to do with her talents, she would shine. Oh, yes, she was a daughter that any parent would be proud of.

His face grew more anxious as he thought of Debbie, so vulnerable, so unsure of herself. She was as intelligent as Vicky, he had no doubt about it, but she lacked her elder sister's confidence. He must help her to make the most of herself; she needed constant reassurance. And last, there was little

11

Felicity-Flea as the others called her. His face relaxed; it was hard not to smile at the thought of his youngest daughter, so passionate and impulsive, so funny and full of odd ideas. An original, she was. And very loyal.

As he thought of them, all so different, so individual, he told himself that no marriage which had produced such interesting and loving children could be regarded as a complete failure.

One good thing about the war, Felicity thought as she walked back home from the village shop, was that it had made children have sweets. Before the war she'd hardly ever been allowed them, but now she had this ration card and spent hours trying to choose between jelly babies, mint humbugs, toffees and liquorice torpedoes. There was chocolate as well but a chocolate bar was two weeks' ration, which meant eating just a tiny bit each day, which was really too difficult.

She loved Mrs Bushell's bright little shop with the jars of sweets and bottles of Tizer on one side and the Post Office counter on the other. Mrs Bushell was never grumpy and didn't mind how long children took to do their choosing while she got on with jobs like hitting with a rubber stamp all the mail that came through a hole in the wall from the letterbox outside. The only thing she grumbled about was how fiddlesome were the little triangles of sweet coupons that had to be collected and counted and sent off to the Ministry. Felicity wasn't sure what the Ministry was, but it seemed to be in charge of everything.

It was very still, this late July day. Nobody was about in the High Street, the school was deserted now that the holidays had come, no rowdy boys chased round the playground. The evacuees had come and gone. They'd arrived when the war started, but nothing had happened, so they'd gone back home again. She'd been afraid that her own family would go back too, because she loved living in Netherby; she loved their rambling old house, called Beckside because the stream was nearby, she loved the big garden with its paddock and the lawn where they could play croquet. And all around were fields of cows, very big black and white ones with huge brown eyes around which flies clustered on warm summer evenings. Debbie had been scared of the cows at first and said they ought to be chained up, especially at night, because she could hear them after dark munching at the grass, tugging at it as if pulling it up by the roots, so they'd do a lot of damage if they bit you, she'd warned Felicity. But even Debbie had got used to the cows now.

But most of all, if they'd had to go back to

13

Gradby, she'd have missed playing by the stream, lower down where it widened and flowed under the packhorse bridges. When they first came here, before the war, their mother used to send them down there for the day with Sarah so that she could get on, she said, without having them under her feet. Sarah said that if she was the mistress she'd have come down to the stream for the day herself and let the maid get on with the housework.

Sarah used to bring a picnic which they'd eat sitting on the grass bank that sloped gently down to the edge of the shallow water, which was so clear that you could see every little pebble at the bottom and the tiny fish which darted about above them. Caddis worms crawled slowly along encased in their armour of tiny stones and broken shells, so well disguised that she'd probably never have seen them if Arthur hadn't pointed them out. He knew a lot about nature, Arthur did. It was Arthur who noticed the trout lying very still in the shadows beneath one of the slate bridges and made himself a rod out of a bamboo cane and a piece of string with a bent pin on the end. He wanted to put a worm on the pin as bait but Debbie had cried and said it was cruel to the poor little worm, who'd never done them any harm, so Sarah gave him bits of ham instead. But Arthur never caught a trout all the same.

14

Then Sarah had been taken away in an ambulance and never came back because of the war, and now the evacuees had gone because nothing dangerous seemed to be happening. Grown-ups called it a phoney war, which she'd thought was just their grand way of saying funny war, but Vicky had laughed at her, and Debbie, who was on Vicky's side at the moment, had called her a baby.

She would ask her father about it when he came at the weekend. He didn't come very often now that he was working in London doing something called National Security, which had to do, she thought, with arranging air-raid shelters, but it was all very secret, so he didn't talk about it. There was a notice on the buses which said, *Careless Talk Costs Lives*, with a picture of two women gossiping on the bus and an evil-looking man sitting behind them and listening to every word they were saying. So she knew that if she talked about her father's work, Hitler might hear her and know where the shelters were and drop bombs on them. And it would all be her fault. So she didn't ask any questions.

Vicky and Debbie had promised to play croquet with her this afternoon, she remembered as she turned up the road to the house. 'On the first day of the holidays, we'll play with you,' they'd said. 'That's a promise.' They'd found the croquet set in a

15

toolshed in the garden of this house on the day they moved in, a set just like the one they'd played with at Northrop when they'd gone there before the war. It was a long time ago but she could remember quite clearly the great house with the wide steps and rows of windows where the wounded soldiers lived. Before the *last* war, the grown-ups told them, their own family had lived there: Aunt Diana and Great-Uncle Charles and Great-Aunt Elspeth and several others who were dead. There were lots of photographs of the dead ones, including one of her mother's mother, Selina, who was killed in the war. Everyone said that she was very beautiful. With a name like Selina, Felicity thought, you'd have to be beautiful.

They also said that Vicky was just like Selina. She knew that her eldest sister was a beauty because everyone said so, but she'd never realized that it was only because she'd got it off her dead grandmother.

It was quite steep, this last bit of the road, but she hurried now that she'd remembered about the promised croquet. They hadn't played with her for ages; first of all it was exams and revision and homework, then they were busy with sports day and practising high jump and long jump. They'd told her not to nag and that she'd understand better when she was old enough to go to the big school.

16

She pushed open the heavy five-barred gate, on which was carved, not very clearly, the word *Beckside*, then climbed up so that she could ride on it as it shut, which it did with a satisfactory shudder and clunk as the latch closed. Once in the garden, off the road, she could eat her first sweet. Eating in the street was common, Vicky said.

She stood savouring the moment: she had a paper bag of sweets in her hand, her father was coming in two days' time and her big sisters were going to play with her. Never mind the war, Felicity Crawley was in a state of pure bliss.

Still sucking her liquorice torpedo, she wandered round the side of the house. Debbie and Vicky were lying on the travelling rug, Arthur was doing something to the lawnmower.

'Can we play now?' she asked her sisters, standing over them.

'Oh, must you go on about croquet? Can't you play by yourself?'

'I always do, but now you're on holiday you can play too. Anyway you *promised*.'

'I'm going to wash my hair,' Vicky said, getting up.

'But you *promised* ...'

'When I promised, I didn't know that I'd need to wash my hair,' Vicky told her.

'I think I'll do mine too,' Debbie joined in. Then she got up and they both walked away towards the house.

'I'll give you a game, Flea,' Arthur said, wiping his hands on a rag. 'I think this is all right now,' and he pushed the blades of the mower so that they whirled round so quickly you could hardly see anything but the movement of them, the way it is with insects' wings.

'Best of five games, Flea?'

'Oh, thank you, thank you.'

She rushed ahead of him to get the balls and mallets out of the shed.

'Shall I go first?' she asked, knowing that it was an advantage to go second and wanting to be sure that he won at least one game.

'All right, but you're bound to win anyway,' he said, smiling his good-natured smile. 'You're really too good for any of us, and you don't even seem to try. I spend ages taking aim and even then I miss. You just whack the ball and it goes through the hoop. I don't know how you do it, Flea.'

She basked in his praise; he was her knight in shining armour, he was the best brother anyone ever had. He was her champion. When she couldn't start school in Gradby because she had swollen glands, and had to do sums at home, he was the one who had taught her that if you added nought to a number it stayed the same, when she'd thought that in sums of addition the number at the bottom always had to be bigger than the one above because that's what addition meant and Vicky had said she was stupid, but he had taken her into the garden and taught her by putting into her hand berries which he'd picked off a tree, which was brave of him because they weren't allowed to pick anything in the garden. He was good at everything, Arthur was, good at school, good at sport, good at mending things. And she wasn't any good at anything except croquet. And yet he bothered with her.

She tried to lose, playing with deliberate carelessness, attempting to go through hoops at impossible angles, but however wildly she hit the ball it always seemed to go through the hoops. She just didn't seem able to lose however hard she tried.

'I give up,' he said. 'You win five nil.'

The other two reappeared.

'No hot water,' Vicky said. 'So we thought we might as well come and play. Let's not play partners, it takes too long. You go first, Felicity,' she added, helping herself to the yellow mallet, 'because you're the youngest. Here's the blue.'

It was nothing to do with being youngest, just that Vicky knew that it was a disadvantage to go first and risk having all the others hitting you. Felicity knew it too, but agreed without demur, knowing she could win whatever Vicky did.

She got through the first hoop and the

second and was well out of their way by the end of her first turn. Arthur and Debbie got through the first hoop and missed the second. Vicky missed the first. Very soon Felicity was nearing the last hoop and the winning post.

'We haven't much hope, have we, Debs?' Arthur remarked to his younger sister. 'She's just brilliant.'

'Well, she does get lots more time to practise. She doesn't have homework like us.'

Felicity was taking aim; the hoop was a long shot. Normally she'd have taken one shot to get in a good position and then get through next turn, but she was so well ahead that she could afford to take risks. She hit the ball hard and watched as it went straight and fast and then clean through the hoop, without touching either side.

'Through,' she called out. 'So I get another turn,' and she took aim at the winning post.

She was just about to hit the ball when Vicky said, 'It didn't go through the hoop. If you can't win without cheating, I don't want to play with you,' and threw down her mallet.

Felicity stared at her. How could her clever big sister make such a mistake?

'It's not true,' she shouted, outraged. 'It did go through, straight through.'

Debbie and Arthur walked slowly across to her.

'We didn't see. I'm afraid we were talking and not watching.'

Vicky shrugged.

'Well, I saw,' she said. 'She missed the hoop and I'm not playing with a cheat.'

Rage welled up. Rage overwhelmed her. Rage at being falsely accused, rage that anyone should even think she *needed* to cheat.

'I'm not a cheat, I'm not, I'm not,' she yelled, flew at her sister and hit her.

Vicky drew herself up, the picture of injured innocence, of quiet dignity.

'You should never strike a young woman there, Felicity,' she explained, laying one hand on the breast where the puny blow had landed. 'It can cause disease and death.'

Disease and death! Oh, what had she done? Tears of repentence prickled Felicity's eyes. She had alienated herself from her big sister whom everyone admired because she was so clever and beautiful and somehow always right, and she, merely her scruffy young sister, had endangered her with disease and death.

The tears overflowed at the horror of it. She could hardly see her sister standing there but reached out to her saying, 'Oh, I'm sorry. I shouldn't have hit you. Oh, Vicky, I'm so sorry.'

Vicky looked down at her, her martyred face assuming a look of angelic forgiveness.

'It's all right, Felicity. The pain will soon

wear off. I forgive you, but never do such a thing again. Promise?'

So Felicity promised and waves of relief swept through her because she was forgiven and at peace again with her sister as she walked with her back to the house, leaving the other two to put away the remains of the ruined game.

Two

Usually they all went to meet him at the bus stop, but this Saturday morning Vicky and Debbie were washing their hair, which always took ages, so Felicity and Arthur walked alone down to the village.

'It's the best time, isn't it?' Felicity said suddenly.

'How d'you mean, Flea?'

'Well, I was thinking, from the minute Daddy arrives it gets nearer the time for him to go, so we've got less and less time with him, but now it's still all there.'

Arthur laughed and said she was a funny old thing. She didn't mind; in fact she quite liked the way he said it and anyway they were nearly at the bus stop now – she could see

22

the roof of the little stone shelter – and in five minutes they would hear a heavy kind of grinding noise, like some great animal struggling up a hill, and the orange front of the Pennine bus would appear round the bend in the road. And their father would be on it.

In fact it was a minute early so that the bus had to stand there, shuddering and juddering as the driver kept revving the engine in case anyone came running up to catch the bus into Pendlebury. Not that she cared; her father was here, had handed his case to Arthur and picked her up and given her a hug, told her she was getting too heavy for him now and put her down again. Hand in hand they walked back to the house.

She never liked the next bit and it was no better than usual: the ritual of the kiss. Her mother would appear in the hall and they would look at each other and her father would say something like, 'And how are you, Celia?' very politely and kindly and her mother would say something like, 'As well as can be expected, thank you,' and hold up her face to be kissed. And somehow the kiss her father put on that cheek wasn't at all like the kisses the rest of them gave each other; it was more like the little rubber stamp Mrs Bushell put on letters in the Post Office, something official which had to be done.

At supper that night they discussed where

they would go tomorrow. They always went off for the day with their father, their mother wanting to have the house to herself so she could get on. She did a lot of getting on.

'We could climb Sawborough,' Vicky suggested.

Sebastian shook his head.

'It's too far for Debbie and Felicity,' he said.

'I don't see why we should always be held back by them,' she objected. 'Why do we always have to take them? They could go somewhere else, nearer home.'

'They can't go somewhere by themselves,' Arthur told her. 'We've got to stick together.'

'Of course we have. I think you're being jolly mean and selfish, Vicky,' Debbie told her.

She was on Felicity's side now, having quarrelled with her elder sister about the ownership of five precious hair grips, the last ones left from before the war. There'd be no more for the duration. No more elastic bands for plaits either.

'I don't mind where you go,' their mother put in sharply. 'So long as you go off for the day so I can get on without you under my feet.'

'How about going up the lane and then across the side of Southerby, cut along the escarpment, then drop down to the beck and picnic there?' Arthur suggested.

24

'And paddle?' Felicity put in.

'And we could build a dam like the one at Furzebridge.'

'Where's Furzebridge, Debbie?'

'*Oh, Flea,* you *remember,* when we went to Northrop and the cousins told us how the boys built this dam before the last war? And Mummy picnicked there when she was a little girl, didn't you?'

Celia hesitated. She never liked to be reminded of Northrop and her Arndale relations.

'I can't remember much about it,' she said at last. 'I was younger than Felicity at the time.'

The children stared at her, trying to picture her as a child, younger even than the youngest of them. They failed. Sebastian too looked at her, so hard of face now, no trace of the pretty, rather delicate girl he had married. He wondered, as he often did, at the change in her and if he were to blame for it, although reason told him that the girl was mother to the woman.

He looked at his children and wished he could spend more time with them, now when they needed the kind of guidance Celia would not be able to give them, but he knew that the war might keep him from them for many years yet. And then, how would divorce affect them? *I must not do anything to harm them,* he thought, as he had often done before, *I must never let them down.*

Their mother had their sandwiches ready and packed into the rucksack before breakfast the following morning and saw them off with evident relief. She's always glad to see the back of us, Felicity thought, especially me. Not that she minded, not really, she told herself as she toiled up the steep hill that led up the dale, because she loved to be out here and this was her favourite walk.

There were high drystone walls on each side of the lane, with fields and a few little copses beyond them. Southerby, green and grey and dotted with boulders, rose on the left and Thornborough, darker and more wooded, on the right, familiar hills because she could see them from her bedroom, though they looked a bit different from here.

The high walls were often frustrating because the others would talk about something in the fields which she couldn't see. She'd climb up the wall to look and they'd tell her it didn't matter, it was only a flock of rooks or some rabbits that had gone now anyway. But it mattered to her to see what they'd seen and she'd get left behind and had to run to catch up because they wouldn't wait.

She walked now between her father and her brother. Arthur had the big rucksack on his back and her father was carrying the travelling rug over his arm. It was brown, quite old and getting thin. Sometimes when they were packing up after a picnic, Sarah used to let Felicity lie in it, then she'd hold one end and Arthur the other and they'd swing her backwards and forwards. She loved the feel of it, swaying from side to side, in the exciting semi-darkness of the folds of the rug, which had a warm, grassy smell.

'When is Sarah coming back?' she asked now.

'She's joined up,' her father told her. 'She was in the isolation hospital with diphtheria for a while and then she was moved to another one until she was better and now I think she's in the Land Army.'

'Will she be there for the duration?'

'Yes, Debbie.'

'She'll come back to us after the war, won't she?'

'We can't be sure of that, Flea,' he told her, knowing that what the last war had done for footmen and butlers, this war would probably do for the resident maid.

'There's the Post Office van, right at the end of the lane going up to the Thorntons' farm,' Arthur said suddenly.

They all looked and nodded, except Felicity, who couldn't see over the wall.

'Where?' she demanded, standing still. 'I can't *see*.'

'Oh, for goodness' sake, it's only a *van*.

Don't be so silly. You've seen a van before,' Vicky said and walked on.

But her father stopped and helped her on to the wall so she could see the little red van winding its way up to the farm. And he told her all about a great man called Roland Hill who had invented the Royal Mail a hundred years ago so that it cost the same wherever you sent a letter. It was a penny in those days and was tuppence halfpenny now but it still cost the same however far the letter had to go.

She sighed deeply as he helped her down off the wall; she loved it when he told her all these stories and often wondered how he knew so much.

They soon caught up with the others, who were waiting at the brow of the hill. It was breezier up here.

Her father paused and took deep breaths. 'Oh, the air here is so good,' he said.

'You could put some in jam jars and take it back with you,' Felicity suggested.

'You could breathe in great gulps of it before you get on the train tomorrow and take it back inside you,' Debbie counter-suggested.

They were all subdued by the reminder that he was leaving tomorrow.

So, 'Come on, let's just make the most of today,' he said, setting off again.

This was the best bit of the walk, Felicity

thought. The long trek up the lane was over and they were perched up here on top of the world. Well, of this part of the world anyway, because mighty Sawborough towered ahead of them. One day when she was older she would climb up there. Meanwhile she was content to walk along the top of her smaller world, her head tipped back, the sun on her face, the wind blowing through her hair and her father's hand in hers.

Arthur too was contented with his lot. Usually there were four females and just him in the family. Today there were three girls and two men. If you went by weight there was probably less of girl than of man. He laughed aloud.

'What's funny?' Debbie asked.

'I was just thinking that if we put father and me on one side of a weighing scale and you three on the other, we'd probably weigh heavier. So you may outnumber us but you don't outweigh us.'

'You're right,' his father said. 'And I've read that if you put all the animals in the world on one scale and all the insects in the other, they'd outweigh the animals.'

'What, even counting all the rhinos and elephants?'

'Yes, Debbie. You see, the animals are only on parts of the surface of the world, whereas insects are everywhere, underground and in the air.'

'What about birds? Birds are animals.'

'Oh, yes, they'd go on the animal side of the balance.'

'But you couldn't catch them,' Felicity objected. 'They'd fly off the scales. And anyway, where would you get scales big enough for all the animals?'

'Oh, don't be so silly, Flea,' Vicky told her. 'It's just a *theoretical* balance.'

That was the thing about Vicky. She knew all these long words, which made you feel silly and babyish.

'We're nearly at the stile now,' her father said to distract her.

'A bit further along,' she corrected him.

She knew the way well. A little further up the lane, they'd come to a stile into a field which had lots of boulders, some dark and some pale: millstone grit and limestone, Arthur called them. They'd walk across the field to a little gate at the far corner and up the next field, which was steeply terraced by glaciers long ago, he said, and over another stile from the top of which you could see for miles. From here the lane was just a narrow ribbon of grey and green and you could see how, soon after you'd left it, it became a track which led to the Thorntons' farm. You could see the beck meandering down to the village, taking its time with many a detour, sometimes widening into a pool, before going on its leisurely way down to Netherby.

After the stile, there were no more fields, just the open side of Southerby where it was easy to lose the little path to the escarpment because there were so many sheep runs, which looked like paths but weren't. Unless, of course, you were a sheep.

The older two were soon well ahead. While Felicity struggled up the steep hillside, Arthur and Vicky positively ran all the way. They were sitting down resting on this side of the escarpment by the time the other three climbed over the last stile and caught up with them. Whereupon Arthur and Vicky promptly got up and set off again.

'That's so *mean*,' Debbie shouted. 'You've had your rest and we want ours now. You should have *waited*.'

'It's all right, Debbie,' her father told her. 'The three of us can rest for a moment.'

So they sat down on the grassy slope while the others set off for the escarpment.

'Look, there's the van going back,' Felicity said suddenly. 'It looks so tiny, just like a ladybird.'

Her father laughed and looked where she was pointing.

'Mind how you go along that ledge,' he called after the others, his eyes still on the little red van.

'Don't worry, we're used to it,' Arthur shouted back. 'It's quite wide you know.'

The ledge, which was their name for the

31

escarpment, was the only flat part of the hill. Nobody seemed quite sure how it had been dug out of the hillside; it was wider than most of the terraces made by glaciers. As you walked along it, the hillside rose steeply to the left while on the right it dropped sharply, briefly levelled and then gave way to a cliff face of scree, which went down in a sheer drop to the green pasture below, which was bordered by the track up to the Thorntons' farm.

It was wide, as Arthur had reassured his father, over a yard wide for the most part, though here and there it narrowed; Arthur went carefully as he led the way, Vicky following, the others still resting.

He was glad to have a moment alone with his sister. He'd tried to get her on her own ever since yesterday afternoon, but she'd been elusive.

'Vicky,' he called back now, over his shoulder, after they had rounded the bend and were out of sight of the others.

'Yes?'

He stood still, then turned to face her.

'Felicity didn't cheat yesterday,' he said bluntly.

Vicky flushed.

'You didn't see. I did,' she told him.

'I didn't need to. You were lying.'

'I was not,' she told him angrily. 'How can you say that? I was looking and you weren't even bothering to see what she was up to.'

'I can say it because I know Flea,' he told her. 'For a start she's easily the best and had almost won anyway. She'd absolutely no need to cheat. But more important I know she's dead straight. She would never lie or cheat. If there's a cheat in this family, it isn't her,' he added pointedly.

Vicky was outraged. How dare he talk to her like this? She whom everyone else admired, who was respected by her peers at school, praised by the staff for her poise, her maturity, who saw herself as noble, who had been chosen to play Portia in the school play.

But a bit of her was also afraid; could he possibly make her confess, force her to apologize? For a moment rage and fear made her quite ugly, as she burst out childishly, 'It's so unfair. You always take her side against me.'

Childish too was the angry push she gave him.

It took him by surprise. He grabbed at the cliffside to his left, clutched at the empty air. The rucksack swung out to his right, seemed to pull him towards the abyss and for a moment he seemed to hang there on the edge. Then, very slowly it seemed, his body swayed, turned and fell.

For a moment he was out of sight, then reappeared, rolling helplessly down towards the scree. He seemed to bounce down the loose stones until he reached the gentle grassland below, where he lay quite still.

Vicky stood terrified at what she'd done, staring down at him. Then she moved the last few steps towards the end of the ledge and leant against the hillside.

Debbie appeared round the bend, Felicity and her father following behind.

They gathered around her.

'Where's Arthur?' they asked.

She pointed. They saw.

'He just tripped and fell,' she said.

'Oh, my God.'

Their father was off, leaping down the slope with incredible speed. The others followed more slowly, stumbling. When they reached him, Sebastian was holding his son in his arms, supporting his head, which was at a funny angle. The rucksack was lying alongside.

'Run to the farm. Ask for help. I'll stay here,' he told them.

Felicity crouched down beside him. Vicky and Debbie ran off.

They were met at the farm gate by Mrs Thornton, who had been filling a bucket at the pump. They gasped out what had happened.

'I'll tell Nathan,' she said. 'He's in the milking shed.'

They heard her telling him to get the van out, saw her opening the big gates as they

34

climbed into the van with him.

'He's down there,' Debbie whispered when they had gone a little way down the rough and bumpy track.

He nodded. 'I can see,' he said.

Not far from the track, on the grassy strip of land below the scree, Sebastian was kneeling; his son lay limp in his arms. Felicity was standing now, head bowed, looking down at them. They seemed so still, frozen like figures in a tableau.

Nathan drove the van off the track to get as near to them as possible. He saw at once that the lad's neck was broken, he told his wife later, but at the time just said to Sebastian, 'I'll help you lift 'im. You'd best be with 'im in t'back. You'll 'ave more room.'

'I want to be with him too, Daddy,' Vicky said in her best tragic voice.

So the two youngest sat in the front alongside Nathan, Felicity nursing the rucksack, while the others crouched in the back, which was furnished with a bench and some sacking. Vicky perched on the narrow seat. Sebastian, ashen-faced, knelt among the sacks, holding his son in his arms.

'What happened?' he asked his daughter.

'I honestly don't know, Daddy,' she whispered. 'I looked around when I got to the end of the ledge to see where he was and he just seemed to lose his foothold and then—' she ended, her voice almost breaking, 'I saw him falling.'

'It's all right, darling. He'll be all right.'

Would he be? Vicky wondered. His eyes were staring at her. Accusing.

At that moment Arthur seemed to move his head and she thought in a panic, *He'll wake up and give me away*, but it was only the jolting of the van that had moved his head.

Gently Sebastian rested his hand on his son's face, closing the lids over those staring eyes.

'Straight to the hospital,' he directed Nathan as they approached Pendlebury. 'If that's all right.'

'I'll tek you wherever you want,' the other replied simply.

At the hospital the children watched as porters and nurses moved their brother on to a stretcher and carried him inside.

'I can't thank you enough, Mr Thornton,' Sebastian said. 'I don't know what we'd have done—'

'It were nowt,' the other interrupted him. 'You'll likely be needing a lift 'ome later?'

'No, don't worry. We'll find our own way back. Can I offer you something for your petrol?'

The farmer shook his head, 'Nay,' he said, 'I'm just reet sorry about t'lad.'

Sebastian couldn't reply, just took his hand for a moment and turned back into the hospital.

36

'I'll go with Arthur,' he told the children. 'Can you just sit here in reception for a while?'

'Yes,' Vicky said. 'We'll wait here. Come on, you two.'

Felicity clung to her father.

'Please let me stay with you, *please.*'

So in the end he took Debbie and Felicity with him and Vicky stayed in the reception. Calm and sensible she was, as she settled down with a magazine and waited for her father and sisters to return.

Arthur had been wheeled away. They waited in a little cubicle nearby.

'Could I have a word with you?' the doctor asked Sebastian. He smiled at the two children. 'I won't keep him long,' he promised.

He led the way to another room in the same corridor.

Sebastian stood looking at him, hoping against all rational hope.

'I'm afraid—' the doctor began.

'I know.'

'How did it happen?'

'He slipped apparently. It's very strange, because he's been there many times and he's a sure-footed lad. Is it possible that he had some sort of attack which made him lose his balance?'

'I can't say. The post-mortem will tell us.'

Post-mortem!

A few short hours ago they were talking of

picnics and now they talked of post-mortems. *His* post-mortem. It was impossible to believe. He saw him again as a toddler, as a boy with a cricket bat, Arthur laughing, Arthur with his lovely open nature. Oh my son, my son. Suddenly he was racked by convulsive, silent sobs. The doctor tried to make him sit down.

'No, I must get back to the children. I must tell them.'

'Where do you live?'

'Netherby. His mother doesn't know yet.'

'Look, I'm going off duty shortly and I live in Lowsham, not far from Netherby. Let me drive you back.'

Half an hour later they set off once again in a stranger's car, only this time without Arthur. Sebastian sat in the back, his arms around the two younger children, who leant against him, shocked and disbelieving. Vicky sat in the front with the doctor, admirably calm and composed, he thought.

He dropped them at the end of the drive, by the five-barred gate, the familiar five-barred gate.

'I'll leave you here,' the doctor said to Sebastian. 'Ring the hospital tomorrow. And of course, the police must be informed.'

'Thank you. Yes.'

'And I can't say how sorry I am.'

They watched the car disappear round the corner of the road. Then they walked up the drive to the house.

Celia heard them coming in.

'You're late,' she began, then stopped. 'Where's Arthur?'

'It's bad,' Sebastian said, then, turning to the others, went on, 'Vicky, take Debbie and Felicity into the drawing-room, or upstairs if you'd rather. I need to talk to your mother.'

Celia heard him out in silence. He tried to embrace her, comfort her, but she drew away and looked at him angrily.

'You can't be trusted to look after your own children,' she accused. 'I manage to look after them on my own here, day in, day out, and you come for a couple of days and they get all silly and excited – and this happens.'

'Oh, Celia, it was an accident.'

'They've been up there often enough and there's never been an accident.'

'Celia, surely we can comfort each other at a time like this. Our son, yours and mine ...'

He couldn't go on.

'The only comfort,' she told him, 'is that if this wretched war goes on he'd have been called up in a few years and probably killed anyway.'

The harsh words went through him. Later he tried to rationalize them: she'd lost both parents and her brother in the last war. Subconsciously she must have had a terror of losing her son in this one. Her dread made those words understandable, forgivable. Thus he reasoned later. But at the time he could feel nothing but horror at her words. He left her and went back to the children.

Confused days followed, days of giving statements, waiting for the inquest, for the results of the post-mortem, which showed that death was caused by the fall, there being no sign of ill health in this young man. Sebastian had prayed that there would be; it would be more bearable if his death had been inevitable, if by this swift death, his son had been spared prolonged suffering. He said this to Celia, who told him it made no difference what Arthur died of. Death is death, no matter how.

Through all this time, Vicky remained calm. She had quickly convinced herelf that it wasn't her fault. It couldn't be, since she hadn't meant to do it, or at least hadn't meant what she'd done to have such awful consequences. It was a small step from there to believing that, since it wasn't her fault, she hadn't actually done anything to cause her brother's fall, had only been the tragic witness of it.

She went quietly about the house, keeping out of the way of her two sisters, helping her mother much more than she had ever done before. They were both impatient with Felicity, who seemed to be making no effort to get over it and would insist on clinging to

Arthur's wretched rucksack. The very first evening, when Celia had rescued the sandwiches from it – sandwiches remarkably undamaged – and put them out for supper, Felicity had refused to eat and had choked when her mother tried to make her.

It had seemed to Felicity that eating them was somehow eating his body; she couldn't get the horrible thought out of her mind. Even her mother's constant reiteration of *'Waste not, want not'* would not shift it.

On the hot summer days which followed, so sunny, so heartlessly bright, she often hid herself away in the long grass at the bottom of the paddock. 'He was my favourite person in all the world and I can't bear it,' she would murmur to herself. 'Why should we all be alive and he be dead? It's so *unfair*.'

Sometimes Debbie came and wept with her, sometimes she tried to be helpful and grown-up like Vicky. They all seemed separate from each other, only their father moved between them, comforting them each separately, trying to enter into how they felt.

'Everybody has different ways of bearing grief,' he told the three of them as he embraced them the night before he left. 'Try to remember, Felicity and Debbie, that Vicky has had the most to bear. She saw it happen. She's the one who's had to make statements. And then he was her twin brother and so the closest to him. So try to be tolerant if she reacts differently from you.'

'Thank you, Daddy,' Vicky said and gave him her brave little smile.

Three

'Twenty-three pounds, twelve shillings and sevenpence three farthings,' Mrs Double said. 'Have you all got that down?'

They indicated by nods and noises of assent that they had.

'To be divided by seven,' she concluded.

There were twelve of them in the class. There had only been six before the new lot of vaccies came. These ones didn't go back home the way the first lot had done; they stayed because the war had really got going now. Some of them had little brothers and sisters in Mrs Penny's infants' class on the other side of the folding doors.

The children found it funny to have teachers called missus. They'd always been Miss before the war. The vaccies still used to say, 'Please, Miss,' and Mrs Double would correct them. '*Mrs Double*, if you please,' she would say.

First there'd been Miss Scott, who'd gone

away to fight in the war, then Mrs Peters, who'd left to have a baby. And now Mrs Double, who'd only just come. She wasn't only a mother, she was a grandmother, so must be very old. She was round and slow-moving and breathed quite heavily as she moved between the desks.

'Oh dear, Felicity,' she was saying now, peering through her spectacles at Felicity's book. 'You haven't got very far, have you?'

Felicity shook her head.

'Now, Felicity, how many times does seven go into twenty-three?'

'Three times?' Felicity offered, after a short pause.

'Good. So write in the three, there beneath the twenty-three. Now how much is left over?'

'Two.'

'Two what?'

'Remainder two?' Felicity suggested.

'Two *pounds*,' Mrs Double said with some irritation. The child used to be quite bright but really didn't seem to be making much effort nowadays. 'And what do we do with the two pounds?'

'Carry them forward?'

'Yes, that's right. But we have to turn them into shillings first so that we can add them to the ones that are already there, don't we? And how many shillings are there in two pounds?'

'Forty?'

'Of course.'

It was easy, why was the child so hesitant?

'And when we add those forty shillings to the twelve that are already there, what do we get?'

'A headache,' one of the vaccies whispered and some of them giggled, but the nice thing about Mrs Double was that she didn't hear very well.

Forty and twelve, forty and twelve. Felicity could hear her brain chanting, over and over again. She stared hard at the page and managed to say fifty-two loud enough to drown the silly chanting in her head.

'Good. Now we have to divide the fifty-two by seven.'

Felicity could not do it. She guessed. Wrongly.

'A lot of you have trouble with your seven times table,' Mrs Double addressed the whole class. 'Now all together, recite it all together. One seven's seven ...'

'Two sevenserfourteen, three sevensertwenty-one, four sevensertwenty-eight,' they chanted raggedly all the way up to 'twelve sevensereighty-four.'

'Good. Now go back to your work. And Felicity, now can you tell me how many times seven goes into fifty-two?'

'Seven sevens are forty-nine and three left over.'

'Excellent. You see, you can do it when you try. And those three that are left over are shillings, aren't they, so how do we turn them into pennies?'

'Multiply by twelve.'

'And three twelves are?'

'Thirty-six,' Felicity said promptly. She never had trouble with that one.

'And we add that thirty-six to the seven pennies we already have. You may write it down if you wish.'

'Forty-three,' Felicity managed without writing down, just counting on her fingers under the desk.

'Good. Now we divide by seven. You've just done your seven times, so it should be easy.'

She managed it.

'Six, remainder one,' she said.

'Good. So write in the six under the pennies. And now do the farthings. You can manage that yourself.'

She moved on to the next child and Felicity sat staring at the farthings.

Remainder one penny made four farthings. Add the three that were there already. That made seven. What happened when you divided seven by seven. Was it one or was it nought?

It was so vivid, the memory of Arthur telling her about noughts. She could see him in the garden, she could see him picking the

45

berries, feel him counting them into the palm of her hand. She could see his smile, hear his voice. She couldn't see the page in front of her any more, couldn't hear the shuffling of the children all around her. It all vanished, the high windows, the big stove with the metal guard in front, the folding doors to the infants' class, the maps on the wall, even Mrs Double; none of it was there. Just Arthur.

Every night she dreamed that he came back and told her she was a silly old thing for believing he was dead. As if he'd go off and leave her behind! And every night relief flooded through her and she ran towards him. Then she woke up and at first it felt lovely and then she remembered. So every day he died again, every single morning. Yet still part of her could not believe she would not see him again. She *must*. He couldn't just disappear for ever.

'Felicity! You are daydreaming *again*,' Mrs Double's voice cut in sharply. 'How many farthings are left when you divide twenty-three pounds, twelve shillings and seven-pence three farthings by seven?'

When Mrs Double had to leave because of an illness called Nerves, she was replaced by Mrs Magthorpe, who wasn't nearly as strict as her predecessor. She had bushy hair and a strong northern accent which was sometimes difficult to make out, but her lessons were much more interesting than Mrs Double's had been.

Her very first one was about teeth. She talked about baby teeth, which most of them had lost by now, and how, if you put them under your pillow, the fairies replaced them with sixpence, which of course they all knew, but it was reassuring to have it made official. She explained how their adult teeth grew into the spaces and then their wisdom teeth would come, though she said they were more trouble than they were worth even though they were supposed to show you were wise.

But even grown-up teeth didn't last for ever, she explained; they either fell out or had to be pulled out and then you had new teeth called dentures. Then she did an amazing thing; she put a finger in her mouth behind her teeth, made them all pop out and laid them carefully on a saucer on her desk. Her mouth caved in a bit but she could speak all right and, pointing with a ruler to the teeth, named them one by one: incisors, canines, molars and premolars. The children all watched and listened with more rapt attention than they had harkened to Mrs Double's lessons and never thereafter did one of them forget the names of their teeth.

She also explained to them why all the weights and measures were printed on the back of their exercise books, something they'd never really thought about before. Once upon a time, she said, everyone used different measurements in different parts of the country, which didn't matter because nobody moved far from home anyway. But when people began moving about more and selling things to faraway places, the government made a law that everyone should use the same weights and measures. But a lot of people didn't like having to lose their old measures, so in the end the government made another law that school exercise books should have lists of the official measures, so that all the children would learn to use them, even if the adults wouldn't. People in England always thought anything new was bad, Mrs Magthorpe said, not like the Americans, who thought anything new was bound to be good. That was because they were a young nation, she said. So Felicity pictured America as a land peopled with children, boys and girls alike clad in shorts, cotton socks and sandals.

Mrs Magthorpe talked more about the war than Mrs Double had done. She pinned up maps to show where Hitler had invaded, shading more and more countries in black until there was only Britain and Russia left fighting Hitler. She said America should join in the war, and when Felicity said how could they since they were all children, she explained what being a young country meant

48

and wasn't cross and even said it was her own fault for not making it clearer.

In the autumn they didn't have nature study, but instead went out to pick rosehips from the hedges for the government to make into rosehip syrup to keep children healthy, because there were no more oranges since the war. There was no more of a lot of other things too, like bananas, and absolutely everything else was hard to get and had to be rationed. Paper was so short they had to write twice between the lines in their exercise books, which was all right if you had neat little writing, but she didn't and her pen nibs always seemed to get crossed so that they spattered blobs of ink all over the page.

'You're the messiest girl I've ever known,' Mrs Magthorpe said, but she smiled and shook her head at the same time and added, 'And what I can read of it is very good, but I'd like to be able to read it all, so could you try a bit harder?' which somehow made it seem possible that she might one day get better.

She was sorry to leave Mrs Magthorpe when she had to move to the big school in Pendlebury, where she had a different teacher for each subject; she went there nearly two years earlier than she should have done, because so many vaccies had come to the little school when the bombing started that it was overflowing. Besides, her mother said, it would be more convenient if all three girls went to the same school.

She was over a year younger than the rest of her class, so nobody expected her to be very good, but when she stayed down a year and was still bottom of the class they began to get cross and some of them said she must try to follow the good example set by her two older sisters, especially Vicky. She did listen to what they said, she did try, but somehow she heard the words the teachers said but couldn't always make sense of them. 'Put your mind to your work,' Mrs Baggs, who gave very boring biology lessons, used to say. 'Concentrate.' The trouble was that Mrs Baggs gobbled as she spoke and her several double chins wobbled in time to her words, so it was really hard to think about what she was saying and not just observe the way she said it. In a lesson on Human Biology she talked about teeth, which Felicity, remembering Mrs Magthorpe's teaching on the subject, felt confident about, so when Mrs Baggs asked which were the last teeth to arrive, she put up her hand and said, 'Dentures.'

Instead of being pleased and nodding, Mrs Baggs turned a peculiar red colour and her chins wobbled like the pink bit that flops about on a cock's head. Then, almost spitting out the words, she ordered, 'Go outside at once, Felicity Crawley, and stay in the

50

corridor until the end of the lesson.'

Afterwards she lectured her on impertinence and said she was lucky not to be sent to the headmistress. But she didn't explain why she was so cross or why the rest of the class had tittered.

She did manage to be one up from the bottom at the end of the year but that was only because a new girl called Maria who came to the school that term was even worse than she was.

The new girl had come from Liverpool to escape the bombs; she'd been evacuated with her school to a castle in Northumberland but had hated it, then her brother was killed in the war, so she and her mother came to Pendlebury. She cried a lot, the new girl did.

When she was sent for by the headmistress, Felicity could hardly walk along the corridor to the terrifying door at which she had to knock, expecting expulsion, but the head only told her to come in and sit down and then she said quite gently, 'You lost your brother, didn't you, Felicity? Maria too has lost her brother and I thought it might help her if you talked to her about it, shared your experience with her.'

Lost. It sounded like mislaid. Perhaps Arthur hadn't been killed, perhaps all those dreams she'd had about his being really alive, the whole thing a mistake, were true.

He'd just got *lost*.

She often thought this, and was full of hope. But at the same time she could see him quite clearly below the scree, his head twisted. And she could see his grave too. Then she knew with awful certainty that he was dead. But the odd thing was that she could feel them both. She knew that if she'd felt them at different times it would be all right, but that it was very peculiar that she could feel them both *at the same time.*

Sometimes she went down to the stream and sat on the bank gazing at the slate bridge where Arthur used to try to catch trout. She would look at it for a long time and then shut her eyes and imagine Arthur there, his long brown legs hanging over the side, the string with the pin dangling into the water, and if she opened her eyes quickly she could really see him. And it was so real that it hurt, so real that she really did see him again. Yet he was gone for ever.

'Well?' the head prompted.

She realized she had been sitting there, looking at the floor and saying nothing while all these thoughts were going round in her head.

'I'll try,' she managed to say.

But she never did talk to the new girl who had saved her from being bottom of the class, because Maria left school, still weeping, the next week.

Four

The war had been going on for so long that Felicity could hardly remember what it had been like before it started. Memories of Gradby were fading. As in a picture in which a few vivid details stand out against a blurred and misty background, some events from the past would suddenly come quite clearly into her mind for no particular reason. Some were good, like the memory of the day Arthur taught her to skip or the afternoon he had made her understand about sums by picking berries in the garden. Others were awful, like the time she was ill and her godmother, Agatha Beale, came to visit her and collapsed on the bed, looking as dead as Debbie's pet mouse. But of exactly when and in what order these things had happened, of what had gone before or come after, she could remember nothing. So she couldn't make a whole picture out of her scattered memories, however hard she tried. But very clear in her mind was the fact that Sarah had always been there and that her father had come home every evening. And that when she talked to him, he had always seemed to understand.

She wanted to talk to him now about so many things, especially about Arthur and how she dreamed about him. She had tried to talk to Vicky about what had happened that day at the ledge, but Vicky just told her to shut up and not be morbid, so she shut up and wasn't sure what morbid meant anyway. Her father never wanted to talk about Arthur in front of Vicky because it upset her, he said, and they must be extra considerate now that she was about to take her School Certificate. He was very proud of her because she always got good reports and was so poised. That was the word they used about Vicky at school, very *poised* for her age, they said. They even awarded her a deportment badge.

She knew that she was scatty by comparison and would never be a bit poised. But it was worse for Debbie because she was nearer in age. Debbie was almost as tall as Vicky, but somehow looked smaller because she didn't hold herself so straight; she had spots and stooped as if she wanted to hide her face. She'd noticed too that Debbie could talk to people on her own, but if Vicky was there she was tongue-tied and awkward. Any strangers who were introduced to them looked from Vicky to Debbie and were surprised that they were sisters; she could guess what they were thinking and knew that Debbie must do the same, though they never said anything to each other about it. And they didn't talk to each other about Arthur either, though she knew Debbie thought about him. She could tell that she did. On Vicky's birthday she'd hidden in the outside lavatory and cried because it was Arthur's birthday too and Debbie had noticed and said she must be careful for fear of upsetting Vicky and spoiling her birthday. But she could see that Debbie had been crying as well. But still they didn't talk about him or about why they were crying.

Sarah would have talked about Arthur, she knew she would; Sarah had loved him. It suddenly occurred to her that Sarah wouldn't know what had happened. Sarah wouldn't know that Arthur—Sarah should be found and told.

'Where's Sarah?' she asked her father suddenly.

It was his first visit since Vicky's birthday and they were all having tea in the paddock, all except Arthur, of course. She knew, before she spoke, that her mother would look disapproving and she did. Nonetheless, 'Why didn't she come back when she was better?' she persisted.

'She had to go into the forces when she was well again.'

'I've told you that often enough,' her

mother put in severely.

It was true, she had, but somehow Felicity hadn't believed it.

'Young women like Sarah can't go and be maids any more,' her father was explaining. 'They have to go and do war work if they haven't any children to look after.'

'But she had *us*,' she exclaimed indignantly.

Her father smiled. 'Of course, darling, and I know she loved you all, but she had to go and do her duty.'

'And that's enough of that,' her mother put in sharply. 'It's in the past.'

Vicky glared at her youngest sister and Debbie said nothing. She knew they would not be any help, Vicky always taking care not to annoy their mother and Debbie being too scared to say anything. Soon afterwards both of them went off to do their weekend homework. She stayed and began crawling through the long grass remembering how they used to do that in the Paisleys' garden years ago in Gradby when they were neighbours and the four Paisley children used to come round, mostly on Sunday afternoons, to ask if they could come out to play. Celia would say they could go so long as they played quietly and respected the Sabbath. But Mrs Paisley didn't seem to worry about respecting the Sabbath. In fact she didn't seem to respect anything much, not even clean hands and saying thank you. She and Mr Paisley used to disappear upstairs and leave the children to get on with it, with a vague instruction not to hurt themselves.

The Paisleys' garden was wild, quite unlike their own neat and tidy one. The best thing in their own garden in Gradby had been the climbing frame that Sebastian had made for them. The Paisley children said the Crawley children were jolly lucky to have an architect for a father, who could make useful things like climbing frames; their own father was a bank manager and couldn't make anything, they said.

One of the games they played was tracking, which involved wriggling along the ground on your stomach so that nobody could see you. You had to move very slowly or the long grass waved above your head and gave you away. Felicity relived those games now as she crawled through the grass in the paddock and curled up in the extra-long patch in the corner, feeling warm and sleepy. Next week Farmer Coltby was going to come and scythe it and take it away for his cattle. After that she wouldn't be able to lie hidden in its depths; it would be all short and stubbly, sharp and newly shaven, as she remembered it from last year.

She realized she must be invisible to her parents, because she heard her father say, 'Celia, why didn't you let Sarah come back to say goodbye?'

'What was the point? I'd sent all her belongings after her and she was joining up in a few days.'

'It would have been a chance to thank her for all the work she'd done for us.'

'She was paid.'

'But, Celia, she'd been with you for so long and she was so loyal. I remember how distressed she was when you were hurt in that accident with the boiler. And how she spent her savings on a wedding present for us.'

'She didn't have to.'

'Of course not.'

There was a pause, then he added, 'It would have been good for the children to say goodbye.'

'Nonsense, it would only have upset them, especially Felicity. Sarah always spoiled her.'

She wanted to jump up and say it wasn't true. Sarah didn't spoil her. Instead she began to crawl away, not wanting to hear any more, but stopped because she was afraid they'd see the grass moving and she'd get into trouble. So she lay still.

Her mother made some comment about the milk. She was angry because the law said it had all to be pasteurized, whatever that meant, and put into bottles. Her mother liked the way the farmer brought the milk round in a churn and ladled it out into the milk jugs she left ready in the scullery.

Felicity agreed with her; she loved the blue and white jugs with their little muslin covers, edged with lace and weighted down with blue beads, that kept the flies off.

'There's nothing wrong with the milk,' her mother was saying. 'And he always gives good measure.'

'But you see, Celia,' her father replied in his extra-reasonable voice, 'it simply isn't safe. A great many farm families lost children through tuberculin-infected milk.'

That word, *lost*, again.

'Oh, the government will always find excuses to back up whatever they want to do.'

'It isn't a case of excuses, it's medical facts. America has been pasteurizing milk for years, ever since it was proved that tuberculosis could be caused by cow's milk.'

'Oh, *Americans*,' she said scornfully.

'And you can't have forgotten how ill Felicity was for nearly a year with swollen glands, which is a form of it.'

Felicity hadn't known that; *they might have told me*, she thought indignantly. *They were my glands, after all.*

'She got over it and didn't need to be operated on.'

'She was lucky.'

It was always like this when they argued. It was like this after Vicky's birthday treat to the pictures in Pendlebury to see *David*

59

Copperfield. It had been wonderful and so had been the ride back on the bus in the dark afterwards. The bus was blacked out with stuff like netting stuck to all the windows, but there was a little hole through which she could see the stars as she sat with her sisters on the long bench at the back of the bus. Her parents were sitting in front of them.

'Of course, Dickens wasn't very good at depicting young women characters,' her father had said. 'They're always very weak.'

'Oh, no, he got them just right,' her mother contradicted. 'All women were like that in his day, very weak and dependent.'

They went on and on about it, like they always did. It didn't seem to matter what the subject was; it could be the war, or the milk or Sarah; he only had to say something for her to contradict it. It seemed to Felicity that if he'd said the opposite, her mother would have contradicted that too, as if it wasn't actually about any*thing*, but about themselves that they were arguing. It seemed that just being together made them argue. Sometimes he fell silent and said no more, but at others he quietly persisted, not angrily, just with a kind of dogged politeness which, she was beginning to realize, her mother found much worse.

'You read about Agatha Beale's trial?' he was saying now, as he sat with her mother in

60

the garden.

'I did. It was in the *Yorkshire Post*. The court got it all wrong, of course. Agatha was – and is – a law-abiding, God-fearing woman. That is why I chose her to be Felicity's god-mother. She was quite innocent.'

'But the facts are incontrovertible, Celia. By acting as she did, she might have killed herself and the vicar and many other people.'

'She merely suggested to the vicar, who was driving, that if he had true faith he would take his hands off the wheel and let God do the steering. *You* may not under-stand it, but I do. She has the faith that moves mountains.'

'But when he refused, she tried to pull his hands off the wheel and then she hit him and—'

'It was only a little tap on his head, such as she might have given a child at Sunday school.'

'A tap? She knocked him unconscious.'

It was at this point that Felicity burst out laughing. Quickly she converted it into a cough and a sneeze.

'What are you doing, hiding in there?' her mother called out angrily.

'I was asleep,' she said, getting up and stretching. 'I've just woken up,' she added, yawning hugely, which seemed to reassure them. That was the odd thing about grown-ups: they knew so much and were so power-

61

ful, but sometimes could be so easily deceived.

Vicky did well in her School Certificate, as everyone had foretold. In two years' time she would take her Higher and then be all set for the university. Vicky's future seemed to be mapped out already and she would do great things once the war was over. Not that the war showed any sign of getting over. Hitler hadn't come here after all, but had invaded Russia instead; night after night there were descriptions on the news of the awful things that were done to the Russians, implanting terrible pictures in her mind.

Sometimes she listened to the news by herself, if her sisters were doing their homework and her mother was busy. She would sit opposite the wireless cabinet, watching it as she listened, amazed at the amount the newsman knew. She was on her own when he told how someone in an occupied Russian village had shot a German soldier, so the Germans rounded up everyone in the village and made one of the men stand in the centre of the square, where they burnt him very slowly, turning on him torches with flames not quite hot enough to kill him. Soon he was slipping in his own fat as he melted, like meat in a slow oven, and all the time he danced to try to escape the heat and uttered cries unlike any other human sound.

And everyone had to watch and listen as he slipped and danced and in his agony scream- ed his inhuman cry.

If Hitler came here, it would be like that. Yes, it could be like that in Netherby.

She didn't want to picture it, didn't want to keep remembering it afterwards but couldn't help it; it was as if her memory had a separate life of its own.

Once the Nazis took a Russian woman and told her that if she didn't give away the names of people fighting them they would put out her little girl's eyes. So in the end she did tell them, but they blinded her daughter just the same.

She was looking out of the window as she listened to that broadcast, knowing that if Hitler had invaded England instead of Russia, it could have happened here, here in their own back garden. It could have been her own mother, who was even now hanging out some washing, unaware of what they had all been spared.

Mr Churchill made great speeches praising the Russians, and Mrs Churchill had a special Aid to Russia Fund which raised millions of pounds and even Netherby raised nearly fifty pounds for her at the village fête. It wasn't enough, Felicity thought, nothing was enough to stop such terrible things hap- pening here.

But the next year the Russians began to

win and the German invaders were pushed back – like Napoleon had been, her father said – and on every news on the wireless there were reports of salvoes of victory by great Russian generals like Marshals Voroshilov and Zhukov and Vyshinsky. She remembered those names for the rest of her life, just as she remembered the names of newsreaders like Alvar Liddell, because they gave their names now, so that people would recognize their voices if the Germans invaded and tried to put in imposters pretending to be British newsreaders. There seemed to be no end to the wickedness the enemy would get up to.

That autumn Farmer Coltby didn't just scythe the grass, he ploughed up the paddock so that they could grow vegetables. He said it was better soil than up there on the grazing land which the Ministry was making him plough and plant corn on. When her father came up on one of his rare visits, he explained that it was necessary because we couldn't import wheat now there was a war on, and we had to grow our own. But her mother repeated what farmer Coltby had said, that it was ridiculous to plough up grazing land, only a thin layer of soil on top of stones, any fool could see it was no good.

So they argued about that too and she could hear their voices droning on as she lay in bed, because one of the things about this

64

house was that the wooden floor of the bedrooms was the ceiling of the downstairs rooms, with no space between, so you could hear sounds up and down very easily. She couldn't hear their actual words but could hear the high-pitched anger in her mother's voice, answered by the quieter, more re-strained tones of her father. On and on until she wanted to scream at them to stop.

They grew a lot of things in the paddock. Sometimes she worked with her mother on it while the other two did their homework. In the spring they raked and hoed and dug a trench to plant potatoes. They didn't talk much, not like she and her father would have done, but somehow it was easier to get on with her mother when they were doing something like this together, something where they didn't need to speak.

They planted strawberries which produced huge crops because the soil was so good and had never grown plants before. In the summer they took basketfuls of them to the farmer, who in return gave them a jar of cream, which they kept covered because farmers were only supposed to make cream for their own use and never sell it, but her mother said giving it in exchange for straw-berries wasn't selling; it was barter.

They used to go to another farm across the fields to buy eggs, which you weren't sup-posed to do, because there was a war on, so they covered the basket with rhubarb leaves in case an inspector saw them. The villagers all knew that there were inspectors everywhere; any strange man was probably one. Her mother said it was ridiculous because at this time of the year the farmers' wives had eggs to spare, so why shouldn't they be allowed to sell a few? Felicity could see the sense of that and enjoyed these outings with her mother, crossing the fields in pursuit of illegal eggs.

They always went in the evening, presumably because the inspectors would all have gone home for supper, and though they didn't talk, her mother sometimes sang. It was always hymns that she sang, and on one lovely, gentle evening when the sun was setting over the quiet fields, her mother, who had a very sweet singing voice, sang 'Now the day is over', and Felicity joined in and thought *she's all right, so long as she's not with Daddy*. And it came to her that what she must do was find a way of keeping them apart, so that they could both be happy on their own, without the other one there to quarrel with.

Five

After Arthur's death, Debbie and Vicky never climbed again on Southerby, once their favourite walk. But Felicity often went back alone; it was somehow comforting to go and sit up there, remembering. If it was sunny, she would lie on the short, warm grass, cropped by generations of sheep, and think about the things he had told her, about the rock formation and the glaciers which had shaped this landscape. He had known such a lot; she wondered how he had found it all out. He was thirteen, which had seemed a great age to her at the time, but as the years passed and she approached that age herself, she wondered at how much he'd known and how well he'd explained it and thought perhaps he would have been a teacher if he'd been allowed to grow up.

Occasionally when she thought like this, imagining the life he might have had, she felt a kind of detachment, a peaceful acceptance, and would be surprised to realize that the tears that were trickling down on to the grass were her own.

Sometimes she had imaginary conversations with him, not as she'd done when she was little, but speaking now as an equal. It was so odd to think that she would soon be older than he was – or had been – and she wondered if you can overtake the dead and, if she ever saw him again in some afterlife, would he be younger than she was, or would he have grown up too?

She worried a lot about the afterlife. When she said in the creed in church that she believed in the resurrection of the body, she really did want to believe it. To think of seeing Arthur again! But somehow it didn't make sense, however much it was reiterated in church. On the rare occasions when she could talk to her father about it, he would say that Arthur's body was gone for good, it was no longer of any use to him. Bodies were for the here and now, he said, useful on earth, belonging to time and space, useless anywhere else. She knew how much he missed Arthur, how he grieved, for he looked so much older and sadder when he came to see them, yet still he couldn't say he believed in the resurrection of the body, however much he must have wanted to believe it.

She never talked to her mother about Arthur; it seemed to be forbidden territory, but Celia knew that she believed absolutely that the dead would be resurrected, body and all. When asked, she said that everything in the creed and the Bible was true and that if you didn't believe it you went to hell.

After much thought, she decided that she had to agree with her father, and took to missing out bits when she joined in the creed at church on Sunday. She still believed in *God the Father Almighty*, so started off firmly enough, but she hesitated over the *maker of heaven and earth* because hadn't Arthur told her how glaciers had shaped the landscape and all sorts of physical forces had helped to create the world over millions and millions of years? So in the end she missed out *and earth* and just left God with the creation of heaven. That, and the *resurrection of the body*, were all she omitted at first. Later she also dropped *born of the Virgin Mary* because she was sure, quite sure, that the boy Jesus must have had a father, a proper father like her own. Maybe in those olden days they just didn't understand reproduction as well as she did, not having had the benefit of Mrs Baggs' biology lessons.

Her sisters didn't miss out bits of the creed; Vicky's voice particularly was clear and strong in announcing to the world what she believed. Of course, they'd been confirmed, so maybe that made a difference. Perhaps she'd understand it all better when her turn came.

The old vicar had retired and the new one was a young man who believed that religion should be fun and argued about like everything else, so when they met for confirmation classes in his study in the vicarage, sitting informally round the fire, he encouraged Felicity to question things. *'There lives more faith in honest doubt, believe me, than in half the creeds,'* he told her, poking the fire to make them all feel at home. He said that the others, who were mostly silent, should join in such discussions. But after a few weeks she realized that there were limits to his tolerance of honest doubt, for he would answer her queries with remarks like, 'Yes, that's *very* interesting, Felicity, but we really must *get on*,' which was so exactly like what her mother used to say, when she wanted them out of the way, that she knew the vicar didn't want her under his spiritual feet.

Thereafter she was silent, making do with the thought that probably the truth would be vouchsafed to her on confirmation day.

She shivered as she stood in the aisle wearing the white confirmation dress which had been handed down from Debbie after it had been handed down to her from Vicky, like most of her other dresses. She didn't mind having third-hand cast-offs from her sisters; in fact it made her feel more grown-up to think that Vicky had worn this when she was thirteen, which she'd thought very old at the time, and now she'd reached that great age herself. She shivered, not because she was cold in her thin white dress, but because she was excited at the thought that something momentous was going to happen. When it was her turn to kneel before the bishop, surely she would understand, see everything clearly and no longer through a glass darkly, as it said in the Bible.

It didn't happen; she felt the pressure of his hand on her head and nothing else. The disappointment was bitter, but she tried not to show it as she walked down the aisle after taking communion, knowing that her mother and sisters were watching her. Her godmother wasn't there; as a result of an unfortunate car accident some time ago, her mother said, Agatha Beale was still being detained in Gradby.

Later that year her father came up for one of his rare weekends and by a wonderful piece of luck his visit coincided with the annual village fête, which was the best day of every summer. For a start it was always sunny and the grown-ups were always in a good mood. Some of them even dressed up and joined in the procession through the village, like the time the village carpenter, a very neat and tidy man, dressed as a tramp, all ragged, with his shirt tail hanging out of his torn trousers and a battered old saucepan dangling from a piece of string round his middle. And his spotless, house-proud wife blacked her face and went as a sweep. Next day they were back to normal, as if it had never happened.

The first time she'd gone in the procession, she'd been dressed as Alice in Wonderland, with her hair loose down her back, and had suddenly felt her head being pulled backwards. It was Mrs Coltby's pony, supposed to be Black Bess with Mrs Coltby on its back disguised as Dick Turpin, which was tugging as it took in mouthfuls of her hair.

''E thowt it were straw,' the farmer's wife explained, and then, seeing her tears, gave her a sweet.

She was much older now, of course, and went as a suffragette with a placard demanding *Votes for Women* hung around her neck. Vicky was a beautiful Queen Elizabeth: tall and stately, her golden hair piled on top of her head, despite the lack of hairpins, she looked truly regal, everyone said. Debbie wasn't so convincing as Queen Victoria; she really wasn't fat enough and looked too nervous.

They processed from the far end of the village, past the green and the cross and the church, all the way down to the big house at the far end. The fields were covered in stalls; apart from boring things like plant stalls and bric-à-brac, there were always bran tubs and hoop-la and bowling for the pig. But this year there was something different. There was a tent where you could buy a stamp from the vicar for sixpence and then stick it on a huge bomb case so that the money would go to pay for another bomb to beat the Germans and you'd know it was your bomb because it had your stamp on it. She took her sixpence, bought her stamp and took her time choosing exactly where to put it on the big iron shell which would one day house the Netherby bomb.

They all walked home together that evening, Vicky and Debbie slightly ahead, Vicky still dressed as Queen Elizabeth, for which she'd won a prize of half-a-crown. Debbie had sneaked home and changed out of her uncomfortable Victorian dress into a cotton frock which had been handed down from Vicky, though Felicity could see that it didn't look as good on her as it had done on Vicky last summer; Debbie didn't seem to fill it out in the way Vicky had done. But, though sorry for her sister, she felt very content as she walked home, her hand in her father's and the light breeze soft against her cheeks, which still tingled from the day's sunshine. It was a peaceful feeling, especially because they were all chatting in a friendly way, her mother telling them that her tea tent had made £15.18.2d, which was far more than any of the stalls, her father wondering how the postman would cope with the pig he'd won, her mother explaining that he'd probably give it to a farmer and in exchange be given half of the meat when it was killed, which was against regulations, but then some of the regulations were so stupid that it was your duty to disobey them.

They all agreed with her, Vicky turning round to say so and then announcing that she was going to the dance in the village hall that always rounded off the evening of the fête. Her mother said it was disgraceful that last year the dancing had gone on a quarter of an hour after midnight and so broken the Sabbath. But her father pointed out that if God didn't acknowledge the existence of Double Summer Time, the Sabbath would not begin until two o'clock the next morning. They all laughed except her mother, who couldn't say much because she'd always been against Double Summer Time on the grounds that it was unnatural and against God's order of things. She agreed with those farmers who ignored it and kept what they called God's Time. So she stayed silent now but looked grim and the atmosphere changed and wasn't happy any more.

Evidently sensing this, her father remarked conversationally, 'It's a shame there had to be that tent with the bomb case, when everything else was so good. It's horrible to encourage children to stick stamps on a bomb that's going to kill other children.'

'Nonsense!' her mother exclaimed. 'Where's your patriotism? You're so *soft*,

74

Sebastian. A man with any spirit should be delighted to do anything to kill Germans.'

It wasn't just about the bomb, Felicity realized; his funny remark about God and Double Summer Time still rankled with her mother. So they went on about it and by the time they reached the gate at the bottom of the drive, they were both silent and the air tense between them, and she knew that if she tried to make it better by saying something, she would only sound silly and probably make things worse.

About the bomb, she wasn't sure which side she was on.

'But we've got to beat them, haven't we?' she said when her father came up to say goodnight to her. It was still daylight; Double Summer Time meant that it was never dark when she went to bed nowadays. 'I mean, otherwise they'll beat us, won't they?'

He came and sat down on the side of her bed.

'Yes, darling,' he said. 'I think it's what we call a just war. Much more than the last war, for it's like the police having to act to stop a thief or a murderer.'

He paused, then went on, 'But never forget, Felicity, that most of the German families are like ours, their children aren't responsible any more than you are. So, yes, this war has to be fought, but not in a spirit

75

of hatred for all Germans. And we certainly shouldn't encourage children like you to revel in it.'

'So you don't think the vicar should have had that tent with the bomb case in it?'

He hesitated.

'I'm sure he meant well,' he said at last.

She'd always thought that when the war ended, it would be sudden but it wasn't. On the first of May they heard on the wireless that Hitler was dead and everyone went mad with joy, even her mother, for it seemed that the war *must* be over, but no, somebody called Admiral Doenitz, whom nobody had ever heard of until now, so christened him Admiral Doughnuts, took over in Germany instead. But then the next day, Wednesday, Italy surrendered and everyone said that it must mean the war was over. But it wasn't. Then Berlin fell, but still the war wasn't over. Then on May 6th she heard John Snagge on the wireless say that all the Germans in Denmark had surrendered and again everyone said the war must be over, but still it wasn't. That was on Sunday, which would have been a lovely day, she thought, for a war to end. But it wasn't until Monday that they heard it, having sat staring at the wireless all the evening. At last it happened, the war was officially over and the next day was to be called Victory in Europe

Day and was to be a national holiday and so was Wednesday, too. Furthermore, they were told that night on the news, that, 'Until the end of May you may buy cotton bunting without coupons, as long as it is red, white or blue and doesn't cost more than one and three a square yard.'

Most people didn't wait to hear that; the church bell was ringing and everyone had run out into the street, and they were all shouting and hugging each other and kept saying, 'It's over, it's over, no more blackout, no more bombs,' and they said it in that order because in Netherby everyone had been more frightened of the ARP men than they had of bombs, because only one had fallen and that was in a field miles away from anywhere, whereas the ARP men were there all the time, banging on your door if they could see the tiniest bit of light, threatening penalties and telling you it would be your fault if Hitler bombed the village and killed everybody.

It was the women who made plans for the celebration. The next day her mother sent Debbie and Vicky into Pendlebury to get the bunting which had somehow miraculously appeared in the draper's, so that the Women's Institute could make flags for the children to wave, and red white and blue cloths to put on the trestle tables for a great tea party. Felicity was sent across the fields with half-a-crown to buy eggs and realized when she was nearly there that she'd forgotten to bring rhubarb leaves to cover them, then remembered she didn't need them now that the war was over.

The trouble was that she couldn't imagine what peace would be like; it was easier for Vicky and Debbie because they could remember what it had been like before the war, but she hadn't anything to go back to. It was only as she sat down with her sisters at the street party the next day, and saw the amazing spread – because everyone had given their rations of butter and margarine and sugar to make cakes, and their points to make jellies – that she thought, this is what peace will be like, marvellous food all the time, and said so, but Vicky told her not to be so silly, of course rationing would go on for a while, because the food couldn't just reappear overnight, could it?

In the evening they climbed up Westerbirt, where all day long the men had been gathering firewood into a huge pile, so now all the young people, and some of the old ones, gathered up there impatiently waiting for darkness to fall so that the bonfire could be lit. Somebody said they should have made an effigy of Hitler and put him on it like they did the Kaiser in the last war, but others joined in and said it would be a waste of clothes and anyway he was dead and burning in hell.

She didn't hear any more because suddenly the fire was ablaze and a great cheer went up and people were singing 'There'll always be an England' and 'Auld Lang Syne' and any other cheerful song they could think of.

They stood for a long time watching the fire, feeling the warmth of it on their faces, until the heat drove them back. Vicky and Debbie began remembering bonfire parties they'd been to before the war, but Felicity had never seen a fire at night and watched in silent wonder as it roared and crackled in the clear night sky, shooting flames up and out of sight, lighting up the faces of the bystanders when it flared, leaving them in the shadows as it died down, only to flare up again and transform them in its shifting light.

And everywhere else they were lighting beacons too; all the other villages and market towns and even little hamlets had their bonfires, so that it seemed as if a whole chain of beacons had been lit. An old man standing near them said it was like the bonfires that had been prepared a hundred and forty years ago in case Napoleon invaded. He said his grandfather had told him how he had seen them being built when he was a little boy.

Felicity pondered these words as she

walked with her sisters back to the village, reluctantly leaving the last smouldering ashes of the bonfire. She was enthralled by the idea of all the changes that had happened since the old man's grandfather had seen the beacons; if people who'd lived in 1805 could be dropped down now into 1945, they'd see changes they couldn't believe in. They wouldn't know what cars were, or aeroplanes or trains or how to use gas cookers or Hoovers or typewriters. Yet each little year was a tiny link in a chain, which joined the past to the present, and the changes must have seemed imperceptible as they were actually happening, year by little year.

She was shaken out of her reverie by hearing Debbie shout, 'Look at that!'

Netherby, nestling in the dark valley, seemed ablaze. As they hurried towards it they could see that everyone had turned on their lights and flung back the curtains, so that every window was brilliantly lit. Some had torches which they waved in the sky and others had candles in jam jars. Somebody had rigged up Christmas tree lights in the chestnut tree by the church. Netherby was celebrating the end of the blackout; there would be no more tripping over kerbs and bumping into trees on dark winter nights, no more missing the footpath and falling into the beck, no more reign of terror by ARP men. They looked rather sad now, the ARP men, standing there, not sure whether to join in. They seemed older and less fierce and it was hard not to feel sorry for them because they were suddenly just like everybody else and not important any more. The stick, which one of them always carried, seemed less like a weapon now, more like a prop for his gammy leg.

Even more startling than the lights was to see usually sedate men and women doing the hokey-cokey down the village street, winding round the cross on the green, flinging their arms, legs, hips and any other bit of them in and out as they sang. Everyone seemed to want to make as much noise as possible; the village hall piano, dragged out into the porch, was being loudly played by the church organist while her elderly father beat a drum he'd had in the last war. Children banged dustbin lids and nobody told them to stop.

There was less excitement when the war with Japan came to an end three months later. On a hot day in August, Felicity saw the word Hiroshima in a great headline in the newspaper and wondered how to pronounce it, so went to ask her father, home for the first time in six months. Evidently this huge bomb had been dropped on Japan, bigger than all the other bombs put together.

Naturally it was the cause for another disagreement between her parents, she thought afterwards. Then she corrected herself – getting words right was beginning to matter to her – it was just the *occasion* for argument, because they'd have found something to disagree about anyway.

Her mother was jubilant like most other people. The war would now end and the wicked Japanese should be made to suffer like the wicked Germans. She heard her saying so as she lay in bed that night. It was a stuffy night, all windows wide open and her parents sitting just below hers in the garden.

'But it's a great city, Celia, full of women and children. They'll be incinerated, blinded, skinned alive, and who knows what the effect will be on future generations.'

'Good. It was time they were taught a lesson.'

'It could have been demonstrated, dropped on some uninhabited island.'

'Well, the war is over, that's the main thing.'

There was a pause; she could imagine her father about to say more, then restraining himself. Perhaps he would give a little shrug, perhaps his mouth would turn down for a moment in a subconscious grimace that said it was hopeless to argue.

'So what do you plan to do?' her mother

asked.

'I must stay in London. The devastation is terrible, Celia. It's a great chance to rebuild something better because not everything that was destroyed was good and—'

'So you won't be going back to Gradby?' her mother interrupted.

'No. Did you want to? Are you disappointed?'

'No, I don't want to leave here.'

'Really?' he was more surprised than he should have been, Felicity thought. That her mother had settled here was obvious, but then he didn't see her as much as she did, so couldn't be expected to know.

'So you wouldn't want to come to London?' he was asking.

'No.'

That didn't surprise her either; she had heard her mother refer to the capital as 'that sink of iniquity'.

There was a pause, then her father said, very carefully, very gravely, 'I think in that case it would be as well if we separated.'

'I'll never divorce you, if that's what you mean. I gave you the chance once and you didn't take it.'

'But, Celia, you know that we haven't been happy for a long time—'

'*I'm* all right.'

'We'll talk about it another time,' he said, sounding suddenly very weary.

'There's nothing to discuss, as far as I'm concerned,' she said, and there was the sound of cups being gathered together and carried into the kitchen.

Six

'The war may be over,' they heard an old woman say in the shop when they went to buy a bottle of Tizer for their picnic, 'but it doesn't seem to have made much difference to the rations.'

'Butter still only four ounces a week,' Mrs Bushell agreed, 'and they talk of rationing bread now.'

'It's no better than it was,' the old woman said.

Felicity felt she would burst with rage, but managed to contain it until the three of them were out of the shop.

'It's *wicked* to talk like that!' she exploded once they were out of earshot. 'I mean, *everything*'s different. There aren't any bombs any more and—'

'We didn't have any bombs in Netherby,' Vicky said. 'Don't get so excited, Flea. It's childish.'

'All right, we didn't have any bombs, but we had the ARP and the blackout and we never knew if parachutists would drop down on us and anyway, even if *we* didn't have any bombs, what about the people in towns bombed every night? And the men who were killed fighting?'

'She didn't say she wanted the war to go on, Flea, she just said peace hadn't made much difference to her.'

'But, Vicky, it *has*. Buses aren't blacked out any more and the towns and villages have got their names back again and they've put the signposts up so you know how to get to them—'

'She probably knows how to get to anywhere she wants to go anyway.'

Oh, Vicky was so cool and so logical but she, Felicity, just *knew* she'd got it all wrong.

'Well, I just feel that it's as if all this is ours again,' and she spread out her arms to embrace the lane down which they were walking, the fields all around them, the trees beyond, the beck that awaited them, sparkling in the sun, and the place beside it where they would have their picnic. 'It's as if,' she ended passionately, 'our country *belongs* to us again.'

'But,' Debbie objected, 'there still aren't any hair slides or bananas.'

It was no good arguing against the two of them. She gave up and just said, 'I can't remember bananas. What did they taste like?'

'Well,' Debbie said slowly. 'They tasted like, well like, you know, bananas.'

'That's a lot of help,' Felicity told her. 'I'll go and put the Tizer to cool,' and she ran on ahead, jumped down the bank to the beck and, by the packhorse bridge, jammed the bottle between the stump of an old thorn bush and a large stone.

There was a flat stretch of sand and tiny pebbles down there, which made it seem like a miniature shingly beach. The water was shallow as she squatted on her haunches, gazing into the beck. There was an island which she used to jump on to when she was little, and make up all kinds of stories; she used to stand on it and imagine that it was her own country with the sea all around it. Now it was just a little island which she could reach in one stride.

How everything has changed, she thought, looking up at the bridge where Arthur no longer cast his home-made rod, which had seemed so impressive at the time but which she now knew could never have caught anything, not even a bullhead, let alone a trout. And the family had changed, Arthur gone, Sarah gone, her mother and father – she didn't understand what was happening, but it was certainly going to be different.

Yet nothing had changed down here by the

beck. Caddis worms still crawled slowly across the pebbles, dragging their burden of sand and twigs, while minnows darted past them, unencumbered. Dragonflies still swooped down, flashes of brilliance over the water. Pond boatmen still looked like miniature oarsmen as they rowed their way across the stream, and water skaters still skimmed its surface. There must have been generations of them since she first came here all those years ago. Sometimes it seemed heartless of nature to go on as if nothing had happened. Sometimes it seemed reassuring; if things were going on just the same *here*, perhaps somewhere – anywhere – Arthur might be going on too.

Today was one of the reassuring days; it was soothing to be here by the stream, feeling the sun on her head, prickling her arms, warm on her back even through her Aertex blouse.

'You'll peel,' Vicky called across to her. 'You should put some oil on.'

'Too sticky,' she called back.

Vicky was sitting under the weeping willow, writing her diary. She wore a big straw hat. It was a battered old thing, which would have looked awful on anyone else, but somehow everything looked all right on Vicky.

Higher up, on the grassy bank, Debbie was lying on her stomach, exposing her back to the sun in the hope that it would cure her spots. She was wearing a triangular garment on her front. She'd spent ages making it from a pattern she'd read about in a Make-do-and-Mend article in the paper. The article explained how you could make the sun top by using any bit of material, even old blackout material, just by cutting it into a triangle with the top chopped off. The base of the triangle should be your waist measurement and you turned it up and threaded some tape through it. The top was your neck measurement and you did the same at that end. Then you tied the top tape round your neck and the bottom one round your waist. Debbie had read all this out to them and shown them the picture of the pretty girl wearing the finished article.

But it hadn't turned out at all like the picture. It looked awful on poor Debbie; the curtain material was baggy yet stiff and the sides gaped.

Felicity was sorry for her; somehow nothing Debbie ever did seemed to turn out quite right. Yet she went on thinking that it would, every time. Perhaps it was just as well; it would be worse for Debbie if she didn't even have hope.

'You mustn't wear it where anyone can see you,' Vicky had ordered.

'It'll be all right to wear it down there by the beck,' Felicity had pointed out. 'Hardly anyone comes that way.'

So Debbie had carried her sun top with her, then hidden herself behind the wall when they arrived and put on her new creation. At least when, silently, she lay herself down on her front, the dreadful garment didn't show.

It wasn't only about clothes that things always went wrong for Debbie, Felicity thought, watching her sister as she lay there. Nature too seemed to have it in for her, giving her spots and then, last winter, inflicting worms upon her, like some Old Testament plague. And only on *her*; why the little threadworms should have taken up their abode in Debbie and not in her sisters was evidently a medical mystery.

Poor Debbie had felt like an outcast; her towel had to be kept very carefully away from everyone else's and her white knicker linings had to be boiled in a special pan.

'I wish I could swallow some poison and kill them,' she had said desperately as she sat, pale-faced, on the edge of the bed while they waited for the doctor

'Oh, you mustn't,' Felicity had implored, panic-stricken. 'It would kill you too.'

Vicky had told them not to be so silly, pointing out that there wasn't any poison in the house anyway and asking them if they didn't realize why their mother had got the enema out of the airing cupboard.

It was a sinister thing, the enema; an object of horror which lay curled up and snake-like in a box with a cellophane front so you could see its horrible rubber coils, like entrails, with a bulb at the end, which was for squeezing. Poor Debbie had had to lie on the bed and have soapy water pumped into her bottom. Afterwards she'd said it didn't really hurt, just made her feel as if she was going to explode.

No, what really hurt, Felicity knew, was the dreadful indignity of it; it wasn't the sort of thing you could imagine anyone doing to Vicky, even if worms had dared to invade her beautiful body.

It had, indirectly, been the occasion of yet another disagreement between their parents because, as the doctor left, after purifying Debbie's entrails in this ghastly manner, they had heard their mother say, 'If this health scheme which the government is plotting goes ahead, we want nothing to do with it. You will please send your bill as usual.'

She had said the same to Sebastian when he came up later in the year and he, of course, had said the opposite. It was a good scheme, he said, long overdue; everyone should pay into it and be treated free when they needed it. It was just like any other insurance, he said, only for everybody, which was why it was called National Health.

Celia didn't listen.

'I don't hold with socialized medicine,' she kept repeating.

In the end it had all fizzled out, because next time the doctor called she said she'd only be taking National Health patients anyway but would try to find another doctor for Celia and her family.

They could see that Celia was taken aback, because everyone knew that Dr Mack was the best in the land and even Debbie didn't want anyone else for a doctor. So in the end Celia gave in and never mentioned the subject again.

It was so hot by midday that they had to eat their picnic in the shade of the willow tree. Crickets had started to sing in the long grass, but the rest of the animal world was silent; in the field the sheep sought out the shade of the walls and lay inert against them. The lambs, which looked bigger than their mothers since shearing, ceased their bleating. The cows clustered under the trees and the young colt stayed alongside its mother, instead of prancing about the field as it usually did.

Felicity, barefooted, went down to the beck to retrieve the bottle of Tizer. Vicky poured it out into the mugs. It was ice cold so that you shivered as it slid like a little glacier down your warm, dry throat.

'Oh, lovely,' Felicity exclaimed. 'Everything's lovely today.'

Vicky sighed.

'I just can't wait to get away,' she said.

The other two stared at her, shocked. They knew she was leaving the next day, of course, to go to London, staying for a few days with their father in his lodgings and then going to Cambridge, but they'd thought she'd be a bit sad about going away from them and from Netherby.

'I'm going to help Daddy find a flat,' she said. 'And I'll be like his hostess because Mummy doesn't want to come. And I'll choose something really nice so you can both stay there too. Of course, I shall spend my vacations there and some weekends.'

It all sounded very grand; Debbie and Felicity listened in surprise but not disbelief. Neither of them could have dreamed of doing such a thing, but when Vicky wanted to arrange something, she always got her own way.

'I don't understand,' Debbie began, and stopped. 'I mean, if Daddy has to work in London, why doesn't Mummy go too?'

'She doesn't want to.'

'How do you know, Flea?'

Felicity hesitated. She couldn't say she'd heard them talking about it; it would sound like eavesdropping, which it wasn't really because if people choose to talk under your open window on a summer night when you're lying quietly in bed, they're *making* you listen. You can't help it. Well, you could get out of bed and get into a cupboard or something, but you'd probably get into trouble for doing so. Or you could stuff cotton wool in your ears, if you had any cotton wool, which she hadn't. Cotton wool was far too precious and was kept for emergencies in the medicine chest with the lint and the bandages.

'Because it's obvious,' she said at last. 'She likes it here and she doesn't like London, because of its wickedness.'

'Flea's right,' Vicky surprisingly said. 'They live different lives and should be divorced.'

'*Divorced?*' Debbie could hardly get out the dreadful word. 'But they couldn't do that.'

'Why not? People do.'

'People like lords and film stars and Americans get divorced, not people like us.'

'Yes, they do.'

'All right then, tell me one person we know who's been divorced,' Debbie demanded, assertive for once.

Vicky tried – and failed. 'Well, I don't actually *know* anyone, not personally,' she said.

'There you are then. It doesn't happen.'

'It does, Debbie, it's just that we don't happen to know anyone who's done it. Besides, everyone says that what happens in America first, happens in Britain next. As we get more sophisticated, divorce will get more common.'

Debbie didn't reply, silenced as usual by Vicky's superior knowledge of the world.

Instead she turned to Felicity and said, 'Oh Flea, wouldn't it be awful to have divorced parents? Nobody at school has divorced parents. I can't bear to think of it,' she added desperately.

'No, it wouldn't be dreadful, Debbie,' Felicity tried to reassure her, 'not if they were better apart.'

'But where would *we* belong? I mean, home is where they *both* are.'

'Well, they haven't been together for six years, so it wouldn't be very different,' Vicky told her.

A false argument, Felicity knew, and Debbie was not misled by it.

'But that was only because of the war,' she said. 'Lots of parents were apart during the war. Being apart because of a war is different from being apart because you're divorced.'

'Debbie,' Felicity said, wanting to get the argument back on the right track. 'We'd still see both of them, only separately.'

'Oh, well, yes, I suppose so.'

Felicity turned to Vicky.

'There is just something,' she said. 'I mean, she may not agree to it.'

She couldn't very well say she knew her

mother wouldn't have a divorce, because she'd heard her say so in the garden that evening.

'I know,' Vicky agreed. 'But she'll come round to it. It would be different if she was prepared to try to make a go of the marriage, but she isn't. She doesn't even pretend to want to live with him. She'd be happier if it was all settled. They're just incompatible, that's all there is to it.'

As usual, Vicky made everything simple.

'And don't worry, you two,' she said in her most adult voice, as if they were both years younger than she was. 'I'll find Daddy a really nice flat and you shall come whenever you like.'

'So when you go tomorrow,' Debbie said, 'that's really the end, isn't it? There'll just be the two of us here.'

And when Debbie leaves school, Felicity thought, *there'll just be me.*

Somehow, after that, nothing seemed much fun any more; they talked in a desultory way as they drank the Tizer, finished their date sandwiches and rock cakes and scattered the crumbs. And when Debbie said, 'Shall we go back now?' Vicky promptly agreed. 'Yes, do let's, I've all my packing to do ready for tomorrow.'

Debbie, crimson-backed, went behind the wall to remove her sun top, Felicity helped Vicky to pack away the picnic things, then they all walked slowly down the lane back to Netherby, not saying much.

It seemed to Felicity that in the term after Vicky had left, school work suddenly became more serious; already they were talking about that dreaded certificate and muttering about working on the syllabus. Fortunately this coincided with everything beginning to make more sense, she realized one morning, quite suddenly. Well, not quite everything, because science was still meaningless, but French and Latin could be got right if you spent time on the agreements, and English she loved and history too. Geography was bad because it mattered to be able to draw neat little maps and she still got into trouble for being untidy.

The head sent for her one day and to her horror she saw that all her exercise books, every subject, were laid out on her desk.

'I want you to look at these pages,' the head said.

They did look awful, blotched, the writing all over the place, slanting sometimes one way, sometimes another.

'It isn't just that your writing is illegible,' the head was saying, 'but it also looks illiterate. Look at it and give me your opinion.'

She presumed that the head wanted her opinion about which was worse, illegibility or the appearance of illiteracy. She'd have thought it worse to be illegible, because surely it didn't matter much about *looking* illiterate as long as you could read it. So she said so.

Apparently that wasn't the kind of opinion the head was soliciting. She had a vague notion that the head always found her exasperating.

It was with the head that she started her School Certificate scripture lessons the next year. They were a select little group and at first the head, like the vicar at confirmation classes, encouraged discussion. Gradually, like the vicar, she seemed to decide the advantage of free discussion could be overrated. After a particularly long argument about faith, in which the head said that since we all have to take on trust things we don't understand, like electricity or the wireless, we should also be able to take the existence of God on trust. The rest nodded, but Felicity pointed out that the logical deduction from that was you could believe absolutely anything. Moreover, although the head might not understand the working of the wireless, plenty of people did and could explain it to her.

It was a hot afternoon; the head sighed, and said, 'That is enough, Felicity. St Matthew is a very long gospel and we really must get on.'

Somehow from the time of that unfortunate business of the false teeth, she always seemed to be in trouble with authority. Vicky seemed to know what they were getting at so instinctively said what they wanted to hear, which made them consider her very responsible, so they let her do as she liked. Debbie never argued with them, just complied. But she, Felicity, though she wanted to oblige, somehow never seemed quite able to get it right.

Debbie had a very good report at the end of the year; it was prophesied that she would do well in her Higher and for her Conduct she had the single word *excellent*. Felicity's marks were good too, but her Conduct said, *Felicity has an independent and thoughtful mind but must learn to conform.*

'There, that's what I'm always telling you,' her mother said angrily, holding up the report as if it justified all the criticisms she had heaped, to no avail, on her youngest child's head. 'You just won't *give in*, will you?'

Seven

They sat, Sebastian and Diana, leaning against the sea wall, sheltered from the gale-force winds. Barbed wire and land mines, designed to deter invasion, still decorated the beach. Below them the sea crashed angrily at the shore as if determined to tear it to pieces, then retreated, growling and frustrated, dragging the shingle with it, only to return again, the waves roaring in, crashing against the rocks and then hissing as they slithered back after each unsuccessful onslaught.

'It's different now,' Diana said.

He nodded, knowing what she meant: war had made permissible things previously unthinkable. But now peace had broken out, bringing back with it the conventions of peacetime. For both of them they were more than conventions, these assumptions, they were moral absolutes. Things were back to normal after abnormal times.

They sat, remembering those times when love and death had seemed intertwined: that first night when the bombs fell on his parents' house while they made love in the shelter, knowing that if they'd stayed in the house five minutes longer they would both have been dead. That was how it was when war could suddenly burst in, smashing what had seemed calm and secure. That was how it had been a few weeks later when they'd walked on a clear-skied afternoon in Sussex, breathing in the fresh country air, rejoicing in a day out of London. In a little wood they had lain down on lush and mossy grass, gazing up through the pattern of branches at the pure blue beyond. It was very still, only the sounds of birdsong, of insects in the grass, of bees droning busily in the bushes; in this murmurous wood, war seemed far away. Suddenly they heard a deeper, louder droning and the sky was alive with aeroplanes, turning and diving, making patterns in the sky as, fighting, they plunged and twisted. The air exploded with sound, with the rattling of machine guns and the shrieking wail of sirens; then the bombs began to fall, thudding down, so that the trees shook and the earth quivered. They'd stayed locked together, mouth to mouth, looking into each other's eyes, curiously calm, awaiting death. But death moved on, the sounds faded, the sky cleared. And they made love there, under the trees. And it seemed right, natural, love and death. Then they walked out of the woods and saw that, over the fields, buildings were burning, ambulances arriving, and they ran across to help the injured and seek out the dead.

That was how it was then, with danger ever present and love equally present, vital and assertive. It was no time to plan any kind of future together, just brave the present. But now a different reality prevailed, peace had returned, bringing back the rules.

'I'm going to see the solicitor tomorrow,' he told her. 'About the divorce.'

'But will she agree to it?' She couldn't say her cousin's name, not in this context anyway.

'She's implied that yes, if she was paid a certain sum.'

He had realized in the last few years that Celia had begun to show symptoms of her aunt's miserliness, pressing him for small sums, for anything which could be construed as a necessary extra, although he paid her a generous allowance. So he had suggested that a payment, secret of course, because illegal, might make divorce more acceptable. And she had agreed.

'And the children, Sebastian, what about the girls?'

She was looking anxiously up at him, fearing to do anything which might upset his children. She seemed more worried about them, Sebastian often thought, than

Celia was.

'I think they'll understand. Felicity has actually said to me that we're nicer people apart from each other. And of course, Vicky is quite grown up now and very understanding.'

'And Debbie?'

'I think she'll be guided by Vicky. She usually is. But she's insecure. I honestly do think that you would help her a very great deal. In fact I think all of them will benefit. I know that sounds a selfish thing to say—'

'No, my darling, it's not selfish. I only want to do anything I can to help them, not hurt them in any way. And not have them feel any divided loyalty. I want to encourage them to see their mother as often as they can. I want to work with her if possible.'

He doubted if it was possible, yet he was reassured by her words. Taking her head between his hands he turned her face towards him so he could look into her eyes.

'I love you,' he said simply. 'And want only to be with you for the rest of my life.'

They sat close together, unmoving for a while until she broke the spell by asking, 'They're good, are they, the solicitors?'

'Baintree and Dalton. They specialize in this sort of thing. A chap in the Ministry gave me their name. I said I was enquiring for a friend, of course.'

'Of course.'

★ ★ ★

The offices of Baintree and Dalton might have been used for a set for a play about a Dickensian firm of solicitors. There was a dustiness about their offices and everything in them. Dust lay deep on the linoleum in the waiting-room and danced in the rays of light which filtered through the dirty window. Dust rose from the moquette cushion of the chair when Sebastian sat down; he could feel dust in his nostrils as he waited, and he sneezed as he followed the elderly secretary up the narrow uncarpeted stairs to Mr Baintree's equally dusty office with its piles of faded papers and beribboned documents.

Mr Baintree, however, was anything but dusty. A clean-shaven man, he had a sharp little face and penetrating eyes. Though in his fifties, his face was remarkably youthful and unlined. Sebastian, shaking hands, decided he liked and could trust him.

He sat down opposite him on the other side of the desk, where Mr Baintree pulled a sheet of paper towards him and sat, pen poised.

'Married?'

'Well, yes,' Sebastian said, thinking it an odd question to ask a man seeking divorce.

A slight smile.

'I was enquiring as to the date,' Mr Baintree said.

103

'Oh, yes, sorry. 1926.'

He felt foolish, realized that he was hating this.

'Children?'

'Three.'

Oh, Arthur, my first-born, what would you have thought of your father now?

'And your wife is seeking a divorce?'

'No, I am the one seeking it. We are totally incompatible.'

The solicitor smiled, sat back in his chair and made a steeple with his fingers.

'I think, Mr Crawley, I have some explaining to do. The only grounds for divorce are adultery, desertion without cause, cruelty and insanity.'

'But if two people are incompatible, can't they agree to—'

Mr Baintree held up his hands in horror.

'If you are suggesting that people might *agree* to divorce, I must warn you that such a thing is collusion and if the King's Proctor got wind of it, your decree nisi might never become absolute.'

'It seems ridiculous. I mean, it's against all common sense. If people are incompatible, if the marriage has broken down, surely that should be the only sane reason for divorce?'

'That may be what the future holds, Mr Crawley, but it is not in the here and now. I must remind you,' he went on sharply, 'that we are not speaking of what *you* might regard as common sense. We are speaking of the *law*. In the absence of any conjugal offence by your wife – and I take it your wife has not committed adultery ...'

Would that she had, Sebastian thought to himself. 'And there is no chance that she will,' he said aloud.

'Then in the absence of any conjugal offence by your wife and any cruel behaviour by you to her, you have two options: either you leave her and allow her after three years to petition for divorce on the grounds of desertion—'

'She won't do that,' Sebastian interrupted. 'She wants us to live apart but she won't seek divorce on the grounds of desertion.'

'Then she must petition for divorce on the grounds of your adultery. I expect you know the procedure?'

'Vaguely. I believe you go to a hotel with some woman and the hotel bill is proof of infidelity.'

'About fifty per cent right,' Mr Baintree said, looking at him with an examiner's eye. 'You and the woman you refer to may sit up all night playing patience, or she may go to bed and you may sleep in a chair. That is up to you, but in the morning you must be in bed together when the maid brings in the tea, so that later she can be called to identify you and give evidence.'

'And how does one find such a person?'

The solicitor hesitated, then, 'Do you wish to remarry?' he asked.

'Yes.'

'The lady you wish to marry might possibly ... ?'

'Absolutely not. I shouldn't dream of asking her.'

'Then I'm afraid I can't help you,' Mr Baintree said, suddenly more formal. 'You realize that by even discussing the possibility of practising this deception on the court we are committing an offence? Adultery as grounds for divorce should be adultery, not some faked transaction in a hotel with a lady unknown to you.'

'I see.'

'I should point out to you,' Mr Baintree said very solemnly, 'that these rules exist to protect the public and uphold the sanctity of marriage.'

Unable to think of a suitable reply, Sebastian got up to go. They shook hands very formally, but as he opened the door for him, Mr Baintree said, 'I have heard there is a very respectable typing agency which has a department specializing in personal services. By name of Glossop, I believe. Good afternoon, Mr Crawley.'

No office could have been more different from Baintree and Dalton's than that of the agency run by the Glossop sisters. No dust dared inflict itself on the ante-room where Sebastian, whom nervousness had made early, waited for his appointment. The patterned carpet had a newly hoovered look, the paintwork gleamed, the chairs, modern and uncomfortable, might have come straight from the factory. There was a faint smell of disinfectant about the whole place.

On the highly polished table an array of brochures was laid out; seeking distraction, he picked one up and learned that he could have typing done for one shilling and six-pence per thousand words, a carbon copy being provided for a mere ninepence. Any-thing from a couple of pages to the manu-script of a full-length book could be man-aged by Glossop's agency, whose employees' work was swift and accurate. Estimates could be supplied immediately and work could be posted to any address in the United Kingdom if required.

It all seemed far removed from talk of dirty weekends in Brighton. It occurred to him suddenly that he might have made a mistake; perhaps Baintree was only telling him about an agency which did confidential work of a personal nature, maybe typing reports on staff that businesses did not want to be seen by their own typists. Yes, personal services, in this clean and businesslike room, were much more likely to mean something like that. He'd better get out before he made an utter fool of himself, he thought, standing up, hesitant, wanting to leave but held back by the thought that he might be losing his only chance of ever being married to Diana.

As he stood, uncertain, the door opened and a woman came in, introducing herself as Miss Glossop. She was tall, elegant, fortyish, dressed discreetly in grey. She looked exactly as a woman who ran an efficient secretarial agency should look.

'Come through to my office, Mr Crawley,' she said, after they had shaken hands. Her voice was well modulated, her vowels immaculate.

Her office too was immaculate. She sat down at her uncluttered desk and he sat, facing her, wishing she was a man; to talk of such things to this very respectable woman went against everything in his nature and upbringing.

'Mr Crawley,' she began, sounding brisk and businesslike. 'You mentioned when you made this appointment that you had need of our personal service. I take it you are seeking a divorce?'

Oh, the relief! He wouldn't have to explain.

'Our personal department is experienced in these cases. I imagine you are not?'

'Not at all, I'm afraid. But my solicitor has explained something of what is involved.'

'You are aware then that you will sign the hotel register as Mr and Mrs Crawley and that you will share a bedroom? In the morning the maid will come in and see you in bed together. Try to make an impression on her so that later, when she is called to give evidence, she will be sure to remember you. Our employee will be able to give good advice on how that is best done.'

'And this employee? How shall I—? I mean, do we meet beforehand?'

'You will travel to Brighton together. I have already given the matter some thought and I am going to ask Miss Agatha Kibble to come down to meet you.'

Agatha! Ill-fated name. A mad fear that he would be confronted by Agatha Beale momentarily flashed into his mind.

'Is that all right, Mr Crawley? You look troubled.'

'No, it's fine. I'm sorry,' he added, realizing he was grinning at the nonsensical idea of Agatha Beale in such employment.

Miss Glossop rang a bell and a girl appeared.

'Ask Miss Kibble to step down, would you, please, Betty?'

The girl nodded, disappeared and in a remarkably short time there was a knock on the door and a woman whom he took to be this other Agatha came in.

He was relieved to see that this woman, with whom the law was forcing him to spend a night in Brighton, in order to uphold the sanctity of marriage, was a pleasant-looking person, not much younger than himself. She was neither dowdy nor too smart. Her expression was open and friendly as she shook hands with him.

'How do you do, Mr Crawley?' she said.

Her voice was warm, with a slightly northern accent.

'You will travel down together,' Miss Glossop said. 'Have you a date in mind, Mr Crawley?'

'As soon as possible. I'd like to get it over as soon as I can,' Sebastian said and then stopped and added apologetically, 'I'm sorry, Miss Kibble, I didn't mean to be discourteous. I mean, it's very kind of you to help in this way.'

He was floundering but Miss Kibble cut in to put him at ease, 'It's a business arrangement, Mr Crawley,' she said gently. 'I understand that.'

'And what travel arrangement have you in mind, Mr Crawley?'

'Oh, I'm afraid I hadn't thought about that yet. Where do you think?'

'Victoria Station under the clock,' she told him promptly.

Sebastian said very little after that except to agree to the arrangements suggested by these two obviously capable and well-organized ladies.

'Then I think you may go now, Miss

Kibble,' Miss Glossop dismissed her after everything had been settled.

'Now,' she said, after her employee had gone. 'Do you feel that Miss Kibble meets the standard of your requirements?'

'Oh, yes indeed.'

He hesitated, feeling he should show more enthusiasm, but aware that he had no idea of what were the standard requirements of somebody being appointed to this job. It wasn't like praising a secretary for her fast shorthand or accurate typing.

'She seems a very pleasant person,' he added at last, aware that it wasn't an adequate response.

Miss Glossop, however, seemed to find it perfectly acceptable.

'Good,' she said. 'Then nothing remains except that you fill in this form. It is pretty straightforward stuff but you must sign that you understand that all our transactions are confidential and that you have no redress against the agency if anything should go wrong. You also agree to our terms, which are twenty-five guineas with a further ten guineas to be paid when the divorce is de-clared absolute. I think you will find that our terms compare favourably with other similar agencies, some of whom demand a deposit in case of any damage to the woman who is hired. You understand my meaning?'

He did. He was appalled, first by the casual

way she referred to other agencies as if these businesses had sprung up like mushrooms in the dark world of divorce, and then by the idea of anyone damaging one of her employees.

'But I choose *my* clients with care, Mr Crawley. I have an instinct about whom I can trust. You are an honourable man. Shall I help you fill in the form?'

So it was that on a Friday afternoon two weeks later Sebastian Crawley found himself sitting on the Brighton train, trying to concentrate on reading a report on the rebuilding of central London while opposite him sat Miss Agatha Kibble busily knitting.

It was a strange-looking garment, so when the train stopped outside Croydon and he caught her eye as they both looked up, he asked her what it was.

'An elephant,' she told him. 'I knit toys for children. I began in the war making toys for my own children when there were none in the shops. I went to jumble sales and bought old woollens and unravelled them, you know. Everyone was doing that. Good as new when you've washed it, unravelled wool is. So that's how I got the wool for a few pence. It's the stuffing that's the problem. Kapok's that expensive, when you can get it, which you usually can't. So I just cut up old rags that my friends give me.'

He nodded.

'Of course, my girls are long past that age now, but I kept up soft-toy making as a little business. I make for friends and one or two shops, nothing grand, you understand, but it helps me earn a bit extra, since my husband was killed.'

'I'm sorry. Where?'

'Very early in the war it was. Dunkirk.'

'I'm sorry.'

What a brave person she was, he thought, looking at her; a widow who had kept her home going by this innocent work of making toys for children.

'Of course,' she went on. 'It's nothing like the money I earn at Glossop's. Peanuts really, compared with the hotel jobs.'

'No, I suppose not.'

Another inadequate reply, he thought, but then what could anyone say in response to such a remark? Would anyone looking in the train window and seeing this pleasant lady knitting toys imagine that her other job was accompanying gentlemen to Brighton so that they could sit up in bed in the morning when the maid brought in the tea, to enable a divorce which would not damage the sanctity of marriage? Baffled, he returned to his report.

As they approached Brighton she put her knitting into a canvas bag with wooden handles and allowed him to lift her case off the luggage rack.

'Do you know Brighton well?' he asked, and instantly regretted it as being a stupid thing to ask in view of her trade.

'I've made several visits,' she replied matter-of-factly. 'But not of course to *this* hotel. That wouldn't be wise.'

'No, of course not.'

He was surprised, when he signed the register as *Mr and Mrs Crawley* at how guilty he felt, and even more surprised that the disloyalty he felt was to Diana and not to Celia, the rightful Mrs Crawley. Guilt persisted as he followed the thin little peaky-faced maid, who looked about fourteen, up the stairs to their bedroom.

After she'd gone, suddenly radiant because he'd put half-a-crown into her hand, he stood awkwardly by the bed, surveying the room. It was shabby, of course, all hotels were run down, unpainted since before the war. The curtains were frayed, the carpet grimy, the cretonne covers of the two armchairs faded, the chaise longue in the window had a battered look, but it was a spacious room with a view over the sea.

'Is it all right for you?' he asked.

'A bit parky, isn't it?' Agatha Kibble said. 'We could do with the gas fire lit.'

I must follow her example, he thought, as he fed shillings into the gas meter and lit the fire, just be matter-of-fact about all this, not show any embarrassment over what is essentially a business deal. He pushed the two armchairs near to the fire and they both sat down.

'Oh, you can't be choosy about hotels nowadays,' she said. 'At least they've got back to bringing up morning tea. It was a problem in the war when there was no maid bringing in the tea, nobody to witness you in bed with the client. A lot of hotels made guests make their own beds and collect their own breakfast on a tray, so you couldn't get the evidence, you see.'

'Of course not. I hadn't thought of that.'

'Well, with so many hotels requisitioned during the war, there weren't many to stay at anyway. But of course there wasn't the demand for personal services in the war, people weren't so bothered about divorce, they'd other things on their mind, but trade's looked up now the war's over. They're kept very busy at Glossop's.'

So he was one of many. Did that make it better or worse? Stop thinking like that, Sebastian Crawley.

'I think I'll go for a stroll,' he said. 'Would you like to come?'

'No, I've a bit of a sore throat. I think I'll stay here by the fire. The room's hotting up nicely. Then I'll go along to the bathroom before the rush.'

It was a miserable evening as he made his way along the front towards Rottingdean. The air had that penetrating damp chill that seeps into the bones. There was no wind; it was cold without being bracing. Nature was subdued as he walked alongside the whimpering sea under a leaden sky.

Few people passed and those who did were all huddled into their clothes and did not glance at him. He longed for Diana. If only she were here with him now. They'd never gone to a hotel together. Their meetings had never been planned or lasted long. They'd had none of the domesticity of this evening with Agatha Kibble, sitting by the gas fire.

'Oh, what a ludicrous situation,' he said aloud.

Then he must accept it as such, he realized, accept it for what it was: just the first necessary step to get the divorce and free him to marry Diana. They did things in a more civilized way in America and one day the law here would be reformed and this nonsense would stop, but for now he must go along with it. More cheerful, he turned and walked briskly back to the hotel.

The room was warmer, the shabby curtains closed, a bedside lamp glowed through its shade of torn parchment. Agatha had changed for dinner into something more appropriate for a co-respondent: a pre-war cocktail dress.

'I didn't give money for it,' she explained when he complimented her on it. 'The woman gave it me in exchange for clothing coupons. She was desperate to buy a New Look costume. Rich people prefer coupons to cash nowadays.'

She watched as he took his sponge bag, towel and a clean shirt out of his case, then said, 'If you give me your pyjamas, I'll put them on the bed with my nightie. I don't know if they turn the bed back but if they do, it'll look better to see the night things laid out together. Enjoy your bath, Mr Crawley.'

The bathroom was large and cold, the water tepid. He wouldn't be tempted to linger, he thought as he filled the bath up to the five-inch line which had been painted round it to remind people of the regulation depth allowed by the government. All the same he lay for a while remembering that other hotel bathroom of long ago. He remembered the shock of opening the door and seeing Diana standing there in her dressing gown, Diana by then the wife of the great and good Dr Bramley. He remembered her body, her lovely pale body lying across his knees, he felt again that tearing loss when she left him, like the terrible shock, four years earlier, when she had told him, as they sat by the lake at Northrop, that she was married.

Agatha Kibble was wearing more make-up, he noticed, as she took his arm to go down to dinner.

'You must act the part, Mr Crawley,' she told him gently but firmly. 'Remember we are here as lovers. That is the impression we must aim for. And from now on I shall call you Sebastian.'

The dining-room was vast, the furnishing drab, the tables far apart. It was very quiet, the sort of place where diners speak in whispers. As elsewhere, the staff were either very old or very young and would be until men and women were demobbed from the forces to fill the gap. An ancient waiter led them to their table.

He hovered by them after they had sat down and said in his thin dry voice, 'I have to tell you, Sir, that if you and Madam have bread with your soup we are not allowed to serve you pudding. You may wish to discuss this,' and he withdrew and crawled, tortoise-like, across an expanse of parquet to the next table.

'There's a big decision to make,' Sebastian said, smiling across at her.

'It says it here anyway,' Agatha replied, pointing at the warning at the top of the menu.

By order of the Ministry of Food, not more

than three courses may be served at a meal including only one dish of Meat, Game, Fish or Egg. Bread counts as one dish.

'I think I'll have soup without the bread, then,' she went on. 'It might help my throat.'

'It's still sore? I'm sorry.'

'Oh, it'll be better when the cold comes out. First stage is always worse. Oh look, snoek's on the menu. I've never had it.'

'It looks like meat and tastes like fish,' he told her. 'I don't know which it is, only that it comes from Holland and you can get it off the ration.'

The waiter had returned and was standing by them, head bowed over his order book as if in silent prayer.

'Then I think, darling, I shall try snoek,' Agatha exclaimed.

Sebastian looked at her in astonishment that she was addressing the waiter in such affectionate terms, then realized she was addressing himself, her supposed lover.

Rising to the occasion, he replied, 'Certainly, my darling, and I shall have the omelette.'

Agatha nodded her approval after the waiter had gone. 'But you might look at me a bit more gooey-eyed,' she suggested.

Despite the fact that there wasn't much to eat, the meal seemed a long-drawn-out affair, the waiter taking so long to crawl across to them with the various courses, with the half bottle of wine which was all they could be allowed, with the jug of water which was the only thing not in short supply. This was just as well, as Agatha knocked her glass over and the waiter and a young lad spent a long time mopping up, finding another cloth, relaying the table while Agatha apologized profusely, 'Silly me, oh, silly me,' she kept saying, looking at the two men in turn, her eyes wide and her voice positively flirtatious.

She relaxed when they'd finished and said to Sebastian, 'That was so they'll remember me. It's very important to be remembered. You might need his evidence.'

'Of course,' he said. 'That was very thoughtful of you,' and hoped she wouldn't find it necessary to upset the coffee as well.

A very small fire was burning in the guests' lounge. He paused by the door, but she said loudly, 'I think I'd rather go straight up to bed, darling,' and set off towards the stairs.

A few elderly heads turned. Embarrassed, he followed her.

The faded bedcover had been turned back, his blue and white striped pyjamas were on one pillow, her pink nightie on the other.

'I think I'll go to bed early,' she said. 'My cold's beginning to come out,' and she sneezed as if to prove it.

'I'll go for a walk,' he said. 'Just a turn around the block.'

He didn't go far; it was too miserably cold, but he lingered in the bar when he got back, fearful of going up too soon and finding her half dressed. They had run out of alcohol so he had a soft drink and sat for a while looking at a newspaper and then, remembering he should be playing the ardent lover, ran upstairs with what he hoped the receptionist would regard as a lover's impatience.

Agatha was in bed, eyes closed, snoring gently. He went and sat by the fire and picked up the report, which he read for an hour while muffled coughs and snorts and sneezes came from his paramour's bed. Evidently the cold was coming out in a very satisfactory manner.

Towards midnight he pulled the chaise longue nearer the fire, took off his jacket and shoes, lay down and arranged his coat around him. Thank goodness for the long, thick pre-war overcoat, made to withstand northern winters. It shouldn't be too bad, he thought.

In fact he slept only intermittently, aware of the catarrhal snoring from the bed and the chimes of some grandfather clock on the landing. At six o'clock he awoke feeling very cold. The coat had slipped off and the fire had gone out. He searched his pockets and found he had no more shillings.

'Wod is it?' she asked adenoidally from the bed.

'I've run out of shillings.'

'Look id by bag.'

He found the shabby little bag and opened it, hating the idea of taking her money. There were a few shilling pieces in her purse. He took them, fed them into the meter and replaced them with a ten shilling note.

Soon, he thought as he lay listening to the gentle hissing of the gas fire, I must get up and put on my pyjamas for the benefit of the chambermaid. I must make sure she has a good look at both of us. What should I do? Spill the tea? No, better just give her a larger tip than she'd expected. That's the kindest way to get her to remember me.

Having settled that in his mind, he relaxed and slept hard until Agatha's voice said, 'Wakey, wakey, Sebastian. It's gone eight o'clock, time to get into bed and ring for tea.'

When the girl came in, Agatha asked her to draw back the curtains; she herself snuggled up to Sebastian so that when the daylight streamed in it lit up this vision of a very loving couple. She then asked the girl her name.

'Martha, madam.'

'Well, Martha, could you hand me that little hanky case that's on the chair? Thank you so much,' and she smiled, took a handkerchief out of the case and blew her nose.

'And may I give you this?' Sebastian said and handed the girl two half-crowns.

'I think she'll remember us, Mr Crawley,' Agatha said after she'd left. And she moved away from him and reached for her tea.

Eight

'There's a college dance at the end of term. You really must come up for it, Debbie. You'll have finished Higher by then.'

'A dance? Oh, I don't know – I mean, I haven't got a dance dress.'

'Don't worry, I'll see to all that,' Vicky told her, airily sweeping aside what seemed to Debbie to be insurmountable difficulties. 'You can go to London for a couple of nights, stay in the flat, then catch a train to Cambridge.'

The flat that Vicky had helped her father to choose was grander than anything Debbie had expected and rather more expensive than he had intended. But Vicky saw herself acting as her father's hostess in its light and spacious rooms, so unlike the dark, low-ceilinged ones of the old house in Netherby, which she now viewed with some contempt.

And a lovely place to bring her university friends when they came to see her in London.

The flat was in Hampstead. The owner of the large house had converted it into two, living on the ground floor herself. The Crawleys had the two upper floors and the use of the garden. Their father's room was on the lower of the two floors, with the bathroom, lavatory and kitchen. The girls' rooms were upstairs, Vicky had the biggest, overlooking the garden and with the luxury of an inbuilt gas fire, easily the best room, as befitted her seniority. Debbie had a long room in the eaves, with two dormer windows. It was a dark room with no outlook, but she said she liked it for its character. There was a little room which Felicity could have when she came to visit.

Her father put Debbie on the train, carefully choosing a *Ladies Only* compartment for her. A grey-haired lady sat in the corner seat, knitting. She smiled at Debbie and went back to her grey sock.

Debbie opened her book, *Brideshead Revisited*, which Vicky said everyone, but simply everyone, was reading, so though Debbie hadn't actually seen anyone doing so, she felt she ought to read it herself.

It was a slow train; at the second of its frequent stops, a young man dashed across the platform, seized the door handle, wrenched it open and leapt into their compartment just as the train was pulling out. He looked at them, he looked at the *Ladies Only* sign and seemed about to throw himself off again. He thought better of it and instead overwhelmed them with disjointed apologies. 'I'm so sorry. Just didn't see. Promise get off next station. Change compartment. Do apologize. Didn't intend.'

They reassured him that they understood, told him not to worry, and the woman returned to her knitting and Debbie to her book. The next stop wasn't long in coming and, still flustered, he jumped down and ran off to find another compartment.

'A nice young man,' the knitting lady said. 'But careless. He should have looked.'

'But I was so sorry for – I mean, it's awful, isn't it? when you do something like that and feel so silly. And people staring ...'

'He'll recover, don't you worry,' the knitting one told her, and thought what a funny, nervous creature the girl was.

'How far are you going?' she asked.

'Just to Cambridge – I'm not at the university,' she added quickly, fearful of misleading. 'But my sister is and I'm going to her college dance tonight.'

'Well, I hope you enjoy it.'

'Oh, I'm sure I shall,' Debbie told her, though she wasn't at all sure really; part of her was dreading it.

★ ★ ★

She didn't see Vicky on the platform at first, and even when she stepped forward from a group of men, Debbie didn't for a moment recognize her. Vicky looked like a picture in a fashion magazine, standing there in her long New Look skirt and feminine little jacket with sloping shoulders. As she walked the few steps towards her sister, Debbie was very conscious of her own utility skirt, short and straight, and her unfashionable square-shouldered coat, horribly aware that she was letting Vicky down in front of her friends.

She found herself standing on the platform and being introduced.

'This is Max, Debbie, and this is Giles, and this is Tim and this is Alan.'

There seemed to be an awful lot of them and she was afraid she would get in a muddle with their names.

'We just came along to keep Vicky company, hope you don't mind,' the one called Alan said as he walked alongside her, while the others strode ahead with her sister.

He took her case, though she explained that it was quite light and she could manage, really she could.

'Will you be coming up here when you leave school?' he asked. 'Of course, it's a long way off. When do you take your School Cert?'

'Oh, no,' she told him. 'I've just taken

126

my Higher.'

She felt sorry for him. It's awfully embarrassing when you mistake someone's age. And, of course, Vicky did look a lot older, especially now that she was wearing lipstick and powder. But he didn't seem very put out, just said, 'Oh, really? I thought you were a lot younger than Vicky, that's all,' and went on to talk amiably about something else.

Vicky had lodgings, which she called her digs, not very far from college. She warned Debbie that her landlady, a fearful old snob, who gave herself ridiculous airs and graces, was expecting them to tea.

After all the awful things Vicky had said about this Mrs Geekie-Noble, she was astonished by the extremely flattering way she talked to her landlady, smiling at her with what seemed like genuine affection, admiring various ornaments in the room, telling Debbie how fortunate she'd been that Mrs Geekie-Noble allowed her to stay here, how sorry she would be to move into college next year.

Tea was brought in by the landlady's companion, Miss Midgely, a little brown mouse of a woman who clearly lived in terror of her employer. Tea was poured out of a large silver teapot from whose spout a silver strainer dangled. Hot water was in a taller silver pot standing on a little burner, all carried in by Miss Midgely on a heavy silver tray. She went out and returned with a cake stand, on one shelf of which were some biscuits and on a lower one a chocolate cake and buttered teacake under a silver dome.

The tea ritual was a strain. Mrs Geekie-Noble held forth with some long tale of her Georgian silver teaspoons, believed stolen but miraculously restored to her on the death of a cousin, to which Vicky listened with rapt attention, nodding now and then, saying, 'How *fascinating*,' exactly as if she really meant it.

Afterwards she thanked her landlady effusively, Debbie murmured her thanks and, noticing Miss Midgely struggling with the tray, went to open the door for her.

'She can manage,' Mrs Geekie-Noble told her sharply.

When they were back in her bedroom, Vicky laughed and said, 'I did warn you she was awful, didn't I? All that ghastly furniture and those hideous ornaments. If she tells me once more about those wretched Georgian silver teaspoons I shall scream. And look at my bedroom. It's big, it could be all right, but it's ruined by that hideous green screen and blue lino and the purple bedspread and the horrible old leather chair and just about everything she's put in it.'

'But Vicky, you were so, well, *extra* nice to her, I mean, not just ordinarily polite, but really as if you thought she was wonderful. I began to think she wasn't the same one you'd told me about.'

'Oh, I butter her up, of course I do. She can be useful. I mean, she's let you have that little attic room tonight and sometimes she even turns a blind eye if I come in after half past ten when I haven't had late leave.'

'How late is late leave?'

'Eleven fifteen. It's ridiculous. Miss Midgely has to keep a book, would you believe.'

'I thought Miss Midgely was much nicer. I felt sorry for her.'

'There was no need to rush to help her, Debbie,' her sister told her seriously. 'Mrs Geekie-Noble likes to keep her in her place.'

'But—'

'Mrs G-N has come down in the world, she's only got her pretensions left. Miss Midgely represents the servant class for her.'

'Poor Miss Midgely!'

'She's come down too. She kept house for her father, an academic, who died leaving her nothing but a few debts. Alas, poor Midgely,' she added lightly and gave a little laugh.

It was new, that laugh, amused but slightly contemptuous, and she talked differently too; a very slight drawl had entered her voice, which made her sound even more grown-up and confident than she already was; she was so sure of herself and of everything really, Debbie thought.

'Now about that dress,' Vicky was saying. 'I thought this one might do.'

From her wardrobe she brought out a long dress of pale-blue lace over a deep-blue taffeta underskirt. It was lovely, quite breath-takingly lovely, Debbie thought and, to her surprise, it still looked lovely when she put it on. She looked in the glass with disbelief. Her big blue eyes stared back at her, their colour somehow heightened by the blue of the dress. A little ruching and some clever darts made her breasts look plumper than they really were. She hardly recognized her-self. Blessedly her spots were much better now; they'd moved off her face on to her back. Apart from a tiny one on the back of her neck, they wouldn't show at all. And even that one, she thought with uncharacter-istic optimism, might have gone by tonight.

Vicky also was looking at the reflection with surprise; she had the puzzled look of one who, intending a foil, has created a competitor and can't understand how it has come about.

'We have to share a bath,' Vicky told her that evening when they started getting ready for the dance. 'The hot water only runs to one.'

She scattered some bath salts into the water, climbed in and lay back relaxing.

'I'm getting awfully fat,' she remarked.

'You keep saying that,' Debbie told her, laughing because she had referred to it several times already. 'Of course you're not. You're a lovely shape.'

'No, honestly, Debbie, I'm getting too fat to get into some of my clothes.'

'Well, you've got plenty. Where did you get the clothing coupons?'

'Daddy gave me some of his and one or two men did too. Men don't need so many clothes as girls. It was really very unfair not to give women more coupons than men.'

'Just like Mummy always says that people who live in hard water areas ought to get more soap coupons than people who live where there's soft water?'

'Yes, and anyway men are given free demob suits when they come out of the forces.'

'Oh, Vicky!' Debbie exclaimed, shocked. 'They deserve them! Just think what they'd been through!'

'Oh, well, there is that, I suppose. Could you give my back a wash?'

'There are really two quite different groups of men in Cambridge now,' she explained as her sister rubbed. 'There are the older ones who should have come up when war broke out, so they're five or six years older than the rest. Then there are the boys straight from school, who'll have to do their two years in the army when they go down, but they seem

131

so *frightfully* young.'

'But they'll be the same age as you, Vicky.'

'Girls mature earlier; a girl of eighteen is much older than a boy of eighteen. Everyone knows that,' she added, getting out of the bath.

I didn't, Debbie thought, and wondered if next year, when she was eighteen, she would suddenly be mature.

'I much prefer older men,' Vicky said. 'And, of course, *physically* they know their way about much better than young boys.'

She gave a knowing little look and Debbie supposed that, having found their way around battlefields, the older men must have developed a better sense of direction.

'Yes, I can understand that,' she said solemnly, as she got into the bath.

'There'll be fourteen in our party tonight,' Vicky told her. 'Five other girls, some of the men who came to meet you at the station and a couple of others.'

'Will Alan be coming?'

'Yes. Why, do you fancy him?'

'Oh, *no*!' Debbie exclaimed, horrified. 'It was just that he was very kind, you know, talking to me and carrying my case.'

Vicky nodded and then said suddenly, 'Debbie, I've got a problem.'

'Oh yes?'

'Could you help me about something?'

'Anything,' Debbie said, scrubbing her

knees.

'Well, the thing is, I've tried on the dress I was going to wear and I just can't get into it. The zip won't fasten. I wonder if you'd mind wearing it and I'll wear my other one that you tried on?'

'All right,' Debbie agreed, as she got out of the bath, though she was disappointed.

'The one I'll lend you is very pretty. It's pink, such a flattering colour. Goodness, you haven't stayed in long.'

The water had been tepid, but not wanting Vicky to feel guilty about staying in so long, she only said, 'Oh, I've finished, thank you.'

'And since you're a bit thinner than I am, it should fit you perfectly.'

'Thanks, Vicky. I'm sure it will be all right, but honestly, you don't look a bit fatter than you were.'

Her sister, standing there naked, seemed to her to have a perfect figure, she could have modelled for a statue of the most beautiful woman in the whole world. No wonder all these men admired her, she thought as she cleaned the bath.

Vicky brought the pink dress up to Debbie in her little attic bedroom.

'Here's the petticoat that goes with it,' she said. 'Hope it fits.'

It fitted perfectly.

'There,' she said. 'I knew it would do. Now for the dress.'

She stood her sister in front of the pock-marked looking glass and slipped the pink dress over her head.

It had a boned bodice and was strapless.

'Oh, I can't wear it!' Debbie exclaimed. 'I can't possibly wear it. My back's all spots.'

'Oh, they won't show. I'll cover them with talcum powder.'

'But they will show, they will. Oh, please, Vicky, can't I wear the other one?'

Vicky's face assumed a martyred look.

'I can't get into this one,' she said. 'I did think I'd explained that. But, of course, if you feel you really prefer the other one, I'll just stay here. You can go on your own, the others will look after you, I'm sure. All I ever wanted was for you to have a lovely time.'

She gave her sister a sweet and loving smile. 'I don't mind, really, Debbie. It will probably do me good to have an early night.'

'But of course you must go.' Debbie was almost in tears as she begged her sister to go to the dance. How dreadful, how unforgivable it would be to spoil Vicky's party at her own college dance.

'Well, if you insist,' Vicky said more cheerfully. 'I'll tell you what I'll do. I'll put some calamine lotion on the spots now, and it'll dry by the time we go out, and they won't show at all. It's marvellous stuff. I had a spot on my chin a few days ago and it covered it up beautifully.'

'Oh, did it? Oh yes, thank you, please put it on for me.'

She'd been so worried about her back that she hadn't realized that the front looked awful too. The bodice was boned and stood out in front of her flat chest: two little unfilled saucers of pink satin. There were rosebuds round the top, made of a darker shade of pink material. She could imagine how prettily Vicky's breasts would have nestled there.

'I don't fill them,' she moaned miserably.

'Oh, we'll soon fix that,' Vicky reassured her. 'A couple of hankies will work wonders.'

For years afterwards, Debbie tried to forget the misery of that evening. All the inadequacies which the blue dress had hidden were revealed in the pink, magnified a thousandfold.

In her own room with the pock-marked glass, she hadn't been able to see the results of Vicky's ministrations with talcum powder and calamine lotion; in the triple mirror in the ladies' cloakroom, their failure was cruelly revealed; blobs of the lotion, pink and dry, crowned each bumpy spot, set off by the whiteness of the talcum powder which separated them. She might have asked Vicky to help her wipe it all off, but she'd disappeared quickly, 'to find the others', she said.

Other girls in the cloakroom looked at her

sympathetically and smiled. She went into one of the lavatories and tried to wipe off some of the lotion, screwing her head round to see over her shoulder in a vain attempt to mitigate the disaster.

The girls must have thought she'd left the cloakroom, because she heard one say, 'Poor thing, but honestly, if I had a spotty back like that I wouldn't dream of wearing a strapless dress, would you?'

She didn't want to embarrass them by reappearing, so waited in the lavatory, tears running down her face, until she heard them leave.

'Oh, here she is at last,' Vicky called out when she joined them. 'You've been titivating for ages, you vain little thing.'

She put her arm round Debbie's waist and drew her forward.

'Now who doesn't know my sister?' she asked. 'You don't, Simon, or you, James, but I think everyone else remembers you, especially Alan,' on whom she bestowed one of her knowing looks.

'What would you like to drink?' one of the men asked her, sounding so sophisticated, like somebody in a play on the wireless. 'What's your tipple, Debbie?'

She really didn't have a tipple, she said, but a glass of cider would be nice. Vicky asked for gin and orange and she wondered if she should have done the same, but was distracted by the arrival of others. They were girls, but Vicky still seemed to be the queen of the party.

'It's nice to be in a group like this,' one of the older men remarked. 'At May Balls before the war we all stayed with one partner all the evening, I seem to remember.'

'Much nicer, I do agree,' Vicky exclaimed. Then she added, 'Though I'm not sure that Alan and Debbie think so,' and bestowed another knowing look on them.

Debbie felt herself blushing furiously, could feel the blood throbbing in her neck, in her face, everywhere. Whatever would he imagine she'd said? Alan merely looked embarrassed.

'Oh, look, she's blushing,' Vicky said, and they all looked at her and laughed.

Alan avoided her after that and the others took turns, out of kindness, to dance with her, all taking care, she noticed, not to put their hands on her back, which now, in her imagination, seemed to be a mass of repulsive, suppurating sores.

In a haze of misery, the evening dragged on its weary way. The hankies Vicky had given her to stuff into her bosom were worse than useless. They fell out or sat there drawing attention to the deficiencies of her bosom. In the end she took them out. At supper she dropped a large piece of a bread roll which fell into her bodice and settled in one of the empty cups. She saw that the two men sitting opposite her noticed it, exchanged glances and tried not to giggle. To make it worse the roll was buttered and left a greasy smear on the pink satin.

'I do like the pink of your dress,' one of the men said kindly towards the end of the evening. 'That colour suits you.'

'Thank you. But it's not mine. It belongs to Vicky.'

'I know. She wore it last week at my birthday party.'

'Oh, no, she couldn't have. She's too fat to get into it. She told me.'

'Vicky fat? What nonsense she talks. And I promise you she did wear it and looked smashing in it too. And so do you too, of course,' he added, chivalrously.

They all grumbled that the dance had to stop at midnight.

'And this nonsense of needing a late pass to be out until eleven fifteen,' Vicky said.

'But I hear you have an understanding landlady, Vicky. Aren't you lucky?'

'It's not luck,' Vicky contradicted. 'I cultivate her and it's jolly hard work. Debbie will tell you how hard I try.'

'Your sister,' one of the men remarked to Debbie, 'can charm the monkeys out of the trees.'

'Oh, yes I know,' Debbie agreed loyally.

They all went on complaining about the

university's rules. But Debbie, who knew she couldn't have endured another ten minutes of this tormenting evening, blessed the name of whoever invented the rules and wanted only to escape to her bed in the attic.

'Next time you must stay longer, darling,' Vicky said as she saw her on to the train the next morning.

She insisted on putting Debbie's case on to the luggage rack for her and then, 'Here's something for you to read,' she said, putting some glossy and very expensive-looking magazines on the seat. 'I'd better be getting off,' she added as the guard blew the whistle.

They went out into the corridor. Vicky kissed her and jumped down on to the platform.

'You did enjoy it, didn't you, darling?' she asked anxiously, looking up at Debbie, her eyes wide with sisterly concern, as the train began to move.

'Oh, yes, of course I did. It was all lovely,' Debbie called down to her. It would have been awful not to enjoy it after all the trouble Vicky had taken, even getting up early this morning to see her off when everyone else was lying in bed. 'Thank you for everything,' she added as the train gained speed. She leant out of the window and waved and went on waving even though Vicky had left the platform without a backward glance.

139

Nine

'It's a ridiculous idea of your father's, this flat in London. He should have stayed in lodgings like he did in the war,' her mother said, angrily scraping carrots in the sink. 'If he's got money to burn he could send more up here. And you needn't think you can go gallivanting down there either – not that they'd have room for you.'

'There is a little room I can have, Vicky said.'

'Oh, it'll be the smallest, don't you think otherwise, my girl. Vicky will have the best, she's always been your father's favourite. I've told Debbie that often enough. And Debbie's the one who needs extra care, being sensitive and wanting to please, not like some I could mention.'

Felicity said nothing. That was her policy. She'd dreaded the years ahead without her sisters but had soon decided what to do. She would retreat into work, she'd become such a horrible little swot that she'd hardly need to see her mother except at meal times. She'd work every evening and every weekend, except for walking on the hills and the occasional game of croquet against herself.

She had also decided what she would not do: she would never argue. So she didn't point out that constantly telling Debbie that Vicky was their father's favourite didn't do her confidence any good, even if it had been true, which it wasn't. She knew that he loved them equally, but she also knew that Vicky was always special just because she was Vicky. And always telling Debbie she was sensitive didn't help either; Debbie had taken to backing away from anything a bit difficult, with an expression on her face which clearly said, 'Oh, I can't do that, I'm too sensitive.'

She'd got better marks in her Higher School Certificate than Vicky had, but refused to try for a university place.

'But you got distinctions in German and French *and Latin*,' Felicity had told her in exasperation. 'Vicky only got a credit in physics.'

'But she got a distinction in chemistry and biology. And maybe physics is harder than Latin.'

'Nonsense. You know that's not true. You've just got this thing against universities.'

She couldn't understand her elder sister's strange new aversion to college life.

'I just know I'd hate it,' Debbie told her,

beginning to sound tearful. 'All those clever people. I wouldn't fit in. It's different for Vicky.'

'All right. I'll shut up about it.'

'Thank you, Flea. It's so awful the way the staff go on about it, as if I was letting them down. I sometimes wish I'd got worse results so that they wouldn't expect me to try for university.'

'Oh, Debbie, that's *terrible*. You mustn't wish that. You'll do something else with those results that's just as good as going to a university.'

And so it had proved. Her father found there was a secretarial college in Hampstead which included a three-year language course. There Debbie flourished, being easily the best in her year at languages and constantly praised.

'Just think,' she'd said, awestruck, 'I shall be able to type in French and German.'

'Well, please write to me in English,' Felicity had requested. 'And please, no Latin shorthand.'

'I promise.'

She had kept her promise and every week posted a letter typed on the second-hand Remington portable which her father had bought her. Sometimes they didn't make sense, because Debbie was very honest about not looking at the keys, which she covered up with a converted shoebox.

142

Felicity loved those letters; they helped her keep another of her resolutions, which was never to look miserable, even if she felt it, because she'd get into trouble for that too.

But sometimes, when her mother was out, she'd go and look in their empty bedrooms: Vicky's very plain and grown-up, Debbie's full of dolls and teddies and all kinds of childish junk. It would seem very quiet as she stood there, the silence somehow heavy, almost tangible. Both beds had dustsheets over them as if their occupants were dead.

When it happened it was totally unexpected. 'I'm going with the Mothers' Union excursion to Iona at Whitsuntide,' her mother said. 'You'll be going to stay in London while I'm away.'

For a moment, she couldn't believe it. 'Are you sure?' she'd asked before she could stop herself.

'*Am I sure?*' her mother repeated, exasperated. 'Of course I'm sure, child. I'm not in the habit of making things up. You'll travel as far as Gradby with the vicar's wife. She'll see you across to the LMS station where you get the train to King's Cross. Your father will meet you at the other end.'

'Thank you,' Felicity said, aware that it was an inadequate response but instinctively knowing that it wouldn't be wise to sound too pleased.

It was the only time she'd been on a train, except for that time years ago, now very hazy, when they went to Northrop, and she enjoyed every minute of it. She'd brought a book with her, but was too excited to read. It was enough just to stare out of the window and watch the countryside slip by, this lovely green and grey countryside, so familiar to her for as long as she could remember, but somehow different seen from this angle. She could see how the shadows of clouds chased across the hillside, see the back of Thornborough, which looked smaller from here than it did from the village. She saw the way that drystone walls gave way to hedges and fences as they moved south.

The changes were more marked after she'd changed trains at Gradby. The wide open spaces disappeared; sometimes the towns were so close that they seemed to run into each other and there were rows and rows of houses backing on to the line, amazingly near it. She could see their little gardens, their sheds and greenhouses and people standing there who looked up at the train as it rushed past. Washing was hanging out in some of the gardens; surely it must get covered in smuts and be dirtier when they took it in than it had been when they put it out?

As they approached London she could see what seemed like endless warehouses, and sheds and criss-crossing railway lines, all on such a gigantic scale she could hardly take it in. She hoped they'd be sure to meet her at the station; she, who could find her way easily across miles of hills and dales, would be utterly lost in this maze of buildings, with nothing natural to guide her.

Of course they were there; her father, easily discernible in a crowd because he was so tall, and Debbie alongside him. They hugged each other and she was filled with this huge, unusual happiness and walked between them, each hand in one of theirs, blissfully content with her lot.

'Vicky's away staying with friends for a few days, but sends her love,' Debbie said. 'She'll be home before you go back to Netherby.'

Home Debbie had said, and said it so naturally, as if she really felt at home here and not in Netherby any more. That was new, Felicity thought, and put it away to think about later. They led her to the underground and she sat between them as the train rattled along in the bowels of the earth. She'd imagined that London would be like Gradby only bigger and couldn't get over the immensity of it, the way it went on and on, station after station. She couldn't stop remarking on it, chattering away ten to the dozen, Debbie told her afterwards. Well, she had been behaving like a Trappist monk for quite a long time, so must have quite a bit of chatter saved up. Not that she told her sister that.

The advertisements intrigued her. She laughed at the one opposite which ended:

Remember that
You'd look prettier
In a hat.

'Before the war, everyone wore hats,' her father explained. 'But of course that all stopped and now the milliners want women to go back to wearing them.'

'Do you think they will?' she asked in alarm. 'I hate hats.'

He laughed. 'Fear not, little one,' he said. 'You won't be coerced into wearing a hat.'

He laughed a lot, she noticed. In fact he was much more like he used to be and Debbie too was much more fun. 'Can't wait to show you the flat, Flea,' she kept saying.

'You show your sister round, Debbie,' her father said as he opened the front door. 'I'll put the kettle on for tea.'

So Debbie led her from room to room, amusing them both by pointing out the obvious. 'Your bedroom's awfully small, Flea,' she said, standing in the doorway of a room almost entirely filled with a bed. 'We could take your bed into my bedroom if you like. I've got heaps of room.'

They'd got the bed jammed in the doorway, when their father called to them, so they left it there, stranded half in and half out like an ungainly animal wedged in a hole.

Her father had become much more domesticated, she noticed. That evening he made them scrambled dried eggs.

'I haven't yet managed to turn them into *boiled* eggs,' he told her as he measured out the egg powder. They laughed and tried to think of ways of making egg shells to wrap around the reconstituted powder. Felicity thought of the illicit farm eggs and wished she could have brought some. Fancy, a ration of only one egg a week!

She was in charge of making the toast but, distracted, burnt it. She tensed; she'd only been trying to help and now she'd spoiled everything.

'Don't look so tragic,' her father said. 'It scrapes off,' and handed her a knife.

As she scraped the black off into the sink, she realized that something which was a major crime in her mother's house wasn't necessarily one anywhere else. It was a strange, airy feeling.

'I can make a passable stew too,' her father was telling her. 'It takes the entire meat ration but we eke it out for days afterwards with vegetables.'

'I've brought my card,' she said, handing him the week's emergency ration card.

'We'll get extra milk for Flea,' Debbie pointed out, 'because she's still a school-child, so we can make a rice pudding. Daddy makes super ones.'

'The secret,' he told them solemnly, 'is that extra pinch of dried milk.'

'The real secret,' Debbie said, 'is that we've got this very good cookery book called *How to Make Your Rations go Further than You Thought Possible*.'

Their father smiled.

'The title isn't exactly pithy,' he said, 'but the recipes are good.'

'We shan't need to cook tomorrow, because we're going out,' Debbie said.

'Where?'

'Oh, sorry, darling, we haven't told you. We're going to Oxenhurst to see my parents, your grandparents.'

'I was christened at Oxenhurst Church,' Debbie said.

'You howled,' her father told her.

'I remember that. The water was cold.'

'And you bit the vicar.'

'I remember that too. He tasted horrible.'

'No, you don't. I made the biting up.'

They were all laughing and again Felicity felt that lightness, as if her spirit was being lifted up. It wasn't just that it was different here, they became different people, Debbie and her father. Oh, she'd like to be here for ever.

'And of course, your grandparents were there that time we went over to Northrop just before the war for your Great-Uncle Charles' birthday.'

'Yes, I remember,' Debbie began slowly, 'going to that house, what was it called?'

'The Dower House?'

'Yes, that's right, and we looked at photographs and they said that Vicky was just like her beautiful grandmother.'

'Well remembered, Debbie. She was called Selina.'

Even now, after all these years, he found it hard to speak the name of that treacherous woman who had almost wrecked his life. But soon, now that the evidence was in Celia's hands, the divorce process would start and he would marry the woman whom Selina had so wickedly kept from him. He must try to forgive, or, if not forgive, at least feel less bitter.

'I remember that there were some other old people there, but I don't think I realized they were our grandparents,' Felicity said slowly. 'But I remember the croquet.'

'I remember Aunt Diana,' Debbie said. 'I liked her.'

'Did you, darling?' Her father sounded pleased.

'Well, I liked her a lot better than that nanny,' she told him.

'What didn't you like about Nanny Stone?'

'She made me eat the skin on my custard and I was nearly sick.'

'Reason enough,' her father said. 'You're yawning, Flea. Bedtime.'

They told him about the bed being stuck in the doorway and once again Felicity had a moment of panic that she'd spoiled things and would be in trouble, but he only laughed and said he'd come up and give it a shove.

'Come to think of it,' he said, after they'd pushed the bed alongside Debbie's, 'Vicky's room's empty, so you could have gone in there.'

They told him they liked being together, but both of them knew it was an unthinkable suggestion. A younger sister simply did not move into Vicky's special room. She would feel like an intruder and Vicky's wrath would be beyond all imagining.

Debbie's room was long and narrow, built into the eaves, so that you had to be careful not to bump your head on the ceiling when you got into bed, and remember not to sit up suddenly in the morning, she warned her sister.

'But,' she added, 'I do love it up here, all the same.'

Felicity, prowling round the room, nodded and said, 'Yes, Vicky's is big and has the gas fire and all that, but this is cosier. I like all the little unexpected corners and the way that long bookcase fits in under the eaves over there.'

'Yes, Daddy did it.'

She stretched and yawned and began to get undressed.

'Thank goodness we don't have to wear those awful liberty bodices any more,' she said, her voice rather muffled as she pulled a jumper over her head, 'with their fiddly little buttons.'

'Made of rubber, weren't they, those buttons, and used to perish and go all twisted or come off so your stockings went slithering down your leg with the suspender hanging off it.'

'I can't think why they were called *liberty* anything.'

'It's because they're better than what girls had to wear before, stays and corsets and boned collars. It must have been awful. Aren't we lucky to live in modern times? And, Debbie, we don't have to wear those horrible black stockings at school any more. We've got brown ones made of lisle, whatever that is. But they're much better, not nearly as thick.'

'Lucky you! I had to wear them all the time I was at school. I remember how they used to go into holes and we'd have to ink our legs so the pink didn't show.'

'I've still got one pair which Mummy says I have to wear out at home. And they're the only pair that just *won't* wear out. It's

151

jolly unfair.'

'You could make a few holes in them,' Debbie surprisingly suggested.

'She'd notice. Artificial holes probably look different from natural ones.'

But she didn't want to think about being at her mother's home when she was down here, so to change the subject, said, 'That's a pretty BB,' as Debbie took off her bust bodice.

Debbie held it up to admire it.

'They only had a few in at the shop,' she said. 'So I queued for it and bought it with my birthday money.'

She placed it lovingly on the back of a chair and went on, 'Vicky says that girls at college don't say BB, they call it a B squared.'

'That's clever.'

'And in America they call them bras, which is short for brassières.'

'I suppose that's what the French call them.'

'No, a brassière in French is a kind of little vest like a child might wear, a kind of bodice. The French call a BB *un soutien gorge*.'

'You are so lucky knowing languages, Debbie. It's so useful. History and English are no help at all when it comes to things like that.'

Debbie laughed.

'Come on, we'd better go and get washed,' she said, leading the way to the bathroom.

152

And again Felicity thought how much more definite she was about everything when she wasn't overshadowed by their eldest sister.

'Who are the friends she's staying with?' she asked that night as they lay in bed.

'He's called Ferdy and he's having his twenty-fifth birthday party.'

'He's so old?'

'Well, he's done his National Service, or maybe he was in the war. Yes, I suppose he would have been old enough to be called up. He's one of the older ones. Vicky likes them better. She says they know their way around more than the boys straight from school.'

'Way around where?'

'I don't know. Anywhere, I suppose.'

'Tell me about him.'

'Well, they live somewhere in Derbyshire and his father's a farmer. At least not an ordinary farmer, Vicky says, but a gentleman farmer.'

'What does that mean?'

'I suppose it means he doesn't work.'

'You mean he's a kind of squire?'

'Yes, that sort of thing.'

'And what's he like, this Ferdy?'

'He's nice. I like him. He came here one weekend.'

'Does Vicky?'

'What?'

'Like him.'

'Oh, I see. I don't know really. She says he

isn't very clever and he probably won't get a good degree.'

'Yet he invites her to his party?'

'Oh, she doesn't say that to *him*. She'll probably tell him he's brilliant.'

They were both quiet for a moment, thinking about their sister.

'Was he at that dance you went to?'

'Yes, but there were so many men and Vicky seemed to know them all. I don't think he was very special, if you see what I mean.'

'And the dance. Was it fun?'

'Oh, yes, it was super.'

It would have been terribly disloyal to Vicky to say anything else. Of course, Vicky had *meant* everything to be lovely for her, so if there had been any bad moments, when she was among all these people who were older and cleverer than she was, it must have been her own fault. And afterwards, at home, Vicky had been so concerned, so often asked her if she had truly enjoyed it all, that she had convinced herself that she had.

'Oh, yes,' she repeated. 'I had a lovely time.'

They lay in silence for a few minutes, then Debbie asked, 'Did she ever talk to you about sex – Mummy, I mean? And getting periods and all that stuff?'

'No. I just knew what you told me.'

'And I just knew what Vicky told me.'

'So who told Vicky?'

'Do you remember that girl Peggy something, that used to be Vicky's friend, off and on?'

'Yes. Peggy Hazlit. She was a farmer's daughter.'

'That's right. That's why she knew about sex and things. Except that she got it a bit wrong and said that getting the curse was a bit like being a bitch on heat. It isn't, is it? I mean, rather the reverse. But it didn't really matter, because at least Vicky knew what to expect. And later told me and then later I told you.'

'Yes, you did. Thank you.'

All the same, despite the forewarning, she remembered dreading the onset of periods, sure that it would in some way get her into trouble. When she'd found blood on her sheets one Saturday morning, she'd taken them into the bathroom and was trying to wash out the stains when her mother came in.

She'd waited for the skies to fall. But her mother was surprisingly gentle.

'You'll get used to it,' she said. 'It's what women have to put up with, that and intercourse, which is also unpleasant, but necessary if you are to carry out your duty of procreation,' and she gave her an aspirin and a hot-water bottle and let her sit by the fire.

She remembered thinking, as she sat there, clutching the bottle to her aching stomach,

155

how strange it all was. Sometimes in the past she'd been surprised when normally kind people did something unkind, but now she realized that it is just as disconcerting when the normally unkind do something kind.

She thought about it now as she lay listening to Debbie's gentle breathing. Then her own eyelids grew heavy and she drifted into sleep.

Ten

'You're thinking of young Arthur, aren't you?' Arthur Crawley asked his wife as they sat waiting for Sebastian and the girls to arrive.

He recognized that faraway look on her face, as if she was busy in some other world. He got up and stood behind her, resting his hands on her abundant white hair.

She smiled, gently pressed her head back against his hands. Actually she hadn't been thinking about her dead grandson. Not this time; she'd been thinking about her son's dead marriage.

Not that Sebastian had ever talked about it. He had casually referred to his need to

156

stay in London, to Celia's wish to stay in Netherby. That was all. It was enough.

'They'll be here soon,' she remarked, raising her voice when she spoke to him now, since he was getting so deaf, though he wouldn't admit it.

'Wonder what they'll make of this place?' he asked, removing his hands from her head and waving them in the air. 'Not much like our old house they saw last time.'

'Debbie was a baby and Felicity wasn't born, so I doubt if they'll make comparisons.' She hesitated and then said, 'But you're beginning to get used to it, aren't you, Arthur?'

'Oh, yes,' he said without enthusiasm.

He'd never get used to it, he knew that, but no good upsetting Barbara, who said a small place was much easier to run. It only had five bedrooms. Not that he missed bedrooms. It was the outhouses he missed. Not of course that there was much left to put in them now. So a couple of sheds and a garage was probably enough. And there was always that stone shack down by the old croquet lawn. That had miraculously survived. That and a few trees and a bit of the kitchen garden wall.

'We've been so lucky to have this house built when you think of all the delays people in town have to put up with before they can get rehoused. Of course, we'd never have done it without Sebastian,' she added, remembering all the forms that had to be filled in, the applications for planning, the restrictions to be obeyed, the rationing of building materials, as of everything else. She sighed and said, 'We really are blessed and should be grateful. Above all we should be grateful that Diana escaped.'

Her husband nodded.

'To think that she might have been killed,' he agreed, 'just for the sake of coming here to get a few of our old togs ...'

They'd had this conversation many times, but still the guilt was not assuaged.

'I should never have forgiven myself if she'd been killed. And even though it didn't happen, I still can't forgive myself that we let her take the risk of coming back here. After all, we'd had that one bomb. It should have warned us. What were we thinking of?'

'Now come, Barbara, we thought like everyone else that it was just Jerry jettisoning his bombs. Nobody realized it was the start of the blitz.'

'I suppose not. And of course it was Diana who suggested it. All the same ...'

'Jolly sensible girl, that Diana. Must have gone out and done a recce beforehand to see where the shelter was.'

'Don't you think it's time we got rid of it? We could do with the space now we have so much less land.'

'Never,' he told her. 'Might come in handy again.'

She was saved the need to reply by the sight of Sebastian, Debbie and Felicity walking up the drive. She wanted to rush out to meet them but had to wait until Arthur helped her out of her chair. Once up, she was very sprightly and darted to the front door ahead of him.

She saw at once, as she embraced him, that her son was relaxed and cheerful, genuinely so, for the first time in years.

'I won't say *how you've grown*,' she said, turning to her two granddaughters, 'but it's hard not to when I remember what little things you were when I saw you last time. Do you remember going to Northrop before the war?'

'Oh, yes,' Debbie said. 'I remember a huge house with rows of windows and there were soldiers there, weren't there?'

'That's right. Then in the war it became a maternity home.'

'Goodness, did the soldiers have babies?'

Even Felicity realized it was a pretty silly remark and was glad Vicky wasn't there; she'd have certainly given Debbie one of her looks, and poor old Debbie would have gone scarlet and been tongue-tied for the rest of the day.

As it was, their grandma just said, 'No, it was mothers from the towns who took

159

shelter there when they were pregnant and then had their babies and could stay for a while afterwards.'

'Have they all gone now?'

'Oh, yes they all went home when the war ended.'

'So the soldiers are back?'

'No, there are plans for it to be some kind of children's home. But your aunt Diana will tell you about it when she comes.'

She spoke casually but saw Sebastian look up, suddenly alert.

'You mean ... ?'

'Yes, your father has asked Charles and Elspeth to come over with Diana for lunch.'

'Least we can do,' her husband said, 'seeing we went to stay with them for a few weeks at the start of the war and stayed seven years. Don't know what you had against the idea, Barbara. Especially as you're so fond of Diana.'

Sebastian glanced at his mother, who looked away.

'I mean, now Rosie's back to help you there's no problem, is there?'

'It's nothing to do with that,' she told him, exasperated and wishing he'd stop going on about it. 'It's just that, well, I thought the journey might be too much for Charles. Now come along girls and let's get you some lemonade. Only made from crystals, I'm afraid,' she added, leading Debbie and

160

Felicity away. 'There are still no lemons to be had for love or money.'

'I've got a bottle of whisky hidden away, Sebastian,' his father said after they'd gone. 'Kept it for a special occasion.' He paused, looking puzzled. 'The only thing is, I can't remember where I put it. You know, I'm always losing things in this little house, much more than I ever did in the big one. There's a thing called a Drinks Cupboard. Not a patch on the old cellar. Pity you couldn't have built us a cellar, Sebastian. Cupboard indeed!'

Sebastian nodded and then asked as casually as he could, 'And when are the Arndales coming?'

'On the train that gets in at noon. Parker's meeting them in the trap.'

'The car's still laid up?'

'Charles? No, he's all right. At least, if he isn't, nobody's told me. Of course, Barbara did say—'

'No, father. The *car*.'

'Oh, you meant the car. You should have said so, my boy. Oh, yes, that's still laid up over in Broadley, where I put it when the war started. Bit of luck it wasn't here, or Hitler would have got it with all the rest.'

He was quiet for a moment, then, 'You know,' he said thoughtfully, 'I think we all made a mistake changing horses for cars. We'd never be in this mess if we'd kept to

161

horses. They don't need petrol, plenty of horse fuel growing all around us. Don't have to get it from some foreign place. And useful stuff comes out of their backsides. What do cars produce, eh? Exhaust fumes, that's all.'

'Well, horses came into their own in the war, father. If you'd been in London you'd have seen Irish hunters pulling Post Office vans, you know, and there are still plenty of horses and carts around.'

'Good. Hope they keep 'em even when petrol comes off the ration, if it ever does. But the price of 'em, Sebastian! Two hundred and fifty guineas you have to pay for a quite ordinary horse now, and Elspeth told us that they'd paid over a hundred guineas for a pony and trap and even a governess cart costs up to forty pounds. You couldn't give 'em away before the war.'

He looked around puzzled, then said, 'Ah, yes, I remember what I was going to do – look for the whisky.' And he ambled towards the door.

'I think I'll stay outside and wait for them to arrive,' Sebastian told him.

'Good idea. You do that, my boy.'

After his father had gone, Sebastian began pacing restlessly up and down the drive. He hadn't seen her for so long and waiting these few minutes seemed an eternity. But slowly the peace of the morning calmed him. For it was very still. The sky, which had been overcast as they travelled out of London, was clear now, pellucid blue with puffs of white clouds moving very slowly across it, as ponderous as those balloon barrages which used to fill the sky over London.

How untouched by war it was here! In London the debris of war was still visible at every street corner. Trees had perished, nothing seemed to grow except rose bay willow herb, which wreathed every bomb site and derelict building. Here the laburnum was hung with gold, the magnolia heavy with mauve chalices, the apple trees bright with their more delicate blossom, while in the distance wistaria cascaded down the remaining wall of the old kitchen garden. He walked across the lawn, newly turfed and uneven, and stood under the beech tree. He looked up through its branches, branches hung with leaves still only partly unfurled, and tiny pink flowers. There would be an abundance of beech masts this year, he thought, remembering how Partridge, their old gardener, used to grumble when he tried to gather them, proclaiming they were worse to sweep up than the autumn leaves.

Then he heard it, the clip-clopping of the pony, the rumbling of the wheels. For a moment he stayed to watch, wanting to see Diana before she was aware of him, as if stealing a look made it more precious. Then, as she began to help Elspeth down, he ran forward.

'How was the journey, Mrs Arndale?'

'Splendid, dear,' she said, kissing him.

He shook hands with Charles, who smiled his sweet smile and looked puzzled.

'I'm Sebastian,' he told him. 'You must come and meet my two daughters.'

He turned to Diana, longing to take her in his arms. She held up her cheek to him and he planted on it a kiss of the kind any man might give to his cousin by marriage.

'And how is your mother?' their grandmother asked the two girls, as they went in to lunch.

'Very well, thank you,' Debbie said.

'She's quite happy up there,' Felicity elaborated. 'You see, she likes living in the country and she hates London.'

Barbara Crawley looked at her youngest granddaughter with a mixture of admiration and compassion. How clearly the child perceived her parents' situation, yet how sad that, at her age, she had had to acquire such understanding.

Felicity listened fascinated to the conversation of the old people as they talked around the dining-room table at lunch time. She hadn't heard such speech before: the way they said *orf* for *off*, *gals* for *girls*, *lawst* for *lost* intrigued her. And why, since he'd been brought up by parents who talked like that, didn't her father do the same? Did he suddenly change one day when he realized it was funny and old-fashioned? Or did he gradually lose it without realizing?

'They're building in five acre field,' Grandpa Crawley was saying. 'About twelve houses, don't you know? It's going to be called – they did tell me, but my memory's getting so bad. What's that stuff that's used for washing clothes?'

'Persil?' Diana suggested. 'Or Sylvan flakes?'

'That's it, clever gal. It's going to be called Sylvan Close. Ridiculous name, not a tree in sight. They might catch a glimpse of our beech, I suppose, but it's not at all close.'

Felicity laughed.

'So what would you call it, Grandpa?'

'I shall call it Soap Flake Alley.'

'Not in front of the people who'll be living there, I hope, dear?'

'Talked to one of 'em yesterday, Barbara, met her in the lane, moving in soon, she said.'

'You didn't tell me.'

'Didn't think you'd be interested.'

'Of course I'm interested, Arthur, they'll be our neighbours! We must welcome them when they move in.'

'Don't see why, seemed rather a silly sort of woman. Said she was going to plant some newfangled Japanese Cherry tree that does not bear fruit. What's the point of growing a fruit tree that doesn't bear fruit?'

'The blossom is very pretty,' Diana pointed out.

'Can't eat blossom,' he told her. 'Have some more spinach,' he suggested, handing her the vegetable dish. 'Brought it on early, you know. Parker made some cold frames out of what used to be our windows before Hitler visited us. Full of vitamins, good for you now we can't get citrus fruit any more.'

'In the war,' Diana said, 'one of the patients was sent a lemon from America and raffled it. It raised thirty-five shillings for Spitfire Week, I remember.'

'Rosie managed to find four oranges last week,' Barbara said. 'Queued for nearly an hour, poor girl.'

After that the women began telling stories of goodies that had appeared in the shops and been queued for, recounting tales of oranges, lemons, a banana, a pineapple and other exotic fruit, of tins of Spam and un-rationed snoek, until Rosie brought in coffee which they guessed had been fabricated out of a mixture of chicory and ground acorns.

Debbie and Felicity didn't mind; they only drank water anyway.

'So what would you gals like to do now? Go for a walk?' their grandma asked.

'Didn't you say the croquet set had survived?' Diana said.

'Oh yes. It was down in that old brick shed, wasn't it, Arthur?'

'That's right. It was in there with the mowers and so on. They'd all been thrown about a bit and the box was broken, but I remember the croquet set had survived all right. Top-hole game, croquet, though I can't say I ever got the hang of it myself.'

'Do you want to play?' Diana asked them. Then, seeing their faces light up, added, 'No need to ask. I can see you do.'

So she and Sebastian and the two girls left the old people to their reminiscences and walked down to the shed. The girls ran ahead, Diana and Sebastian following, fingers intertwined. It was more than his flesh and blood could bear; he drew her under the beech tree and kissed her.

'The children ... ?'

'It's all right. They're making for the shed. Oh, my darling, isn't this a wonderful day? The girls love you, I can see that. And the agreement must come through any time now. So we really are on our way. It's the first time I've really felt confident.'

She smiled up at him, then he said, 'They're looking for us,' and released her.

So, full of hope on this spring day, sure that everything would work out for them, they walked, not holding hands but close together as two cousins by marriage might walk, towards the croquet lawn, where the girls, mallets at the ready, were waiting impatiently for them.

Eleven

Everything seemed to come alive when Vicky appeared at the flat. It was always like that. As she swept in one afternoon three days later, she seemed to bring with her the glamour and vitality of a different world. And she came laden with presents.

'They had heaps of supplies up there,' she said, putting down various bulging packages. 'Ferdy's father gets them from the farms he owns. Look, they've given me a chicken and some home-cured ham and some eggs and cream. Careful, Flea, keep it upright, the top's not too firm on the jam jar, I've nursed it all the way on the train. Then his mother's given me some fruit she preserved last summer, greengages and plums. Oh, and look, a bottle of wine and a whole pound of butter.'

They gazed at it.

'Four weeks' ration,' Debbie said in hushed tones, awestruck by the sight of it, as it lay in

168

state in the middle of the kitchen table.

'We'll make something special,' Vicky told them. 'Get the cookery book, Debbie.'

'There won't be any recipes with butter and cream in them,' Debbie pointed out, as she handed it to her.

'That's all right,' Vicky said, turning the pages. 'Where it says dried milk, I'll use cream, and where it says liquid paraffin or glycerine, I'll use butter. So what have you two been doing while I've been away?' she asked, looking up from the book.

'Sightseeing,' Felicity told her, 'But all those bombed buildings, it's awful. I'd no idea it was so bad.'

'Oh, they'll get rebuilt,' Vicky told her airily. 'Just a matter of time.'

And somehow it did seem possible that all those piles of rubble, those streets of shattered houses, those bomb sites overgrown with willow herb, would soon vanish and be replaced by new buildings, because Vicky said so. She was so confident you just had to believe her.

They could see their father was delighted to have her back.

'How's my girl?' he asked, holding her at arm's length to admire her new dress, before he hugged her that evening.

'We're dining in the dining-room tonight,' she told him. 'Come and look.'

169

It was all laid beautifully, the wine ready on the side table. Vicky always did things with – what was that word she'd just come across, Felicity wondered – with *panache*, yes, that was the word, panache, with style. What a contrast with scrambled dried egg at the kitchen table, Felicity thought, and knew that Debbie was thinking the same.

'Any news about the divorce yet, Daddy?' Vicky asked as they finished the greengages and cream.

Sebastian hesitated, taken aback by the abruptness of her question. He had talked to her about the divorce, of course, and knew she had discussed it with Debbie, who had probably talked to Felicity, but he didn't know in how much detail.

Then, turning to his younger daughters, he said gently, 'I think you know that your mother and I are planning to part? I just want you to know that you will always have a home with either of us and that we both care for you. You do understand that, don't you?'

They nodded.

'Does anything about it worry you?' he asked, his eyes anxiously raking their faces for any sign of doubt.

'No, we think it would be better for both of you,' they assured him.

'Thank you,' he said quietly, and he looked at them for a moment with an expression

170

Felicity couldn't quite make out, thankfulness, yes, but there was something a little sad about it. 'And now,' he said briskly, 'since Vicky's done most of the cooking, I think the three of us should see to the washing-up. There's an old saying, that "she who wields the saucepan, wieldeth not the dish cloth".'

'You made that up,' Felicity said.

'Maybe I did, but it's true all the same, so let's start clearing.'

'Then I'll go and finish unpacking,' Vicky said. 'It's Saturday tomorrow, so we can lie in. Or are you working, Daddy?'

'No, not this Saturday. We must do something special for Felicity's last day. Come on, you two, we'll talk about it as we do the washing-up.'

They were sitting round the kitchen table having breakfast when the post arrived. Felicity went to fetch it and handed it to her father, who was still in his dressing gown.

'Two for you, Vicky,' he said. 'Oh, and one for me.'

He recognized Celia's writing, very small, very neat. He opened it and took out the single sheet.

Debbie and Felicity watched him, Vicky was reading her own post.

The two of them saw his expression change, saw shock and dismay in his eyes, then he got up and abruptly left them.

171

Vicky looked up, saw her sisters' anxious faces.

'What's up?'

'Daddy.'

'Oh, I expect he's just gone to the lav,' she said, returning to her letter.

'No.'

They knew it was something dreadful, but couldn't explain how they knew, not in words that would sound convincing to Vicky anyway.

They finished breakfast and cleared away the dishes. When he returned, he was dressed.

Felicity put a cup of tea in front of him as he sat down at the table.

'I'm afraid,' he said, 'that my plans haven't worked out as I hoped.'

His voice was calm, expressionless.

'I heard from your mother this morning. She says she has changed her mind.'

'But she can't,' Vicky said. 'I mean, didn't you pay her?'

He sighed.

'I think I must explain to you, Debbie and Felicity, what Vicky knows already. I made an agreement with your mother that I should pay her quite a substantial sum of money if in return she would petition me for a divorce when I sent her the evidence for it.'

Even now, when he was telling them the stark truth, he couldn't bring himself to explain exactly what the evidence was.

'But you won't give her the money now, will you?' Debbie said.

'I have already given it, Debbie.'

He is so trusting, Felicity thought miserably. Her mother would never have been so trusting; she was always suspicious.

'You can ask for it back,' Debbie said.

'No, she doesn't offer to return it.'

'But you can make her. Isn't there a law against taking money for doing something and then not doing it? Couldn't you go to the police?'

He smiled, a resigned little smile, almost a grimace, Felicity thought.

'You see, Debbie, what I was doing was illegal anyway. You're not allowed to agree to a divorce. It's called collusion. No, I've no redress.'

'Why did she change her mind?'

'Perhaps she never meant to keep her side of the bargain anyway, Felicity. She says in her letter that, for financial and religious reasons, she won't be divorced.'

'But why financial?'

'She says that if I die she'll be better off as my widow than as my divorced wife.'

To imagine him dead! Oh, how could she, how could she?

He saw her stricken face.

'Come here, little Flea,' he said, and took her on his knee, just like he used to do when she was little.

'I don't want any of you to be worried by all this. I am only sorry, so, so sorry, that you have to know anything about it.'

'No, you shouldn't be sorry about that, only sorry about what's happening to you. But is it true, that bit about being better off as your widow?'

'Legally, yes, but I've told her I would have something drawn up to ensure she'd be equally well provided for either way, Flea. So I don't think that can be the real reason.'

'It's just spite then,' Debbie surprised them by saying. 'And you should fight back.'

Again that hopeless little smile.

'As the law stands, there is absolutely no way a spouse can be made to divorce.'

'It's so wrong,' Debbie blurted out.

'A lot of people do realize that,' her father told her. 'They think that if you've lived apart for five years, never spending a night under the same roof, that should be a reason for granting a divorce if one party wants it. And there is going to be a royal commission one day, but that takes time.'

'Well, I think,' Vicky said, 'that all you can do is make absolutely sure that you don't stay under the same roof ever, so that if the law is changed you'll have the grounds for divorce of having lived apart for so many years.'

'That's good advice, Vicky,' he said. 'And

174

it's what I intend to do. But I'm afraid it will be hard on you children, no more family Christmases together, family birthdays and so on.'

'It's a sham anyway,' Vicky told him. 'I shall be perfectly happy down here with you.'

'Thank you, darling.' He looked at them. 'I am lucky to have such loyal daughters,' he said.

How lovely it had all been until that horrible letter arrived and ruined it all, Felicity thought on the eve of her return to Netherby. How different everything was now! She was not looking forward to being reunited with her mother.

She admitted as much to Debbie in bed that night.

'Dreading it really,' she said, as casually as she could.

'I bet you are. It's all very well for Vicky to say she's quite happy to stay down here. Of course she is. But what about you stuck up there? Would you like me to come up at Christmas?'

'No, it's all right. You'll be happier here.'

'Yes, I suppose so, but what about you? I can't bear to think of you on your own up there.' She hesitated and then said sadly, 'Everything hurts more at Christmas, doesn't it?'

'Yes.'

Christmas without Arthur, Christmas without any of them now. It didn't matter whether it was death or unhappy marriages, everything hurt more at Christmas.

'Of course, everything might be different by then,' Debbie said.

'Let's hope so.'

'Goodnight.'

''Night, Debbie.'

She didn't sleep but lay staring into the darkness, haunted by the expression on her father's face after he had read that letter. He looked so downhearted, so utterly disillusioned. If only there was someone cleverer than she was to speak for him, somebody who knew more about divorces, somebody who wasn't just a schoolgirl. Someone sophisticated, somebody like Vicky.

But Vicky was too busy enjoying her second year at university. She'd said that her third year would be spoiled by Finals, so she must make the most of her last carefree term, though she might manage to spare a week to come up to Netherby in the summer, but, after that, would have to settle down to hard work and wouldn't be able to spare a moment at Christmas.

Anyway, she told herself, the fact was that Vicky and Debbie were now living in London; she, Felicity, was the one who was at Netherby, the one who could talk to her mother any time, so it really was up to her.

So she lay wide awake, longing to help him, afraid of failing him, as she listened rather enviously to Debbie's quiet breathing as she slept.

The next day her father took her to King's Cross, Debbie and Vicky having decided to make some kind of special dish out of the remains of the chicken.

It was a miserable foggy morning, more like autumn than spring. He talked of other things as they sat on the bus, about her school work, about what she might do when she left school, asked about her friends. She answered as brightly as she could, but she knew that he was trying very hard and that what both of them were really thinking about was the divorce. She wished she was older so that she could have the right words, as Vicky always did; she wanted to do something, say something, anything, that would make him feel better, but she was helpless and could only ache for him.

The train was waiting at the station; he found a seat for her and put her case up on the rack, then they stood for a moment in the corridor.

'You won't let this worry you, will you, poppet?'

'No,' she lied.

He kissed her and for a moment she clung to him, longing to stay here, not to be taken

177

away from him by this train. She could feel the tears prickling her eyes; she brushed them away as he climbed down on to the platform.

He stood at the open window. The guard came along, slamming all the doors. A flag was waved, a whistle blown, the train began to move. She caught hold of her father's hand, held it for a moment, then let go. She leant out of the window and watched him, a lone figure standing in the fog, his arm raised in farewell, until the train rounded the bend and he was lost from sight.

Twelve

Her mother didn't enquire about how she'd spent her time in London, and Felicity didn't volunteer the information. On the train, she'd gone on planning all the arguments in favour of divorce, which she'd worked out the night before, but somehow what had seemed simple on the train became impossible at the supper table; the planned phrases could not be uttered.

It should be easy to explain to her mother, she told herself in bed that night, that if her

178

husband wanted a divorce and her children wanted it too, it might be sensible for her to consider it, at least talk about it reasonably. But in the clear light of day, she knew that it was not in her mother's nature to talk reasonably about anything. The truth was she'd been too scared to talk to her mother, she'd funked it. And she went on funking it for the rest of the week.

On Friday a letter came for her from Debbie, evidently typed with the shoebox covering the keys, in which she said,

I8ve to do a job in the dummer flea to get practival experiende but I8ll try to come up. I8d really loke to come af Cgristmas too, Flee, it8ll be horrud for you but I think i8ll probablu be stayung in Lonson.

No Vicky and now no Debbie! It was definitely up to her alone to fight for her father, she thought as she settled down to her homework that evening. She must find the courage to do it. Then an odd thing happened: planning her English essay on *King Lear*, she found that instead of making notes about the characters of Goneril and Regan, she was making them about the arguments she might put to her mother. And then she began writing what her mother might say in reply, so it turned into a kind of

179

play. And it struck her that if she could pretend she was acting she could say the words she hadn't managed to say when she was just being herself. You're not yourself when you act, so it wouldn't seem so personal, it would be removed from everyday reality. Anyway, she liked acting. Before she went back to her character studies of Goneril and Regan, she made a solemn vow that she'd talk to her mother first thing tomorrow. So, pleased with the whole idea of the play, she returned to sorting out the relatively simple problems of the family life of King Lear.

The next morning the idea didn't seem quite so brilliant as they sat down to breakfast. The stone-flagged floor, the glass-fronted cupboard with the pressed leaves, didn't look like a stage set. They just looked like the kitchen, not at all removed from everyday reality. But this time she wouldn't funk it.

So it was in her most grown-up voice, trying to sound rather casual, as if she was just making polite conversation, that she said, as she scraped butter on to her toast, 'I read somewhere that they might alter the law about divorce, make it easier. Something about a royal commission.'

It wasn't exactly untrue, but she kept her fingers crossed under the table just the same. At least she'd broken the ice.

Her mother looked up sharply.

'And what do you mean by that, might I ask?'

The ice was broken, but there was black, cold water underneath it.

'I just thought that if ever you wanted to get a divorce,' she said innocently, 'you might be interested.'

'And why should I be?'

Her mother's eyes were narrowed, angry.

'Well, you live apart and you don't like London and,' she added, diverging from her script but thinking she might as well be hung for a sheep as a lamb, 'you don't like Daddy much either.'

'How dare you?' Her mother spat out the words. 'How dare you? What's it to do with you, child that you are, what your parents feel about each other?'

'Quite a lot,' she said defiantly, and then, recalling that she had vowed not to alienate her mother, she added, 'but it's you I'm thinking of really. I mean, you often say you need more money and you'd get a lot more this way. The article said you could claim something like a third of his salary.'

'And this article. Where is it?'

'It was in a paper somebody left lying on a seat on the train when I came back from London,' she said, still keeping her fingers crossed.

'Well, they should have put that I'd get more as a widow.'

Felicity flinched at the dreadful word.

'Oh, yes,' her mother went on. 'Under the new act a widow is provided for out of her dead husband's pension. I don't hold with this Labour government, but that's one good thing they've done.'

She couldn't bear it any longer, couldn't manage to sound detached and grown-up, like someone in a play.

'But he's *alive*,' she said fiercely.

Her mother shrugged.

'London's an unhealthy place,' she said. 'All those fogs and traffic. It's healthier in the country, so people live longer.'

She didn't know if it was true but fear gripped her all the same, silencing her.

'Besides,' her mother went on, 'I'd get his life insurance money. He increased it when war broke out and everyone thought people in the towns would be killed.'

A little smile of pleasure, of anticipation, played around her mouth.

Then the smile faded and she looked angrily at her daughter.

'It's disgraceful to talk as you have just done. Marriage is *until death us do part*, and I intend to keep my vows as I have always done.'

You must have done all your loving and honouring in secret then, because I haven't seen any of it, Felicity thought but dared not say.

'Yes, I've done my Christian duty,' her

mother went on self-righteously. Then, suddenly getting up and positively spitting out the words, she proclaimed, 'Whom God has joined together, let no man put asunder.' Then, pointing at Felicity, she added, 'And that goes for you too, Miss. So don't go meddling in things you don't understand. And now I've to go to the shop, so you wash up before you start on your homework.'

'Yes, then I think I'll go for a walk.'

'Do what you like. You always do.'

I've failed, Felicity thought miserably, as she took the kettle off the fire and poured its contents into the enamel washing-up bowl, swishing the lump of green soap in its little metal basket around in the boiling water. The water was hard, so the soap didn't make much lather. I've failed, she thought as she pushed the dishes about in the scummy water. Failed, she thought as she wiped the dishes. The word kept going through her head. I've failed him, she thought as a tear ran down her face and plopped into the dishwater. I was bound to fail really, because she's so illogical and illogical people always win because they use arguments other people can't use and it's all so *unfair*.

Only Debbie and Vicky really know what it's like, she thought as she set off on the lane that led up the dale. Nobody else would understand, not that she'd ever talk to anyone else about it anyway. People with normal families couldn't begin to understand. She paused for a moment at the top of the first steep hill and stood looking back over Netherby, a cluster of grey roofs, a church, a few trees: a village full of normal families.

When she reached the top of the dale, where the beck emerged from its underground haunts into the sunshine and began its meandering journey down to the village, she sat on one of the rocks and thought about Arthur and wondered how different it would have been if he had still been here. Would he have seen, as she did, how desperately their father needed to escape? The same age as Vicky, he would have been away at college by now. No, he would have been doing his National Service, probably miles away. Then, as so often happened when she was thinking about him quite calmly, the awful finality of his death suddenly overwhelmed her and she knew that she would soon be wracked with sobs, if she didn't take a grip on herself. So, determinedly she got up, her throat aching with unshed tears, ready to make her way back to Netherby.

She hadn't realized, as she'd sat there looking down at the beck, how the storm had been creeping up; the sky was a heaving mass of curdling clouds, black and grey, very low and menacing. Soon it would be bucketing down, she thought, but just for the moment that eerie light which precedes storms illumined the land below, so that the fields and hills and dipping vales, and even the sheep as they grazed, were touched with something strange. She loved it here, loved it with her whole soul. How perfect it would be to live in a happy home in this beautiful place, oh how perfect it would be. She stood very still, filled with this yearning, knowing she mustn't give in to it, this longing for the unattainable, aware that her mother would call this 'mooching about'.

'She's always mooching about,' she'd heard her mother say to her father on one of those occasions when they talked too loudly under her bedroom window. 'Wasting time, mooching about.'

'Adolescence is a difficult time,' her father had said.

'Adolescence!' her mother exclaimed. 'That's always the excuse nowadays. There was no such thing as adolescence when I was a girl.'

Her father hadn't replied and she had wondered if he was silenced by the harshness of his wife, or just trying not to laugh.

The problem of Christmas resolved itself, or rather nature resolved it by providing, in 1947, the hardest winter anyone could remember; it started early and finished late. By Christmas Netherby was cut off; the snow on the roads was higher than the top of the walls, so you couldn't even see where the road was, let alone drive a bus along it. Everyone, the government said, should stay where they were. So Debbie and Vicky stayed with their father in London and Felicity stayed with her mother in Netherby.

She minded less than she'd expected; it was so weird and beautiful. The snowflakes were huge and lazy; they didn't hurry down, but hung in the air, gliding and floating. If you tried to keep track of just one in all those millions that danced in front of your eyes, you could see that it drifted now upwards, now downwards, now sideways, before gently settling on the ground.

The snow didn't lie deep and thick and even, like it said in the carol. Not for long anyway, for soon the wind came and whipped it up, sweeping it off the middle of the fields, piling it up high against the walls, sculpting it into intricate shapes, scooping out the centre of snowdrifts, making a great overhang above them, like a wave, which stayed there frozen, looking so fragile, as if it might fall at any moment. But it never did, not until a thaw came.

There were thaws sometimes, but they didn't last long, just long enough for the snowploughs to try to clear a way up to the

186

main road, so that when term started in January she could go with the others, newspaper wrapped around thickly stockinged legs under wellington boots, scarves crossed over chests, mufflers on their heads instead of school hats, and walk the mile up to the main road and stand, shivering, waiting for a bus to pick them up and take them to school in Pendlebury. Sometimes by early afternoon the sky would be so overcast, so leaden with snow that anxious teachers would shepherd them on to any available bus to get them home before they were cut off again.

When spring came at last, it came with a rush as if impatient to declare itself. Everything seemed to be bursting with energy; the beck, swollen with melted snow, rushed through the village, lambs skipped like mad things in the fields, leaves didn't unfurl gradually, but seemed to snap open overnight, and bulbs, long hidden under the snow, were suddenly in full bloom. The hedgehog, by whose spines Mrs Pertree had placed a saucer of milk in the morning, turned out, when the thaw came, to be an old lavatory brush.

So the magic time was over and everything was back to normal, but Felicity didn't mind; she was going to London at the end of term to stay at the flat for two whole weeks.

Thirteen

'Come in here,' Vicky said, leading her youngest sister into her bedroom. 'I want to look at your nipples.'

'*Nipples?* Whatever for?' Felicity asked, taking off her blouse all the same.

'Because I might be pregnant and one of the early signs of pregnancy is that the nipples turn brown.'

She had taken off her own top too.

'They look about the same to me,' Felicity said, looking at Vicky's nipples, then peering down at her own. Then suddenly, '*Pregnant!* Did you say *you might be pregnant*?'

'Yes.'

'Oh, Vicky, have you had a secret marriage or something then?'

'No. Oh, do stand still and let me have a proper look. Maybe mine are a little bit darker.'

'But what are you going to do? What does Daddy say?'

'I'm not saying anything to anyone until I'm sure. I've only told you because of the nipples.'

188

'Isn't there a better way than nipples?'

'Yes, there is a test and I'm having it.'

'What do they do? X-ray your tum?'

'No, they take a urine sample and they put it into a frog and—'

'I don't believe it,' Felicity interrupted. 'You're making it up.'

'For goodness' sake, Flea, am I likely to make it up? It's a well-known test. It's called the Hogben test. If you're pregnant the frog has some reaction, I'm not sure what. Maybe it lays eggs, or comes out in spots or something.'

'How do they know the frog wasn't getting spots anyway? Like Debbie? Have you looked at *her* nipples?'

'No, not yet, partly because her skin's darker than yours and mine so it mightn't be so obvious. But I'll ask her this evening.'

'Good. And if you want to look at mine again, they're all yours, Vicky,' Felicity said, putting her blouse back on and speaking as casually as she could, although what Vicky had told her was so unbelievably terrible that she couldn't really take it in and just wanted to get away to be on her own to think about it.

She was glad her father was working late the next two nights, so that by getting up late and going to bed early she managed not to see him; she couldn't have borne to know this awful thing about Vicky when he didn't.

It would somehow be like acting a lie.

'I know what you mean,' Debbie said. 'I'm glad too. Only two days now until Vicky gets the results of that toad examination or whatever it's called ...'

'Frog test.'

'Yes, that's what I meant. But, oh Flea, how awful for the poor little frog, everyone staring at it to see if it's got spots or just a bit of sunburn.'

'Don't worry, Debbie. I expect they're well cared for and put back in a pond afterwards.'

'But just think,' Debbie went on tearfully, 'of the *agony* it must be to have some horrible wee injected into you. I mean, it's not what frogs are *meant* for, is it?'

'Well, I just hope it's more definite than the nipple test. I can't really believe that she might be pregnant, can you?'

'No.'

But by the weekend, they had to believe it.

'It's positive,' Vicky said, 'so I shall have to make plans. I'd better ring Ferdinand.'

Their father wasn't back yet. Her two sisters stayed nearby, hovering near the phone in case they were needed.

Ferdinand told her not to be so silly. It was a false alarm, he said. Don't panic, he said.

For the first time, Vicky looked scared.

Debbie took the telephone. She, who had always been so nervous of speaking up for herself, managed to find voice for her sister.

'It *is* true, Ferdinand,' she said. 'She had the toad test.'

She handed the telephone back to Vicky and the two of them left her talking to her baby's father.

'I'll tell Daddy after breakfast,' Vicky said on Saturday morning. 'While you two wash up.'

They did the dishes in silence, while Vicky and their father were closeted together in the sunny drawing-room.

'We'd better not go in, had we?' Debbie asked in a whisper.

'No, better wait until they come out.'

So they crept past the drawing-room door and went upstairs, where they sat on Debbie's bed, wondering what was being said downstairs.

'He'll be very upset,' Felicity said. 'It'll be awful for him.'

'I suppose it's awful for Vicky too.'

'Yes, but she'll make it work out somehow or other. He'll just blame himself.'

'Why? It's not his fault.'

She shrugged.

'I don't know, I just think he will. He'll think he should have brought us up differently or something.'

'But that's silly. It's not as if we're all three pregnant.'

'No, but I think he blames himself because we haven't got a more motherly mother.'

'That's not his fault either. Well, yes, I see what you mean.'

They heard sounds from downstairs, a kettle being filled in the kitchen.

'They're stirring,' Felicity said. 'Let's go down.'

Their father was standing by the drawing-room window, looking down the garden. He looked very serious, they both agreed afterwards, and anxious.

He hardly spoke until Vicky brought some coffee in, then he said, 'Well, Vicky will have told you her news. Obviously we must all help and support her. Ferdinand has sent a telegram asking her to marry him and she has replied, accepting him. She would like the wedding to be in Netherby—'

'Oh!'

'Yes, Debbie?'

'Nothing, I just thought she'd want to have a quiet little service in a registry office.'

'There is no reason,' Vicky cut in, 'why I shouldn't have a proper church wedding. I should like you two to be bridesmaids.'

'But, oh, what will Mummy say?'

Felicity and Debbie looked at each other, both thinking of their mother's views, her constant denunciations of immorality. She would be furious. She would never agree to this wedding.

'I shan't tell her,' Vicky said. 'And neither

will any of you.'

'But afterwards, won't she guess?'

'I'll tell her the baby's premature. Anyway, I'll deal with that afterwards. I've always been able to twist her round my little finger.'

Debbie nodded. It was true, but it was an uncomfortable truth.

'I shall explain that Ferdinand wants to have the wedding quickly,' Vicky went on, 'because he is moving to a new job which he starts immediately after Finals.'

'Oh, *Finals*,' Debbie repeated. 'Will you be allowed to take them when you're, well, you know ... ?'

'When I'm pregnant? Of course I'll take them.'

'But girls get sent down if that happens,' Debbie persisted, fearful for her sister.

'Oh, *really*, Debbie! Do you think I'm going to tell them? Of course they won't know. I shall still be quite trim, only three months gone, and I intend to keep well.'

'Yes, I see,' Debbie said, wondering how she had so underestimated her sister. Of course Vicky would see to everything and make it all right.

The telephone rang; their father went to answer it.

'Vicky,' Felicity said. 'When you're talking to her, could you talk to her as well about the divorce?' She spoke quickly, not wanting to talk about it in front of her father. 'I did try,

193

but I wasn't much good and she takes more notice of you than of me.'

'Oh, we'll soon sort that out now,' Vicky assured her. 'When I'm a married woman I shall have much more influence over her. I'll explain the advantages of being divorced. I'll speak to her as an equal, with authority. In fact, I shall make it clear that she won't be allowed near the baby if she doesn't act sensibly about the divorce.'

'Oh, Vicky, would you really dare to say that?'

'Of course. And Ferdinand and I will invite you all up for Christmas, but she won't be able to come, because it is important for the divorce that they don't stay under the same roof. She doesn't like going away at Christmas anyway, she's so afraid of pipes freezing and bursting. She'll be just as happy at home with her friends in the village.'

How easy Vicky made everything sound, Felicity thought, remembering her own despair. She was so useless compared with her eldest sister; it was lucky that her father had such a daughter for his firstborn.

'The main thing now is to get the wedding organized,' Vicky said as her father came back into the room. 'I must see to my dress, send out invitations. I shall go up to Nether-by with Ferdinand next week to arrange with the vicar about dates.'

She was so calm, so controlled.

'I'll start making lists of guests now,' she said. 'I'll do it in the dining-room, the table's bigger.'

'I'll come with you, darling,' her father said. 'And I think the first thing you must do is ring your mother and explain about this somewhat rushed wedding.'

They went out together. Debbie and Felicity were left alone.

'Mummy'll guess, won't she?' Debbie said.

'I don't know. She might, but Vicky will persuade her. Vicky can convince anybody that black is white.'

'And charm the monkeys out of the trees,' Debbie quoted.

'I like that,' Felicity said. 'Where did you read it?'

'One of her friends said it.'

'It's true. I reckon she'll carry this off. If it had been one of us, we couldn't have done. We don't look noble enough.'

'If it had been one of us, we'd have been looking ghastly and vomiting.'

'If it had been one of us, everyone would have been shocked and condemning.'

'If it had been us, the baby's father would not have asked us to marry him.'

'No, he'd probably have done a bunk to South America.'

Everyone said it was a lovely wedding in the old church at Netherby. Vicky was demure in white, her sisters in shell pink. The very word *pink* filled Debbie with an irrational fear that she would have to wear some backless garment, but the bridesmaids' dresses, like the bride's, had necklines cut high, and long sleeves. As she stood behind her and heard her make such solemn vows, Felicity was struck, more than she had expected, by the enormity of the occasion. Vicky really was leaving them to cling unto Ferdinand for ever. And when her father, having walked slowly up the aisle with his daughter, said he was the one giving her away, she knew, just *knew* how much the words must grieve him. To give away someone so special, so precious, it must be awful for him. She said as much to Debbie that night, alone in the bedroom they were sharing, and Debbie said she'd felt the same and didn't he look sad, but then they agreed that, really, giving away a pregnant daughter can't be quite as bad as giving away a virgin.

Fourteen

'It's a boy,' her mother said, holding the telegram in her hand, when Felicity came in from school. 'I must go immediately; she'll need a lot of help with a premature baby. There's food in the larder and Mrs Pertree says she'll keep an eye on you.'

Mrs Pertree was solicitous; she was sorry for poor Felicity, stuck at school with important exams, not able to go and see her brand new nephew. She volunteered to stay overnight in case the child was worried about sleeping alone in that rambling house, but Felicity adamantly refused her companionship.

In fact, her mother returned sooner than expected. She wasn't very communicative.

'He's a fine boy,' was all she said, as she hung up her hat and coat in the hall.

'What's he going to be called?'

'Giles Dudley Ferdinand.'

Felicity was disappointed; she'd hoped that Vicky would have put their father's name into it somewhere, but knew better than to say so.

'How much did he weigh?' she asked instead.

'Nine pounds ten ounces.'

'That's quite a lot, isn't it?' asked Felicity, who was not well versed in infant weights.

'It's too much for a premature baby,' her mother said. 'Come and sit down.'

Felicity did as she was told.

'This baby,' her mother began, 'is not, as we all supposed, premature. Vicky has told me that it is full term, conceived nine months ago. That was very wrong of her, she committed a sin. But she is perfectly frank and honest about it and assured me that she had no idea whatsoever that she was pregnant when she was married. Yes, she promised me on her honour that she didn't know at the time. She even offered to swear on the Bible, but of course I told her that wasn't necessary. So you need never mention the subject to her. There must be no scandal. The matter is closed. As far as our friends are concerned, the baby is premature. We owe that little deceit to Victoria.'

'Oh,' Felicity said, remembering the frog test and the nipples inspection.

'Oh, what?'

'Oh, I just wondered if Debbie and I can go and see the baby?'

'Yes, you should,' her mother unexpectedly replied. 'You are both aunts now and should

198

take your responsibilities seriously.'

And so it was arranged that Debbie should travel from London to Netherby after work on Friday, then the two of them would go together to Vicky's for the weekend.

'Good,' Debbie said, when they had found an empty compartment on the train. 'Now we can talk. I didn't dare say anything while we were at home. I mean, it's so odd, isn't it?'

'Not really. We knew Vicky would manage it somehow.'

'Yes, but that stuff about swearing on the Bible. She didn't *need* to say that ...' Debbie's voice trailed off and she shook her head in disbelief.

'I think she *did* need. She always needs to go further than anyone else.'

'A lie would have been enough. She didn't need to sanctify it.'

'Maybe she believes it.'

'Oh, Flea, of course she can't, not after all that business of the poor frogs and your nipples.'

Vicky was waiting for them at the station. They were both taken aback by the sight of her. She had always been beautiful, of course, but now she looked ravishing, aglow with health and well-being. She was wearing a long, deep-blue coat, with sloping shoulders, a nipped-in waist and full skirt which reached almost to the delicate little boots edged with fur. Her hat too was fringed with fur which matched the fur on her pretty little muff. They had never seen clothes like this before, except on Christmas cards.

'Golly,' Felicity said, hardly daring to embrace her sister in case she did some damage, 'you do look super, Vicky.'

'It suits you being a mother,' Debbie remarked, also giving her a careful kiss, fearful of upsetting the hat.

Vicky pulled a face and shrugged.

'The best thing was getting back to being a decent shape again,' was all she said. 'Come on, the car's outside.'

'Goodness, do you drive a car?'

'Didn't I tell you?'

'No, you never write,' Debbie told her bluntly.

Vicky laughed, 'Sorree,' she said and nobody could say that word less apologetically than Vicky.

'I'm always so busy, you know,' she said as they got into the car, Debbie in the passenger seat, Felicity in the back with their shared case alongside her.

'Ferdy arranged for me to have lessons,' she went on as they drove away from the station, 'and I passed my test just before the baby was born. I expect the examiner wanted me out of the way before I popped.'

She was quiet for a moment, negotiating a

narrow bend in the road; they could see that she was a good driver, but then Vicky always had been capable at everything.

'Usually Ferdy drives to work but he went by bus today so that I could have the car to meet you.'

'Oh, dear, did he mind?'

'Of course not, Debbie. He knows I need the practice and, besides, I wanted to bring you back in style. Here we are,' she added, turning up a short drive. 'It's quite a pretty house, but a bit small.'

It didn't look very small, this stone-built house, with its bow windows on each side of the front door, Felicity thought as Vicky stopped the car with a flourish at the top of the drive.

'Ferdy will put it away later,' she said. 'Come on in. I've put some tea ready in the sitting-room and I'll take you up to your room later.'

As they sat drinking tea and eating scones and cake, Vicky again told them that the house was too small. 'It's not really big enough for entertaining,' she said. 'Next year, Ferdy's parents are going to let us move into their big house and they'll find something smaller. They might even move in here. They're really incredibly sweet to me.'

'It doesn't *look* small,' Debbie put in, 'but I suppose you'll need more rooms when you have more children.'

Vicky laughed.

'Oh, one's enough for me,' she said. 'Ferdy's got his son and heir, so it should be enough for him too.'

'By the way,' Felicity put in. 'Where *is* he?'

'Ferdy?'

'No, the baby.'

It struck her as a bit odd that there was no sign of this baby they had come to see.

'He's up in the nursery with Nanny,' Vicky told her. 'She's a marvel. One of the old school, Ferdy's mother says. She was Ferdy's nanny and has retired now but is going to stay for three months until I get myself organized.'

She talked more about the nanny than she did about the baby.

'Do you two mind sharing the guest room?' she asked as she led the way upstairs. 'It's got twin beds.'

'Of course not,' Debbie assured her. 'We always share when Flea comes to London.'

'Can we see the baby?' Felicity asked, dumping her belongings on one of the beds.

'Oh, yes, I forgot. Of course, come along to the nursery. Ferdy's father paid to have it all redecorated. It's really sweet. You'll love it.'

Giles was a plump and placid baby, very like his father, Felicity thought, but didn't like to say, as it seemed a bit of an insult to both of them.

Nanny was a tiny, gentle little woman, but

202

made it plain that their presence would not be welcome when she gave the young master his bottle in a few minutes' time. Meanwhile they were free to gaze at him and even hold out a finger, which he gripped with flattering eagerness.

Ferdy had come in from work when they came downstairs, and was waiting for them in the sitting-room. He greeted his sisters-in-law warmly but the look that he turned on Vicky was one of pure adoration, mixed with a little uncertainty, as if he couldn't quite believe that he had won such a prize.

'And how is my darling girl?' he enquired. 'What sort of day have you had?'

'What sort of day should I have had?' she asked in a tone of affectionate tolerance, which certainly had no element of adoration in it. 'What excitement could there be here? But, of course, it's lovely to have my sisters to stay.'

'Debbie and Felicity,' her husband enthused, turning towards them. 'You must stay as long as you can, as long as you *possibly* can. Vicky will love having you and I—'

'Could you see to the drinks, Ferdy?' Vicky interrupted. 'I'm sure we're all longing for one.'

'Of course, of course. I do apologize. Now what would you girls like? I think we have something of everything.'

Unaware that they had been longing for

203

a drink, unused to having one, they didn't know what to request. Finally Debbie settled for whatever Vicky was having, and Felicity had orange squash. It set the pattern for the weekend, Vicky requesting luxuries on their behalf, Ferdy apologizing and none of them seeing much of the baby.

Vicky drove them to the station on Sunday afternoon. She needed the practice, she told Ferdy, who was worried about her driving in the dark, for although it was only four o'clock, the light was fading early on this murky November evening.

'Well, it's goodbye till Christmas, I'm afraid,' Vicky said, 'if you're sure you can't get up for another weekend.'

'I've got entrance exams,' Felicity told her.

'Daddy's coming up in a couple of weeks and, of course, he'll be here for Christmas. He can have the other spare room.'

'What about Mummy?'

'She's been invited to the Beales', but I wouldn't let her come anyway. It's vital that they don't stay at the same time. The law says you mustn't sleep under the same roof throughout the five years of separation if you want a divorce.'

'People could be in different houses but under the same roof if they were in semi-detached houses, couldn't they? Or flats if it comes to that.'

'Oh, Debbie, you're hopeless. Just stop worrying and leave it to me. I'll see to everything.'

'It's odd, isn't it,' Debbie said as they sat together on the train. 'I mean, how much stuff they have up there.'

'What sort of stuff?'

'Well, all that food and drink. I mean, in London you can't get anything except rations. Just fancy! We had eggs for breakfast two mornings running and there was plenty of butter.'

'They know lots of farmers. I think Ferdy's father owns a few farms and anyway he's a magistrate.'

'Do magistrates get extra rations then? I didn't know that.'

'I don't expect so. I just meant they have all sorts of connections and things.'

'We'll ask next time we go. And Daddy would know. He's coming up next month.'

'Funny to think he's a grandfather. He looks too young for it.'

'He doesn't look so young now, Flea. He looks worried most of the time.'

'About the divorce?'

Debbie nodded.

'But he shouldn't worry, Debbie, because it's all going to be all right. Vicky said so. She says she's got much more influence with Mummy now that she's married and has a baby.'

'How feeble her own efforts had been compared with those of the all-powerful Vicky!

'Oh, yes, Flea, it's bound to be all right if Vicky is seeing to it. She's so good at things and she always gets her own way in the end. I'll tell him that.'

The telegram telling her she had been offered a university place arrived on the same December day that her mother told her she would be spending Christmas with Vicky. The joy she might have felt at the first was cancelled out by the second.

'But I thought you were going to the Miss Beales,' she said.

'Vicky's need is greater,' her mother told her. 'That nanny has had to leave earlier than they all expected. It has to do with arthritis, I believe. So Vicky needs her mother's help.'

There was a look of malign triumph in her mother's eye, but still Felicity could not believe what she was hearing. When her mother went out that evening, she rang her father.

'Mummy says she's going to spend Christmas with Vicky. It's not true, is it?' she demanded.

There was a moment's silence at the end of the line, then she heard his weary voice say, 'Yes, darling, it's true.'

'But Vicky said, *promised*—'

'Circumstances have changed, Flea. Babies are hard work. She needs her mother more than she needs me. You must understand that.'

And when she needed you, she used you, Felicity thought but did not say. She found she could not speak; unshed tears choked her.

'I shall stay at a hotel in the area. I'll join you during the day.'

'I'll stay with you,' she managed to say.

'No, you stay with Vicky as arranged. You and Debbie can help too.'

'Please let me stay with you in the hotel.'

She couldn't bear the idea of his going off at night to some strange hotel, while all his family stayed at home with Vicky.

'No, darling, but thank you.'

There was a pause, then he asked, 'I suppose you haven't heard anything from Oxford yet?'

'Oh, yes, they sent a telegram this morning offering me a place.'

'Darling, that's wonderful news. Congratulations.'

There was such joy in his voice, such genuine delight. He asked a few questions and when they said goodbye, he congratulated her again, adding, 'It's marvellous news.'

'Yes. Thank you,' she said, but she put the receiver down knowing that nothing was marvellous any more.

207

Fifteen

'It was *horrible*,' Debbie said, as they got ready for bed in the same room as they'd had before. 'I mean, Daddy and I travelled up together on the train from London, just like anyone would, but then when we arrived, I got into the car with Vicky to come here and he had to get into a taxi to take him to some strange hotel where nobody knows him.'

'I know. It's cruel,' Felicity said simply.

'Oh, Flea, what can we do?'

Felicity didn't reply. She had thought about it and not much else since she had known that her mother was coming here for Christmas. Christmas had always been the worst time of the year ever since she could remember, but this was going to be the worst one of all.

'We can't do anything. Vicky could, but she won't.'

'I don't understand her, Flea. Why has she changed so, gone back on everything she ever said about the divorce?'

'Better ask her,' Felicity told her.

'Shall we? Yes, let's when we get the

chance. Both of us together. I don't think I'd dare, not on my own.'

'All right, but we'd better go to sleep now, or it'll be Christmas day already.'

So they lay still, not speaking, but sleep did not come easily to either of them, both dreading the morrow.

'He won't be here for at least half an hour,' Vicky remarked at breakfast. 'His taxi's ordered for ten o'clock.'

'Oh, I'd have gone and fetched him,' Ferdy said. 'That would have been much more welcoming, especially on a horrible foggy morning like this.'

'You should have offered sooner,' Vicky told him. 'It was quite difficult to get a taxi on Christmas day.'

When the taxi did arrive, the women were all in the kitchen washing up; it was Ferdy who opened the door. He was carrying the baby, so shook hands awkwardly with Sebastian and led him into the kitchen, where Sebastian hugged and kissed his three daughters and bestowed the obligatory peck on Celia's cheek.

'There, I'm sure you want to hold your grandson,' Ferdy said, handing him the baby.

Giles Dudley Ferdinand, alarmed at being so abruptly handed over to a stranger, especially one newly in from the cold outside world, looked aghast, his lips trembled, his face puckered. He arched his back and gave vent to howls of dismay.

Celia walked swiftly across to him and took him from Sebastian.

'Come to Granny,' she said.

The baby relaxed, snuffled, yawned and smiled.

'That's a lovely smile,' Celia told him and began walking him up and down the long kitchen, murmuring, 'A lovely smile for Granny. Granny loves you,' and other endearments.

Debbie and Felicity watched and heard, as they were intended to. Vicky appeared to be concentrating on arranging around the tree the presents which her father had brought. Only Ferdy, innocent as his baby son, appeared unaware of the tensions all around him.

'Come with me into the sitting-room,' he said to Sebastian. 'Oh, and I must show you the dining-room. Vicky's decorated it so beautifully. In fact, the whole house. She's so clever at these things. Do you see those gourds? And those poppy heads? She's painted and varnished each and every one.'

Afterwards Debbie and Felicity agreed that it would have been much worse without Ferdy's parents. Walter and Letitia arrived for lunch, obviously enchanted with their daughter-in-law, full of praise for the new furniture, the decorations, the meal; in fact, everything delighted them.

'Dear Vicky is such a good homemaker,' Letitia assured Sebastian. 'And she's so clever too. You must be very proud of her, of all your daughters really. And your wife's a wonderful granny, such a worker, she is.'

'Never stops,' Walter agreed.

Listening to them throughout the day, Felicity thought, *they're normal, normal people from happy homes where nobody tries to destroy anybody else. They could never understand a family like ours.*

The fog cleared on Boxing Day, a day of sharp air and bright sunshine. Ferdy's parents suggested a walk.

'Show you a bit of our countryside,' Walter said.

'If you don't mind, I'll stay at home,' Vicky said. 'I'm just a bit tired and I'd like to put things ready for lunch.'

'I'll stay and help,' Felicity offered, pulling a face at Debbie, who looked puzzled, then said, 'Oh, yes. I'll stay too.'

'Isn't that lovely?' Ferdy's mother remarked, smiling benignly at them. 'Three devoted sisters all wanting to help each other.'

So the five of them set off, Ferdy leading the way with his father and Sebastian, the two grandmothers following, taking it in

211

turns to push the pram.

When they had gone and the house was suddenly quiet, Felicity took Debbie's hand and drew her into the dining-room, where Vicky was arranging place mats.

'We want to talk to you, Debbie and I,' she said.

'What about?' Vicky asked, counting out knives and forks. 'Oh dear, some of these forks are very brown. It's egg that does it. I really think I ought to clean them,' she added, going back into the kitchen.

Her sisters followed.

'We want to talk about the divorce,' Felicity said.

'Yes, that's right. We want to talk about it,' Debbie agreed.

'Oh yes?' Her voice was abstracted. 'Now, where did I put the Silvo?'

'Please, Vicky, it's important.'

'I'm sure it is. But so is the silver. Ah, here it is. Now for some cloths. Excuse me, I think there's some in the scullery.'

'I'll get them, then we can talk while we polish the silver.'

'All right. They should be in one of the drawers, but I'm afraid Mrs Dodgson who "does" for me doesn't always put things back in the right place.'

At last the Silvo, the cloths and the forks were assembled. Then Vicky had to go and get newspaper to spread on the table.

'Oh, I do envy you two,' she said. 'You in London, Debbie, and Flea soon off to Oxford.'

'But it's lovely up here, this beautiful house, the baby and Ferdy ...'

Vicky yawned.

'Oh, I know all that,' she said. 'But it's very lonely and I do miss having people around. I can't tell you how *boring* it is up here compared to down south. I'll let you into my secret plan. I haven't even told Ferdy yet, but he'll agree, I know he will. I'm going to find a job just as soon as I can.'

'But the baby?'

Vicky shrugged. 'Oh, I'll make good arrangements. But I met someone I knew at Cambridge and he's looking for someone to help in a research job, only part-time, so it would suit me. It might even involve going to London sometimes. I can't wait.'

Felicity looked at the clock. The others might be back soon.

'About the divorce, Vicky—'

'Yes, what about it?'

'Well, you said you'd see to it, you were the one who said they shouldn't be together under the same roof.'

'Well, they're not, are they?'

'Oh, Vicky, you know that's not what you said. You said you'd have all this influence over Mummy now because of the baby, you said you wouldn't let her come unless she agreed to keep her side of the divorce bargain and—'

'I couldn't stop her coming. What do you expect me to do? Put up a portcullis? Raise a drawbridge every time she appears on the horizon? Don't be absurd.'

And somehow it did seem absurd, put like that.

'But, Vicky,' Debbie put in, valiantly trying to salvage the argument, 'you know how important it is. You can see how drawn and tired Daddy seems, how hopeless.'

'He's not the only one who's tired,' Vicky put in. She sat down and sighed, a martyred expression on her face. 'I'm tired too, very tired sometimes. And I do find all this talk about divorce rather upsetting, so, if you don't mind, we'll just get on with preparing for lunch.'

They didn't talk any more after that, just did ordinary things, like laying tables and peeling potatoes as normal families do.

'She's so *convincing*,' Debbie murmured to Felicity as they carried plates into the dining-room and arranged them on the hot tray which had been one of Vicky's wedding presents. 'Even when she's lying.'

'Especially when she's lying,' Felicity corrected her.

Then they both stood still, looking at each other, surprised at what had been said, as if the words might have been spoken by somebody else.

They heard the front door being opened and the pram being pushed into the hall.

'I'll take him up,' they heard their mother say. 'He's ready for his feed.'

'You are such a stalwart,' Walter said. 'He's a lucky boy to have you for a granny.'

'Oh, well, I couldn't refuse, could I, when Vicky rang begging me to come and help,' their mother replied.

Sixteen

'You're going to love Oxford,' her father had said as he saw her off at the station on a misty October morning. 'It's just right for you. It will suit your free spirit,' he added unexpectedly.

She thought of his words a few days later as she walked in the University Parks. She hadn't understood them at the time; she did now. She *did* feel free here, free of constant disapproval, free of her mother's endless criticisms, free of the need to be guarded in what she said, free of the need to conform at school.

Here nobody judged you; people were free

to be themselves. She'd just passed an undergraduate going down Parks Road reading a book as he walked. At school that would have been regarded as mad and possibly exhibitionist. Here, if you wanted to finish a chapter, you could finish it as you walked and why not?

She liked her lodgings in a big house in North Oxford. There were nine other undergraduates in it: four freshers, three second years and two third years. The third years were remote and, being endangered by Finals, were treated with the respect due to people walking in the shadow of a terminal illness.

The other three freshers were quiet at first, possibly homesick, since it was their first time away from what were obviously happy homes. The second years were confident, happy to explain everything.

'The butter and sugar rations are in the cupboard,' one explained when she came down to breakfast the first morning. Only butter and sugar were left on the ration now, so eight ounces of sugar was put out in a little labelled jar for each of them; likewise four ounces of butter in a little labelled dish.

'You can either scrape a bit on every day and make it last a week or slap it on thick and after three days have dry toast. It depends what sort of person you are. Which are you?'

'I don't know – but I shall find out by the end of the week,' Felicity told her as she carried the two precious dishes over to the dining-room table.

The others were already eating. Two of them were grumbling about having to be in by ten thirty at night.

'It's archaic,' one of them was saying. 'Whoever is indoors every night by ten thirty when they're at home?'

'I am,' Felicity told her. 'There isn't much going on in Netherby at that hour.'

They laughed and asked her about Netherby and then they took to grumbling about parents who made them come home by midnight and wanted to know where they'd been and even shamed them by coming to meet them. She was amazed at the way they grumbled, these girls from happy homes. Whatever her mother did, she would never have criticized her to anyone outside the family, and nor would Debbie. How could these girls from happy homes be so disloyal? Maybe they didn't mean it; it was sometimes hard to tell here if people were serious or not.

She didn't know if Bruce Robert was serious or not when she met him a few weeks later and he promptly told her she was the prettiest and most entertaining girl he'd ever met. Of course, with a name like that it was hard to take him seriously anyway. But he was fun to be with and soon they were walking and talking together, drinking coffee together in the morning, having beer and cider at the Lamb and Flag together in the evening.

'Come to my rooms tomorrow afternoon,' he said one Friday evening. 'I'm going to get some half-price cakes from the cake factory – you know they sell them off cheaply at the weekend? – and crumpets we can toast by the fire.'

'No, I've got an essay to do for Monday.'

'Bring it. I've got one for Tuesday so we'll work together.'

It was the first time she'd been in the rooms of a man's college. Compared with the bedsitters which girls had, these two rooms seemed very grand.

'Why have you got two doors?' she asked as she went in.

'The inner one is a door. The outer one is called an oak, though they may look much the same to you,' he added, closing the outer door and then the inner one. 'That,' he explained, 'is called sporting the oak and it's what you do when you don't want to be disturbed.'

'Because you're working?'

'That and other things, darling Felicity,' he said, taking her in his arms.

Taken aback, she struggled to get free and then realized that it was rather nice as it was, so relaxed instead as he kissed her.

She hadn't been kissed before, hadn't realized it could go on so long. After a while, her head found itself on his shoulder and she realized what a comfortable thing a man's shoulder is, just at the right level for one's head, with a nice kind of hollow for it to fit into.

She could have stayed like that for ever, but he moved her gently over to the big armchair by the fire and settled her on his knee, kissing her the while. And this was even better, she found.

Every now and then they stopped kissing and just looked at each other. He had nice eyes, in fact a nice face altogether, which she'd noticed before, but somehow it looked different now, so close to hers and with this new loving look in those eyes.

She wasn't sure how it happened, but somehow his hand was inside her blouse and resting on her left breast. They lay very still for a while, his hand not moving, until he began very gently to stroke it with his fingertips. Something like an electric shock ran through her, as if every bit of her had suddenly sprung into life. The only problem was that her right breast felt a bit left out of things. He must have sensed this, because he reached both hands inside her blouse and tried to undo her bra. He failed and muttered a curse.

It broke the spell.

She moved his hands away and pulled her blouse back as it should be.

He looked at her and smiled.

'I knew that was pushing it a bit,' he admitted. 'Sorry.'

'Oh, that's all right,' she told him cheerfully. 'It was lovely. I've never been kissed before. I can't think why people don't do it more often.'

He laughed.

'You're priceless, Felicity Crawley,' he told her. 'D'you know that?' Then he went on more seriously. 'But I really didn't know you'd never been kissed or I'd have – well, I'd have perhaps stopped sooner.'

'I've told you it's all right. It was lovely. Shall we toast the crumpets now?'

So they sat by the gas fire eating toasted crumpets and half-price cake before getting out their books and settling down to work.

The weeks passed, this term and the next, the only cloud on the horizon being Prelims at the end of the second term; fail those exams and you were out. They worked hard and neither of them failed.

'Now,' Bruce said, 'we can really enjoy a lovely idle summer term. It's not what the authorities intended, but it's what we're going to do. I shall take you out punting and every day there will be brilliant sunshine.'

It was brilliant when they set off that first day, Bruce expertly punting them down the river.

'You're jolly good at punting,' she remarked.

'I have to admit – since your honesty is catching – that I've done a surreptitious bit of practising,' he told her. 'I didn't want to let you down.'

She smiled and lay back among the cushions, watching the bank glide by, watching the ripples the pole made in the water, watching the punter's rhythmical movements. It was the most beautiful place in the whole world, she thought, and wondered what she'd done to deserve this. And she thought, as she so often did, how unfair life was. If only her father had known happiness; he should have had a real home with a proper wife, so that when the children grew up and flew the nest the two of them would still have each other and it wouldn't seem dreadful to go away and leave him as she had done. There'd be no guilt in it then.

'Penny for them?' Bruce called down to her. 'You're looking too serious.'

She smiled and shook her head. It would be no good trying to explain to someone from a normal home. They belonged to a different world. Anyway, it would be disloyal. Disloyalty, it had always seemed to her, was the ultimate, unforgivable sin.

As if reflecting her mood, the sun went in and quite suddenly rain clouds blackened the sky.

Bruce steered the punt into the side, and moored it under overhanging trees.

'No point in getting soaked,' he said. 'I'm coming to join you.'

And he came and lay beside her on the cushions and pulled a tarpaulin over them just as the first heavy drops began to fall. They lay looking up at the clouds, listening to the steady plop, plop of the rain, which quickened, grew heavier, so that soon they pulled the tarpaulin over their heads and lay entwined beneath it.

'You're better at bra-management than you were,' she remarked a little while later.

'It's like punting,' he told her. 'Improves with practice.'

He put the offending garment to one side and said, 'I can't think why women who have such lovely soft breasts should want to squeeze them into these horrible hard garments. I mean what *good* does a bra do? I'd ban the lot.'

He sounded so righteously indignant that she laughed and laughed.

He asked her to stop.

'Laughter is a non-aphrodisiac, Flea. A man can't make love to a laughing woman,' which only made her laugh more.

'Honestly, I can't stop,' she said. 'If you

222

could see how you look – the picture of injured innocence.'

'Then I'll stop the laughter for you,' he said and turning her head, kissed her hard on the mouth and at the same time stroked her breasts, her stomach, and gently slid his hand down between her legs.

He did not need to part them; she did so herself, willingly.

Then, as she felt his fingers inside her, she drew back, suddenly afraid.

'It's all right, Flea,' he whispered. 'I do know the rules.'

So she relaxed and gave herself up to all the delights, all the new sensations, all the feelings she hadn't known her body possessed, until she became breathless with excitement, could feel her heart beating faster and faster and it all came together in a great explosion of joy and she called out his name in what sounded like a cry for help, as if she was lost from the world. He held her close, he held her tightly to him and she felt wonderfully safe and happy in his arms.

It was quite slow, her return to the everyday, to the remembrance that they were lying in a punt under a tarpaulin and the beating rain was now a mere drizzle. She felt as if she had come down from some great dizzying height to a calmer plateau, as in her childhood she used to come down from the great wild fells to the gentler little hills around

Netherby, whose green slopes were dotted with sheep and boulders, with remote farms and villages and with drystone walls encrusted with lichen which felt rough against your fingers. How strange that the image of it should come back to her so vividly now, as she returned slowly to the familiar world.

She saw that Bruce was watching her intently. She felt suddenly exposed, looked away, hid her face against his chest.

'Don't be shy,' he said gently, oh so gently. 'It was lovely, wasn't it?'

She nodded into his shoulder.

'And for me,' he said.

That was puzzling. She looked up at him.

'But nothing happened to you,' she objected.

'Making you happy is enough,' he said simply.

The rest of the term passed quickly. She enjoyed the work, liked her tutors and her friends, spent time with Bruce, who always obeyed what he called the rules, and was delighted when Debbie wrote to tell her that she had got a new job, about which she'd tell her when she came back at the end of term.

Debbie's typing was perfect now; she had long ago progressed beyond the shoebox stage. Felicity smiled at the remembrance of her and suddenly longed to be back with her father and sister in the flat, back in the real world.

'It's great about the job, Debbie' she said as they sat together in the kitchen on her first day back in the flat. 'Well done.'

She wasn't sure what exactly the new job was; only that it was with a company with offices all over the world and Debbie might work in any of them. It was much better than the job she'd had with the travel agency which closed down because, the manager said, people hadn't yet gone back to travelling the way they'd done before the war; the public had to get used to the idea that you could make a journey without having to fight someone at the end of it, he said.

'They might send me abroad in about a year,' Debbie explained. 'It could be anywhere. You just have to accept the good and the bad postings. I might be lucky and get one in Rome or Paris, but the next might be in somewhere horrible.'

'You mean you might be sent to Timbuctoo?'

'Where's that?' Debbie had asked, surprised.

'Oh, it's just one of those sayings. It means any remote place. But I hope your first job will be somewhere they speak French or German or Spanish, so you can use all those languages you've been working away at for years.'

'Thank you, but it wouldn't matter very

much, because even if I was sent to the Far East, say, they'd still have customers in Europe and letters would have to be written. They buy and sell things anywhere, you see.'

Felicity didn't really see, especially as she couldn't imagine Debbie selling anything, and as for buying things, it always took Debbie for ever deciding. She said so, but Debbie just laughed and said she wouldn't have to buy and sell, she'd just deal with the correspondence.

'It's lovely to have you back,' Debbie said suddenly. 'I'm so glad it's turned out like this.'

She knew what Debbie meant; it seemed to be taken for granted that she would come here now that her mother had taken up semi-permanent residence with Vicky, looking after the baby while Vicky went to work at the research department of a big pharmaceutical company in Birmingham. Vicky didn't mind the journey, she said, and if the weather was bad could always stay the night midweek to cut down on the travelling.

'I don't think Ferdy can like it at all,' Felicity remarked. 'I remember how shocked he looked when Vicky said something about getting a job the time we were there for Christmas.'

'Oh, that awful Christmas!' Debbie exclaimed and shivered at the memory of it. 'Oh, how could she?'

'I don't know. She can do things other people couldn't do.'

'Is it because she's so clever, d'you think?'

'No. Cleverness doesn't make people do bad things. The cleverness is in getting away with it.'

'She does, doesn't she? Get away with it, I mean. Look how Ferdy puts up with it. He marries the brilliant, beautiful Vicky and gets her mother instead, while she goes off to Birmingham. You'd think he'd do *something*.'

'He won't though. He'd be too afraid of upsetting her. He'd end up apologizing.'

Debbie nodded. They were both picturing Ferdy with his eyes of dog-like devotion, doing his Vicky's bidding. And if she kicked him, he would only wag his tail and come back for more.

'He won't be much help over the divorce,' Debbie said. 'Oh, Flea, I didn't tell you. Daddy has been talking of giving up the flat. He says that with Vicky settled and you away at university and me maybe abroad, there isn't any need for it.'

'But where would he go?'

'He says he'd go somewhere smaller, even into lodgings. He doesn't say so but I think the three of us having such an expensive education has used up all his savings. And he has to pay for Mummy's house too. Of course, I can help now I'm earning—'

'And I can take out a loan for my last year.

But I can see what he means, Debbie.'

'But I just think it will be so awful for him to go into some miserable lodgings without any of us around.'

She thought for a moment and then said, 'Do you know what I think, Flea?'

'No. What?'

'That it would be a good idea if one of us got married and made a home for him. Later we could have a baby in it that would really love him.'

'Like Vicky's baby didn't, you mean?'

'Yes.'

They sat quietly for a moment, both remembering what had happened that Christmas when the baby wouldn't let their father hold him.

'Of course, one of us could make a home for him without getting married, somewhere outside London maybe, a cottage maybe, somewhere healthier. Mummy said ...'

'What?'

'Oh, nothing. I've forgotten.'

She couldn't bear to repeat the words her mother had spoken about how their father would die young in London. It wasn't true, of course, and yet he didn't look as well as she used to remember him, so that sometimes she was filled with dread, fearing that her mother might be right.

'I once said to him, Debbie, that if he couldn't marry someone because he could

228

not get divorced, we wouldn't mind, you and I, if he just lived with someone.'

'Flea, you *didn't*!'

'Yes, I did. And I think it would be better than living on his own. And honestly, you know, Debbie, however hard we tried, I don't think we could make a proper home for him, just ourselves. An older woman would do it much better. I mean, daughters are only daughters.'

'What did he say, when you said that, I mean about living with someone he wasn't married to?'

'He just smiled and said no, that would be very dishonourable. He said he didn't think he could love the sort of woman who would agree to such an arrangement.'

'No, of course he couldn't.'

'But, Debbie, what's the alternative? Don't you see, he's trapped. I said so to Vicky. Trapped and despairing, I think I said.'

'What did she say?'

'She told me not to be melodramatic.'

'She would! Oh, Flea, when I think how he stood by her when she was pregnant and did everything ...' her voice broke.

'I know. It's awful. But he's got us.'

Debbie sighed.

'I don't think I'm much of a substitute for Vicky,' she said.

'Don't be so silly.'

'It's *true*. I'm not poised like her and I'm

not so clever.'

'Of course you are.'

'I didn't even try for university. I'm not like you.'

'Well, you've done very well without it. You've got this fantastic job and soon you'll be travelling all over the world, meeting interesting people and going to places other people never get to, like India and China. I'll probably get no further than Calais and I'll have some boring academic job in a stuffy little office and be middle-aged before my time.'

She had pulled her hair over her face, peered at her sister, squinnying over imaginary spectacles until Debbie couldn't help laughing.

'Oh, Flea,' she said, shaking her head. 'You're such a clown.'

'Tomorrow I'm going to be serious and go looking for a vac job,' her sister told her. 'Then he won't need to give me any pocket money next term.'

She found a job more easily than she'd expected; it was as a filing clerk at a building society.

'It's the lowest form of human life,' she told Debbie after her first day. 'I just sit there in front of this great revolving drum with a pile of little slips of paper that the secretaries have typed. Then I have to put the slips into the right place on the drum, in alphabetical order. That's all I do all day, all four hundred and eighty minutes of every day. Well, there is a lunch break and we do sneak off to the lavatory as often as we can. But I don't know if I can stand it for more than a couple of days.'

But she did stand it and earned five pounds a week, so explained to her father that she didn't need pocket money next term. He smiled and thanked her, but gave it to her just the same when he put her on the train that would take her back into her other world.

Bruce was waiting for her at Oxford station.

'I've missed you,' he said. 'Horribly. Don't you think it was just a little unkind not to let us meet all this long vac?'

'No, I was working and so were you and anyway we wrote.'

'Letters are no substitute for this,' he said seizing her there and then on the busy platform.

'Not here – it's public,' she hissed, pushing him away. 'It's the sort of thing people get sent down for.'

'All right. Back to my place.'

'No. I want to unpack.'

So they went back to North Oxford and she unpacked while he wandered restlessly round the room, picking things up and putting them down again in a frustrated kind of way until at last she took pity on him and they cycled back together to his college, where everything continued as before.

How easily she had slipped back into this other world, she thought, as life fell into its familiar routine of essay crises and tutorials, of work in the library interrupted by coffee at the Kardomah, of lectures and concerts, of walks in the Parks and by the river, of going out with Bruce and, of course, staying in with Bruce, of evenings drinking coffee in the common room with the other girls and talking well into the night.

It still amazed her, the way that these girls from happy, normal families talked; they were so confident, so sure of themselves and of life. They thought themselves lucky to be growing up in the second half of the twentieth century when wars were a thing of the past, when years of peace abroad and reform at home stretched ahead in some kind of golden future. They lived intensely in the present, never looked back. They grumbled about their parents but took it for granted that they would always both be there for them, that they would always be together. They were so full of hope; they seemed to have no sense of dread.

She felt as if she belonged to a different and gloomier tribe, but played the part of an inhabitant of their innocent world, a role she had long ago learned to play at school. She knew that out there, off-stage, the real world would be waiting for her at the end of every term, and meanwhile she was on a kind of temporary loan to this one. So she smiled and laughed and joined in, was popular and known as something of a clown. Thus they all got on well together and it didn't occur to her that others might also have dark secrets and be pretending, as she was.

The only thing which upset the even tenor of undergraduate life in the common room was the news that Linda, one of the third years, had been sent down for being pregnant; it cast a shadow over all of them, not because they liked her particularly, but because it brought home to them the fact that such a terrible fate as being sent down actually existed; you really could be driven out of Eden.

It was towards the end of the summer term, on a cold wet Saturday, that Bruce came for her and said, 'Too cold for punting, so it's tea at my place.'

'Crumpets and second-hand cake?'

'Not second-hand.'

'Shop-soiled?'

'You never get it right, do you? The expression, newly minted in America, is *cut price*.'

Later, having sported the oak, consumed crumpets and cake, they were sitting by the gas fire when he said suddenly, 'It's time to think ahead.'

'Yes, Finals next year.'

'Well, there is that of course, but actually I was thinking of something else.'

'Yes?'

'Will you marry me?'

'Oh, no!'

The words seemed to spring out of their own accord. He was shocked by the force of them, looked at her, speechless.

'It's just that, no, I don't want to marry, ever.'

'Why ever not? People do, you know, and it suits them. Nature intended us to be in pairs.'

'But it can be so dreadful, so unbearable and—'

He leant forward and took her hands in his.

'I know' Flea, that you've never talked about it, but I've had the feeling that your father and mother don't get on well together.'

She could only nod at this grotesque understatement.

'But that shouldn't put you off all marriages. I mean, my own parents aren't exactly passionately in love. My father can be a bit crotchety but my mother jogs along with it.'

Oh, the difference between jogging along and hatred! Oh, the innocence of people like

Bruce who don't know *from the inside* what it's like to be in a marriage made in hell. That's what her parents' ill-starred pairing had been. People like Bruce just didn't know the risks. It was all very well for him to say nature intended us to be in pairs, but oh the misery when the wrong pairs are locked together and can't be separated.

'We'll talk about it another time,' Bruce said gently. Then, when she did not reply, he added, 'I'd like to meet your father one day. You haven't talked much about him but I know how fond you are of him; I can see it in your eyes whenever he's mentioned.'

She didn't want them to meet, didn't want her father to think some outsider was important to her. If she had to choose between them, she'd certainly choose her father, which must mean, she realized, that she wasn't in love with Bruce, just liked him and the feel of him.

She made some non-committal reply.

'I've upset you,' he said. 'I'm sorry. Come and be comforted.'

And he picked her up and carried her into the bedroom.

They had progressed this year from the armchair in his study to the bed in the adjoining room. It was only a single bed – narrower than the divan bed in her own bed-sitter, which was of course out of bounds, since there was no oak to sport on the door

– but a lot better than the armchair.

He was very gentle, very tender, and so she gradually got over her panic about his proposal and relaxed in his arms. His voice, which she loved to hear, kept telling her he loved her, and his hands, which she loved to feel, told her the same. When she felt herself slipping at last wonderfully out of control, until she was calling out his name, she almost said the words she knew he longed to hear. Afterwards she thought that if he'd asked her to marry him then, at that precise moment, she might have said, *'Yes, oh Bruce, yes.'*

So she was very glad that he hadn't.

'What are your plans, Flea?' Debbie asked her as she sat on her bed watching Felicity unpack. 'Are you going to get a job again?'

'No, I've got to work – Finals next year.'

How had it happened so quickly? One minute you're a fresher and the next minute a third year. She'd let those golden days in that other world slip past too quickly.

'Well, we can still go out at the weekends, can't we? Surely you will take weekends off?'

'Then you might be posted abroad this year.'

Debbie shook her head.

'I'm beginning to feel that they don't think

236

I'm good enough to be sent anywhere.'

But evidently they did, for the next week they told her that she was being posted to Paris.

Seventeen

Debbie looked more and more miserable as the day of departure approached. Felicity's heart ached for her as she watched her pack the two heavy leather cases, cases their father had had from *his* father, covered in stamps and emblems that bore witness to pre-war visits to the continent. One was called *expanding* because it had two metal runners which raised the height of the lid so you could put twice as much into it. Even so, they both had to sit on it before their father could manage to fasten the locks.

'Do you need so much stuff, Debbie?' Felicity asked. 'Honestly, you'd think you were going for good and—'

She checked herself, realizing that Debbie's eyes had filled with tears because she really did *feel* as if she was going away for good.

Debbie was still struggling to hold back

tears when they reached Victoria Station. Miserably she followed the porter, while her father said, an edge of desperation in his voice, 'You can always come back, darling, if you don't like it,' and Felicity said, 'You will write, won't you?' and would have liked to hold her sister's hand but was afraid that such a demonstration of affection would be too much for poor Debbie, who might just stand still and howl, there in the middle of Victoria Station.

The boat train was waiting. The porter lifted the cases on to the rack, accepted his shilling tip and left the three of them standing in the otherwise empty compartment.

'You've got your passport and your francs, haven't you?' Sebastian asked.

Debbie, speechless with misery, just pointed to the new shoulder bag he had bought specially for her.

'Tomorrow evening,' he said, 'I'll book an overseas call to your hotel. I'll ask for about eight o'clock, but you're not to worry if you don't hear, because sometimes they're too busy to put a call through. And if you have any problems at the hotel they've arranged for you, you must tell your Monsieur Frin at work. He sounds very helpful. But I hope they'll manage to find you a nice little flat very soon.'

'Yes, thank you,' Debbie managed to say. 'They have this personnel department and there are other English girls too, so ...'

She couldn't go on, but fortunately the guard came round telling non-passengers to dismount, so, after a last hug, they got down on to the platform, watched for a moment as Debbie tried desperately to smile at them through the window, until at last, to the relief of all three of them, the train pulled slowly out of the station.

Felicity held his hand as they walked to the bus stop, and kept it in hers as they sat on the bus, as she used to do when she was little. She wanted him to know, but hadn't the words, that she was still there, and always would be, even though the other two had gone, though of course the sadness of parting with Debbie must be as nothing compared with the awful pain of Vicky's treachery.

They didn't talk; it was only when they were back at the flat that Sebastian broached the subject of leaving it.

'The expense really isn't justified now,' he said. 'My idea is that I might find a service flat. They do have partly furnished ones, so I could keep my special bits and pieces, my desk and bookcase and so on. And I'd make sure there was a spare room for you or Debbie when you need it.'

When she didn't answer, he said, 'It makes sense, darling.'

Oh yes, it made sense; but it was the breaking up of the nearest thing they'd ever had to a happy family home, without the tensions and bitterness of her mother's house. She remembered, as she lay in bed that night, the weekends in the garden, only a small garden, but they'd worked in it, played in it, relaxed in it. She remembered their attempts at cooking, the recipes that had gone wrong, the way they'd muddled through. Of course, yes, it made sense for him to go to a gardenless little flat where everything would be done for him, meals prepared and brought to him. But oh how soulless, how sad. It seemed like the end of an era.

She was surprised the next day to have a letter from Vicky. Vicky hardly ever wrote letters, so she opened it with a feeling of dread. She read it and handed it to her father.

'I think you should go, Flea,' her father said, handing her back the letter. 'It seems that Vicky really needs your help.'

Apparently her mother had sprained her wrist and, splinted and taped, had had to go home for a week to rest it. Vicky had managed to get a retired nurse to come in temporarily but she was too elderly to do anything heavy. It would be wonderful, Vicky wrote, if Felicity could come and stay and maybe help a little with the odd jobs about the house.

'But I've still a lot of reading to do before next term,' she objected now. 'I was going to go and work in the Senate House library all next week.'

And now that Debbie's gone, I want to be here with you as much as possible, she thought but did not say.

'You can always take work with you,' her father suggested. 'I don't expect you'll be needed to help *all* the time. But, of course, I do see that you wouldn't be able to concentrate properly. No, it's up to you, darling. You must do what you think right.'

Put like that, she saw she had no alternative but to go.

Vicky greeted her effusively at the station the following evening.

'Darling Flea!' she exclaimed. 'What would I do without you? It's wonderful to have you here. I've really missed you so much and you'll hardly recognize Giles, he's the most enormous two-year-old you ever saw. You'll just adore him and I know he'll love you. You're going to have a wonderful time up here.'

'What exactly do you want me to do?' Felicity asked, not wanting her sister to get away with the pretence that she'd been invited for a holiday.

'Well, the thing is, darling,' Vicky said,

241

steering carefully down the narrow road from the station, 'Nurse Geldard is getting on and really needs a spare pair of hands to help out. You know the kind of thing, like hanging out the washing and so on and maybe taking Giles out for a walk. When he holds hands he does rather drag on your arm, which I think didn't help Mummy's wrist, though she'd absolutely insist on taking him for walks. You know what she's like. Frankly, Flea,' she went on, dropping her voice conspiratorially, 'it's a relief not to have her here. I mean, you know how she does *go on* rather, don't you? It's very boring. You'll be so much more fun to have around and far better company for Giles.'

Felicity didn't reply; it seemed to her that Vicky, by using their mother as an unpaid servant, had forfeited the right to criticize her.

'Don't bother with your case,' Vicky told her later. 'Ferdy can bring it up when he gets in from work.'

Ignoring this instruction, Felicity picked up the case and followed her into the house.

'You're in the room you shared with Debbie,' Vicky told her, leading the way upstairs. 'I'm afraid quite a lot of my clothes have overflowed into your wardrobe,' she added, as she opened the bedroom door, 'but the top drawer of the chest's empty.' And she sat down on what had been

242

Debbie's bed.

'How is she?' she asked. 'I haven't heard for ages. And of course I don't have a minute to write.'

'She loves Paris,' Felicity assured her. 'She's settled in really well and she is so happy in her little flat. She writes about it in every letter. I'm going to see her in the Easter vac.'

Vicky sighed.

'Paris,' she said. 'How lovely. I do envy you both, Flea. I'm very tied, of course, and I can't just take time off.'

'I suppose you could give up your job?' Felicity suggested.

Vicky looked at her sharply.

Then she smiled a sad little smile and said, 'Strictly between ourselves, Flea, I can't really afford to do that. Ferdy's work isn't going too well at the moment, so, frankly, and to be absolutely honest with you, we need everything I can earn.'

Felicity was shocked. Straitened finances were not something she had ever associated with this household. On the other hand, one never could be quite sure with Vicky. So she did not dispute what her sister had said, but neither did she offer sympathy.

'Where's Giles?' she asked instead.

'Ferdy's taken him out for a walk, so he'd be off my hands and I could concentrate on you. Actually Ferdy quite likes taking him out and there's a park with a children's playground not far away. Now come and meet Nurse Geldard and I'll put on a kettle for tea.'

Nurse Geldard was a spritely, talkative little Yorkshire woman, much less decrepit than Felicity had been led to believe. She had put their tea ready on a tray and was doing some ironing when they went into the kitchen. Vicky introduced them and then said she must go and pack.

'I always leave on Sunday evening,' she explained. 'It's a shame in a way, but so much easier than travelling in the rush on Monday morning, and it means I can settle in at the hotel and be fresh for work the next day. Of course, I'm usually at home for a couple of nights. Being away all week because of this conference is very unusual. Now if you'll excuse me I'll just put a few things together.'

'It's a really modern kitchen, is this,' Nurse Geldard told Felicity, after Vicky had gone. 'And that new washing machine's a right marvel. Come and have a look see,' and she turned off the iron and led the way into the scullery.

'It's got this electric mangle, here see, with rubber rollers. You lift it up like this,' she explained, raising the mangle to demonstrate, 'and, when you put the clothes through, the water runs down into the tub below and it all

244

folds away so neatly when you've done, you can use the top for putting things on. There's still the old mangle out in the shed. Your mother said it should be kept because we get so many power cuts and the electric mangle wouldn't be any good then, now would it? Very sensible, is your mother.'

'Oh, you've met her?'

'We had a day together so she could show me the ropes. And she left everything in order and plenty of food prepared in the larder. That's one of her cakes you'll be having for your tea. She's grand is your mother. Vicky's lucky to have her. She can go off knowing all's well at home.'

The days soon took on a pattern.

'You have to have a routine with children,' was one of Nurse Geldard's many sayings. So she fell into a routine of taking Giles to the shop in the morning, bringing him back in the pushchair because it was a long walk, dropping off the shopping, giving him a drink and then setting off again for the park. After that he was put to bed for his rest while she helped Nurse prepare the lunch. In the afternoon she either took him out again or played indoors until tea and bedtime. He was an amenable little boy, very like his father, and seemed not to miss his mother.

'He's a good little lad,' Nurse Geldard said. 'He'll go with anyone, he will. Just as well too,' she added with, it seemed to Felicity, a touch of disapproval in her voice.

In the evening, when Giles was in bed and supper cleared away, Nurse Geldard liked to go to her own room and listen to the wireless.

'I know I'm welcome to sit with you both,' she told Felicity that first night. 'Mr Thorndale has told me so, but we all need our privacy, that's my view.'

So Felicity went and sat with her brother-in-law by the fire, working while he read the paper. To her surprise he disappeared into the kitchen at ten o'clock that first evening and returned with a tray, two cups of cocoa and some of her mother's home-made cake.

'I always did this for Vicky,' he said, 'and still do when she's at home. I like to do these little things for her. So it's no trouble to do it for you as well.'

He smiled, and added sadly, 'I do miss her, you know.'

Remembering what Vicky had said, she sought to cheer him by saying, 'I suppose it helps to have two salaries coming in,' thus implying that it was duty, not choice, which took his wife away from him.

He looked surprised.

'Oh, by the time she's paid for her travel and hotel expenses out of it, there's not much left. And what little there is has to be added to my salary, which puts us into the higher range of taxation, so we're probably

246

worse off in the end. Not that I mind that, please don't think so, Felicity,' he added hastily. 'And of course I pay her expenses so that she can keep what she earns. The main thing is that she enjoys her work and that's all that matters.'

He leant forward to poke the fire and then added, 'She is so talented, your sister, she needs stimulating company, I quite understand that. You see, I'm quite a dull sort of chap really. So I do know what a lucky man I am.'

'I'm staying on a bit next week,' Nurse Geldard told her on Friday evening when Ferdy had gone to the station to meet Vicky, 'just to see your mother back into things. I'll miss you, I must admit it. You've been a grand help. You wouldn't think of staying a few days longer?'

'No, I must get back,' Felicity told her.

She had work to do. Besides, Ferdy wasn't the only one who was on his own in the evening.

As she spoke, they heard the others returning, Ferdy radiant at having his wife back home, Vicky less enthusiastic about it and looking, Felicity noticed, very tired.

'Oh lord, I need a drink,' she said, immediately they were alone in the sitting-room.

'Anything you like, my sweet,' Ferdy said. 'I think we've got most things. How about a dry sherry?'

'I think a brandy would do me good, or some whisky,' Vicky said.

'Are you sure?' he asked, surprised. 'I mean, *spirits*?'

'Of course I'm sure, or I wouldn't have said it,' she told him.

He said nothing, but went away and returned with the brandy.

She rewarded him with a ravishing smile. 'Sorry I was grumpy,' she said. 'Forgive me?' and she turned her face towards him for a kiss.

'You know there's nothing to forgive,' he said. 'And anyway I think I could forgive you anything.'

Embarrassed, Felicity muttered an excuse and left them to it.

She was determined to have one more attempt at persuading Vicky to do something about the divorce, but they never seemed to be alone together. It was not until Sunday morning, when Ferdy had taken Giles to the park and Nurse Geldard had gone to church, that she was able to raise the subject when they were alone in the kitchen, Vicky making a sauce while she peeled the potatoes.

'Oh, must you go on about it, Flea? I've told you there's nothing I can do, and frankly I think he's quite resigned to the situation now. It isn't as if he wanted to marry again.'

'*Resigned*, that's what's so awful. As if he's given up. Vicky, please listen. Look, all the rest of us are so lucky. Mummy's perfectly happy at Netherby, doesn't want him around, you've got everything you want here – husband, son, job – Debbie's happier in Paris than she's ever been, and I'm OK. We've all got things in front of us, but he's the only one of us who's been left alone with nothing, and he's the one who's provided all three of us with what we needed. We *owe* it to him, Vicky,' she added passionately. 'You must see that. Don't you feel you *need* to help him? In this one way *you can* help him. Nobody else can. Only you. And you *promised* long ago. I was there, I *heard* you and I *know*.'

Vicky's face had hardened during this tirade.

'You don't know what you're asking.'

'Yes, I do. All right, you'd risk offending Mummy, maybe losing her help for a bit, but all you have to do is make a bargain with her, as you said you would. Freedom for him in exchange for her being welcome here. She'd listen to you, Vicky. She won't listen to me or Debbie.'

'You and Debbie are so childish, so un-sophisticated. I've told you I can't stop her coming here, she probably finds life easier here, she doesn't have to work so hard as she

249

does when she's at home.'

It's a bit odd, in that case, that it's taken two of us to replace her, Felicity thought but didn't say.

'Things are better as they are, believe me,' Vicky was saying. 'Why upset everything, when everyone is happy as things are?'

'He isn't happy, I've just told you.'

'He always sounds perfectly all right if I ring up.'

'He pretends. Oh, Vicky, if he leaves our flat, it will be awful for him.'

'Nonsense, Flea. Really, he'll be far better off in a service flat, no worries, everything seen to—'

'By strangers.'

'And it isn't as if he wanted to remarry.'

'He should be free to. Then one day he might remarry and be happy, but I think just being free would make him happy. Oh, Vicky, if only for a little while he could be happy, have someone to put him first, the way he's always put us first, to love him as he's loved us ...'

She stopped, almost in tears now.

'Pull yourself together, Flea. You're always so melodramatic, as if he was going to die or something.'

'I think he might,' Felicity whispered, horror-stricken.

'Come here,' Vicky said, putting her arms around her. 'You're getting yourself all worked up over nothing.'

Felicity stayed rigid, not responding to the embrace.

'You've said some rather unkind things to me,' Vicky was saying in a sad little voice, 'but,' she went on bravely, 'I shall put them right out of my mind because I know you don't mean all you say when you get into a silly state about things.'

But I do, I do, Felicity thought. Yet it was true that their father would not like her to upset her elder sister. Upsetting Vicky had always been some kind of sin, only expiated by apology, which led to forgiveness. Now she had committed the sin once again and, even after all these years, the childhood feeling of guilt returned. All the same, she was not going to apologize, even if it meant that Vicky did not forgive her. Even if it meant Vicky conjured up some retribution.

She shuddered and was still, relaxed for a moment in her sister's embrace, then withdrew and blew her nose.

'Now let's get you organized,' Vicky said in a much more down to earth voice, as if everything was now satisfactorily back to normal. 'Look, I'm going to make you sandwiches for the journey and you ought to get packed if you're to catch the two thirty train. I'll make us some coffee.'

Then she was all sisterly sweetness, wrapping up the sandwiches in the neatest of

251

parcels, putting in the last of the home-made fruitcake.

'Was there anything of yours in the wash?' she asked, putting on the kettle to make them some coffee.

'Only my petticoat. It's in the airing cupboard.'

'I'll get it. You put out the mugs.'

She came back carrying one of her own petticoats.

'Yours is still damp, Flea. So I've brought you one of mine.'

'Oh, no. I won't take it, Vicky. I'll just pack mine if it's too damp to wear. It must be nearly dry anyway.'

'But you can't travel without one on.'

'Of course I can. I haven't had one on all morning.'

And she lifted up her skirt to prove it.

'Oh, Flea, it's different on a train. No, darling, I can't have my little sister going on some dirty old train without a petticoat.'

She didn't want to take the wretched thing and have the bother of sending it back, but there was no arguing with Vicky, who insisted on her putting it on, there and then. It seemed she couldn't do enough for her younger sister.

'Thank you so much, Flea,' she said as they stood on the station platform that afternoon. 'I'm so grateful to you, what could I have done without you? You've been wonderful.'

So Felicity was sent on her way, covered in praise, well stocked with sandwiches, the unwilling wearer of her sister's petticoat.

Eighteen

'So how did it go?' Sebastian asked on her first evening back in the flat. 'How were they all?'

'I didn't see Vicky much. She was away at a conference to do with her job.'

'And Ferdy?'

'He's fine.' She hesitated, then added, 'Lonely, I think.'

She didn't say more, not wanting to sound critical of his firstborn daughter.

Sebastian nodded, sad for a moment, as if he understood all too well, then he smiled and said, 'And how did you get on with the elderly nurse?'

'Very easily, because she never stopped talking. I just had to nod or grunt now and then to keep her going.'

'Like one of those toys you wind up and off it goes?'

'That's right, just one turn of the key and she was off. But no, it's sad really. Her fiancé was killed in the first war. They were going to get married on his next leave, it was all planned. She'd made the dress and the day she finished it, the telegram arrived.'

'Poor soul! There were so many like her, Flea, so many young women bereaved, so many young men lost.'

He shook his head, remembering his friends killed in that war, men like Diana's brother Teddy and, oh, so many others.

He looked sad. The room didn't look very cheerful either, Felicity thought, for it was one of those grey, damp sort of evenings which make everything seem drab. She got up and switched on the standard lamp, then lit the old-fashioned gas fire whose porcelain chimneys were wide and curvaceous and had a welcoming, homely look. Soon its flames changed from yellow to orange and it began to make its companionable popping sound.

Her father smiled up at her, stretching his long legs out in front of him towards the fire.

'Was it worse than this war?' she asked.

'It was different this time, Flea, because the war was being carried on at home too, whereas in the first war most people had no idea what it was like at the front. They thought war was something glorious. This time nobody thought that, not once the bombing started. I remember on the first night of the blitz seeing people coming out of the shelters and looking around in a dazed kind of way at streets thick with broken glass and great piles of rubble where yesterday their homes had been. And it went on like that night after night.'

'So it was like that when you came up to Netherby and we never realized? At least I didn't. I used to listen to the news about the fighting abroad, but I honestly don't think I had any idea what the bombing in the towns was really like. It was only when I saw the bomb sites *after* the war that I began to understand.'

'Well, the official policy was not to say anything which might help the enemy and damage our morale at home.'

'But *you* never talked about it either.'

'There was no point in worrying you, darling. Every day I thanked God that you children were safely out of it. Sometimes the whole of London seemed to be on fire.'

He paused. Very rarely did he talk about the war.

'Go on,' she nudged.

'Such strange things happened, Flea,' he began slowly. 'Odd events stick in one's mind. When they attacked the docks, they dropped bombs first and then poured down hundreds of incendiaries so that the contents of the warehouses were thrown up and mingled with the flames. There were pepper fires when one warehouse was hit, and a paint fire which sprayed the fire engines white.'

'And the firemen?'

'Many died, from burns or suffocation.' He shook his head, remembering. 'I often thought that it was as hard for the firemen, the rescuers, the UXB patrols—'

'UXB?'

'—sorry, Unexploded Bomb Patrols, as it was for the fighter pilots and soldiers, who had a human enemy. These chaps at home were contending with exploding gas mains, poisoned air, flying debris, collapsing buildings, and they worked day and night repairing homes and services, struggling to keep life going.'

'Sometimes when you came up to Netherby didn't you want just to stay and get away from it all?'

He paused.

'Well, no, not if I'm honest. I did of course want to see more of you children, but I also wanted to be in London doing my bit, as they used to say, trying to provide shelters, trying to make life more bearable for the homeless. And then, when you saw what other people were doing, well, you'd have been ashamed even to want not to be there with them. They really were heroic, Flea. People who were bombed out during the night would struggle in to work the next day. There was hardly any absenteeism, in fact less than before the war. And often the factories had been damaged too. I remember one where hundreds of thousands of square feet of roof had been blown off and it was assumed the factory would have to close for repairs, but no, the workers, mainly women, turned up and worked, exposed to the elements. They were rained on and snowed on. They worked in raincoats and wellington boots and tin hats in case the masonry fell in. Just getting to work was hazardous. One September day, when the blitz had just started, all the southern lines into London stations were bombed, but somehow most people made it, though they'd have had every excuse not to turn up. I've seen queues maybe a hundred yards long at bus stops, and when the bus came the conductor would try to get them all on. People sat on each other's knees, they squashed together in the aisles and they sat on the stairs. And nobody grumbled as the bus careered along the road, swerving to miss potholes or masonry and often having to alter the route because a road was impassable. People seemed positively to enjoy the challenge. You could hear them say they weren't going to let Hitler control their lives.'

His life in the war had been so different from theirs, Felicity thought; London and Netherby might have been in different countries and I'd no idea what his country was really like as I walked up the dale or played by the beck, no idea at all.

'The evacuees must have known both worlds,' she said suddenly, 'and mustn't it have been horrible for them, being sent away from the towns, knowing that their mothers had been left behind to be killed by bombs and their fathers sent somewhere abroad to be killed by Germans.'

'Did you feel sorry for them because of that?'

'No, I think we just thought the vaccies were lucky because people made such a fuss of them. And anyway, a lot of them left pretty soon.'

'Yes, they tended to drift back to the towns if there was a lull in the bombing and a lot came back after D-Day, thinking it was all over – until the V1s arrived.'

'They were the doodlebugs?'

'Yes, or flying bombs or buzz bombs, people gave them various nicknames. They didn't really buzz, it was more of a fearful clattering noise they made just before they cut out. At first people cheered when they saw them because they saw fire coming out at the back and thought we'd shot down an enemy plane, but of course there was no pilot. When it ran out of fuel, the spluttering noise stopped and there was a sudden, eerie silence. Then it crashed to the ground, with a great roar, a flash and a lot of smoke. It didn't dig in and make a crater like the other bombs, but it scattered glass and debris over a much wider area, so many more people were killed or injured.'

'And I suppose you couldn't shoot them down or they'd just explode anyway?'

'Quite right. Mostly we tried to keep them out with barrage balloons, thousands of them, all round the south of London, like great rubber elephants floating about in the sky. They stopped a great many V1s getting through, but thousands still made it to London. Sometimes sixty or seventy would land in London in one day and, you see, because they were unmanned they could be sent over in daylight, when the streets and shops and buses were crowded.'

'So, did people have to go into the shelters all day as well as all night?'

He shook his head. 'No, people got so used to them that they ignored the sirens, just depended on their own hearing to know if one was overhead, then they'd run for cover, or at least throw themselves down. And one curious result, I've just remembered, was that the blast of the doodlebugs stripped the trees of their leaves, which lay thick on the ground as if autumn had come in June.'

She imagined it; the bare, wintry branches of trees against the summer sky. How weird it must have seemed.

'It lasted about six months but then our

troops on the continent overran the launching sites in the Pas de Calais and the government announced that the Battle of London was over.'

'And was it?'

'No. The V2s arrived the next day.'

'And they were different?'

'Worse, at least I thought so, because they made no warning sound. There was just a sudden bright flash, a loud bang and an explosion. People didn't know what the bangs were at the beginning. No news was allowed to be given about them, so of course there were all sorts of rumours, mostly that they were gas explosions, but in the end the government admitted that it was the enemy's new secret weapon, a long-distance rocket.'

'And it could really travel as far as England?'

'They weren't like any rocket anybody had ever seen, Flea. They were forty-five feet long and the most destructive weapon yet invented. Four of them landed in Croydon and damaged two thousand houses, so you can see what might have happened if it had gone on for longer than six months. As it was, they killed nearly three thousand Londoners and badly injured thousands more.'

'And they weren't given a nickname?'

'No, they were too much loathed, I suppose.'

They sat quietly for a while, Felicity

wondering how it was that they had never talked like this before. Of course, in Netherby she'd been too young, and after that they were all too busy doing other things to reminisce about the war, and her father hadn't volunteered any information. Yet she loved to hear him talk about it now, just as she had always loved to hear him tell tales of the past when she was little.

Sebastian too was reflecting on how different his children's experience of the war had been from that of children in London, though some of them had been remarkably casual about the dangers, playing on bomb sites, running out of shelters to hunt for shrapnel souvenirs to show off in the playground next day, even wanting to stay out of doors when the siren went so they could identify the planes as they flew overhead.

It was good, he thought, that Felicity should have some knowledge of what it had really been like in London and other towns – but not too much knowledge. He had said enough. Besides, there were things he himself wanted to forget, like the stench of dead bodies being dug up by demolitioners maybe a year after a building had been hit, and the smell of bombed sewers. And worst of all the terrible individual memories, like the baby he had seen blown out of a bedroom window and smashed on to the pavement below.

Only half the house was left standing and there was no sign of anyone in it, but he'd found a pillowcase flapping on the pavement, wrapped the little one in it and carried it to an ARP post.

So, 'Well now,' he interrupted the silence to say, 'that's enough about the war. Go on telling me about Vicky's nanny, or rather Giles Dudley Ferdinand's nanny. Did she marry someone else?'

'No, she said she never wanted to after her fiancé was killed. She trained as a nurse, saved up, bought her own little cottage and now has lots of friends and seems to run everything in her village.'

She was quiet for a moment; it had suddenly struck her that women are better than men at managing on their own. Men on their own seem lonelier somehow.

'Penny for them?' her father demanded, noting her abstracted look.

'Oh, I was just thinking I might cook something for you that she told me how to make. She called it Family Favourite but it's really just a kind of glorified shepherd's pie. I was wondering which day you'll be back in time to face it.'

'I don't think I'll be late tomorrow. I'm going to a symposium all day. It's only a grand word for a get-together of all of us who worked in different ways for the disabled soldiers after the first war. You

262

remember I told you how I was involved in rehousing them?'

'Are there many left?'

'Oh, yes, though of course many died young. They didn't have the resistance to fight infections and, you see, there was no penicillin then, no antibiotics, so they succumbed in a way that they wouldn't now. But others recovered well with treatment and were able to live independently, so we don't need anything like the number of special homes we once had.'

'Like the one at Northrop Hall?'

'That's right.'

He spoke casually, but he could not hear the words *Northrop Hall* without thinking immediately of Diana. Thinking of her made him say, 'Flea, I hate to ask you, but did Vicky say anything about the divorce?'

She hesitated. What could she reply without hurting him? How protect him from the cruel truth without actually lying?

'She finds it difficult,' she said at last. 'I mean, she doesn't know how she can help.'

'I understand. Forget that I asked.'

He got up and stood looking down at her.

'Oh, darling, I do hate to think of the three of you being affected by this horrible business of the divorce. It's so wrong that it should cast a shadow over what should be the most carefree time of your lives.'

'Don't worry about it,' she told him,

wishing there was some way she could cheer him, because he suddenly looked so sad and was blaming himself when none of it was his fault. 'Now I'm going to celebrate the end of milk rationing by making us great mugs of cocoa,' was all she could think of by way of consolation.

'All of us here,' the chairman of the symposium was saying, 'remember and revere the great Dr Bramley, without whose inspiration and guidance, I doubt if our whole movement would ever have started.' He paused for the murmurs of agreement, then went on. 'We are very fortunate to have with us his widow, Diana, who shared in his work and carried out what he had planned before his tragically early death. At very short notice she has agreed to come and tell us about the progress made by the men who were moved – or moved themselves – from Northrop Hall at the outbreak of the Second World War. Mrs Bramley.'

Sebastian watched her as she stood waiting for the applause to die down. After the shock of seeing her so unexpectedly there on the platform, he felt nervous for her. He told himself that she must have done this kind of thing before, but love made him anxious nonetheless.

There was no need; she was calm, very composed as she gave a report which must

264

have involved a great deal of work collating facts and figures, yet was humane and sometimes funny and which she presented plainly, in that clear voice that was so dear to him.

He tried to concentrate on what she was saying, but found himself lost in the speaker, not the speech. As she stood there, this fifty-year-old woman, tall, elegant, her abundant hair now streaked with grey, he still saw in her the slender girl who had danced with him in his parents' garden all those years ago. Her lovely face still had that frank and open look which had so contrasted with the sly beauty of her aunt Selina, whom he could never forgive, long dead though she was.

He felt a sudden rush of pride as he watched her. She's mine, part of his mind insisted. Once, in the war, she had been his entirely. She could be his again, if only, if only. Try to concentrate on her report, Sebastian.

He caught glimpses of her throughout the day, endured seeing others talking to her, while he held back, fearful of disconcerting her, watched as other men took her in to lunch, had moments of sudden unreasoning jealousy. But at last, towards the end of the afternoon, as people began to drift away, he was able to seek her out, suggest they might find a quiet corner of the lounge to have some tea. What could be more natural than that he should want to talk to her as one concerned in the same work? Besides, wasn't she his wife's cousin, though that, he knew, was an unworthy excuse. So they sat on a little couch in a far corner of the lounge and talked in the manner that two people who had served the same cause for years might legitimately talk. But they were not discussing homes for the disabled.

'I sometimes think, Sebastian,' she was saying in a low voice, 'that the chance of having a life together has passed us by. We're both in our fifties ...' She tried to go on but her voice was breaking.

Her face was turned towards him, her eyes full of tears. He felt an overwhelming need to take her in his arms and comfort her and only managed to resist the temptation by fixing his eyes on an elderly couple on the far side of the room, concentrating on the old lady's hat, which seemed to be made of felt and cardboard, until the moment passed. Then, turning towards Diana again, he said as calmly and reasonably as he could, 'No, darling, you must never think that. We both have moments of doubt, I know, but we could still have twenty-five happy years together. The royal commission on divorce is being set up at last. They will be taking evidence soon; I'll be allowed to give full details of my attempt at divorce. It's all confidential, of course. I promise you, Diana, that the evidence will be overwhelming.' He was speaking with increasing passion now.

'We're not the only ones caught in this trap,' he went on. 'There are thousands of others out there who will give similar evidence.' He stopped as chrome-plated tea things were placed on a table in front of them by a waitress in a black dress with a frilly white apron. Then, while Diana poured out the tea, he went on, 'I have no doubt whatsoever that divorce reform will come about, everyone acknowledges that the present situation is absurd. One day people will look back on it with disbelief. The law is really making an ass of itself and is beginning to realize it.'

'You sound so certain,' she said, shaking her head. 'But royal commissions take years to report and then it takes the politicians even more years to get the legislation passed. The whole process could easily take up most of our precious twenty-five years.'

'No, I think that once they start this consultation things will move fast. They'll look at other countries too. Americans find it hard to believe that if both parties want a divorce in this country, the law forbids it.'

She looked up at him, half-convinced. He reached out and briefly touched her hand.

'It's going to be all right,' he said. 'I promise.'

She smiled.

'We have so little time together, Sebastian,' she said. 'Let's not waste it by arguing. Tell me, how are the girls?'

'Felicity's back home with me now. Last night I was telling her about what it was like in London during the war. Talking about the V1s reminded me of that time in the British Restaurant.'

'It was weird, wasn't it?'

One of the British Restaurants, which the government had set up to give Londoners a decent cheap meal off the ration for a shilling, was almost next door to the hospital where Diana was working. They'd met there by chance when Sebastian came in after spending the morning and the previous night assessing what should be done with several streets of demolished or badly damaged houses after a prolonged attack by V1s the day before.

Diana, who had also worked all night and morning, called in for a meal before she went to bed.

He could hardly believe it when the nurse in the queue ahead of him turned round and he saw who it was.

All weariness forgotten, enchanted at being together, they'd found a table and had begun eating when they heard the familiar crackling sound of the approaching V1, like a maladjusted motorbike flying overhead. People stopped talking in mid-sentence, all around them everyone sat quite still, forks in mid-air, spoons suspended, silently praying for this sinister pilotless aircraft not to cut out yet. They were frozen like children at a party playing statues. Agonizing minutes later, the sound grew fainter as the doodle-bug flew on. Cutlery moved again, sentences were picked up where they had been left off and nobody mentioned the bomb.

Afterwards he'd suggested they should walk a little in the local park before going their separate ways. They were nearly there when they heard again the discordant rattling sound of another V1. 'Go *on*,' he'd prayed, willing it not to cut out overhead. It went on for a few seconds but then abruptly cut out. 'In there!' he said and pushed Diana into a shop doorway. She lay down and in the split second before the crash came he saw how vulnerable she looked in her light uniform and threw himself on top of her just as the glass and debris began to rain down on them.

Gradually the noise lessened, became more intermittent, and at last all was still. They stood up, taking deep breaths of the dust-laden air. They both had a few bruises and scratches. It was Diana who noticed the blood.

'Let me look at your neck,' she said. 'There's blood coming through on to your coat.'

The thick material had saved him; glass had gone through it so that the cut on his neck was not as deep as it might have been.

'It needs stitches,' she said.

'No, the hospitals will be busy with serious injuries.'

'I know where there's a First-Aid Post,' she told him, 'and that's where I'm taking you.'

Other people were emerging from doorways now and crawling out of cellars, looking around, bemused, then going on their way.

'All right,' Sebastian said, 'I'll go on my own, but you must go back and get some sleep. You'll be on duty in a few hours.'

'And so will you,' she told him, taking his arm.

Their way took them along streets of rubble where a short time ago there had been houses and, somehow more poignant, they saw houses which had been sliced in half so that their rooms were exposed to view, like dolls' houses when their fronts have been removed by children eager for play.

As they approached the First-Aid Post men were already detonating a chimney breast which tilted dangerously over the road. A cat, treading delicately between puddles of water in a street of rubble, searched for the place where its home had been.

The First-Aid Post was busy, so nobody objected to Diana cleaning the wound and stitching it.

'Now I'm taking you back to your lodgings,' she said. 'You're very pale, you know.'

'It's only the dust.'

All the same, it was wonderful to have her so unexpectedly all to himself, so he didn't protest as she took him back to his lodgings, sat him down on a kitchen chair and put the kettle on.

'Sweet tea, that's what you need,' she said. 'Where do you keep it – and some cups?'

'Everything's in that cupboard, but really there's no need,' he told her in feeble protest.

He watched as, with her back towards him she reached up to take things off the shelf. He looked at her neck, her vulnerable neck; the glass would have sliced through that unprotected flesh, he realized with horror, if it hadn't hit him first.

'Oh God!' he heard himself groan.

She turned, put her arms around him.

'What is it, Sebastian?'

'Nothing. I'm OK.'

'You know you probably saved my life?'

'We've survived again,' he'd said, and somehow sweet tea had seemed an inadequate way to celebrate.

'Come,' he said, and led her into the bedroom, where gently, tenderly, he made love to her, mindful of her scratches and bruises and aware of the stitches throbbing in his neck.

They looked at each other now as they

drank their tea in the hotel lounge, both remembering that time seven years ago when death and love had seemed so closely intertwined.

'I'm sorry I was so gloomy before,' Diana said suddenly. 'I've got some courage back now. You're right, it just has to work out for us after we've survived so much, it just *has* to.'

'Thank you, darling, but don't be sorry. I have my bad moments too. And—'

He was interrupted by an elderly clergyman whom they both knew from his years of work for disabled servicemen.

'I just wanted to thank you, Mrs Bramley,' he said, 'before I go on my way. He was a wonderful man, your husband. And a lucky one too, to have a wife so worthy of him. And now,' he concluded as he shook hands, 'I will let you get on with your tea. I am sure you have much to discuss after such an interesting conference.'

'Isn't it strange,' Diana said when he was out of earshot, 'to think that the scheme this symposium has been discussing all day was responsible for both our marriages? I mean, when James wanted me to work with him, we just seemed to assume that we'd have to be married. And it was because you were converting Celia's house into a home for the disabled that you got involved with her.'

'Ironic,' he agreed. 'What traps fate sets for

us! And we walk into them so unwittingly. I can quite see why people used to think of human beings as playthings of the gods, who amused themselves at our expense.'

'And kill us for their sport? No, I don't go along with Shakespeare about that. We *could* have chosen differently. I could have agreed to work with James without marrying him.'

'Yes, and I could have bought and converted Celia's house without involving myself with its owner.'

'Except,' Diana told him, 'that we've missed Selina out of the equation. She wreaked more damage than anything the gods came up with. If she had delivered the note as she promised, if she hadn't lied to you and told you I was engaged, our lives would have been – oh, so different.'

'I know,' he said quietly and then went on, 'Diana, don't you often wonder what her motives were? For years I've asked myself *why*. What did she get out of it?'

'It's gone round and round in my head too,' she admitted. 'And I think,' she went on more slowly, 'that she must have got some sort of pleasure out of it. It gave her a sense of power over other people. And, of course, Uncle William worshipped her, which I suppose convinced her that everyone else should too. I remember when I stayed with her as a girl noticing that she couldn't bear to hear anyone praised except herself. And

273

she didn't mind what methods she used or what lies she told to discredit them. I didn't understand it at the time, but later I thought back on what I'd seen and knew her for what she was.'

'Well, she can't do any more harm now. The evil died with her.'

'I thought the modern theory was that our nature, like the colour of our eyes, can be handed down from generation to generation?'

Then, remembering that Selina's three grandchildren were also Sebastian's daughters, she added, 'But it's only a theory, of course.'

Meanwhile, Felicity had left the library, shopped for supper, caught a bus home and was coming in the front door. She picked up the post from the doormat, climbed upstairs and began to unpack her basket. She had fried the mince and peeled the potatoes before she sat down to sort out the letters.

There was just one for her; she was surprised to see her mother's neat little handwriting.

Dear Felicity,

It gives me no pleasure to have to write this letter, but I found Victoria in great distress when I went upstairs yesterday. I insisted on knowing the reason and, though she was very unwilling to tell me, she did eventually let me know that you had stolen some of her underwear. She said she quite understood how jealous you must be of her, because she has so much and you have so little, but really, Felicity, to steal from her is quite unforgivable, especially after she'd given you, she told me, such a lovely holiday. As she said, she only wanted to give you a little break and spoil you for a few days, and this is her reward.

You must return the garment immediately. It was rather a special slip, she told me, with real lace edging, which had been a wedding-anniversary present from Ferdy. She wasn't sure what else was missing, but this was the one she cared about most. As she said, if only you'd asked, she would gladly have given you anything. It's the stealing behind her back that hurts her. I think if you had seen her standing there, weeping in the airing cupboard, even you would have felt sorry for what you had done.

Despite my deep disappointment in you, I still sign myself,

Your Loving Mother.

For a long time, Felicity sat staring at the letter. At first she felt only disbelief. Her mother or Vicky or both must have gone mad. She would send back the slip with a note saying she was returning the petticoat which Vicky had insisted on lending her. So her mother would know what had really happened.

Then a very cold fear set in: nobody would believe her. Vicky's tale would be believed. After all, they would say, why should Vicky invent a tale like that. What would be the point, what would she gain by it? It was an inexplicable way to behave, so it couldn't be true. That's what normal people in the normal world outside would say.

Arthur would have stood up for the truth but he had left them for ever. At the thought of him, she felt tears of despair welling up. Stop it.

Had Vicky planned it from the start, she wondered, had she forced the wretched garment on her as a trap, or had she just seized the moment when her mother found her on the landing, upset perhaps about something else?

Even her father wouldn't understand. He would think it was some silly muddle be-tween two sisters and maybe Vicky had overreacted, but all would be well if she sent it back with an apology. Yes, that's what any father would think and say. She couldn't blame him for not understanding what Vicky had done. It was inexplicable. And what was frightening, what made her feel cold and alone, was the evil intent behind it.

Debbie might possibly have understood, but Debbie must only be sent the most cheerful of letters when she was settling in to her new life, and she was determined that when she went to stay with her at Easter she wouldn't carry any burdens of anxiety in her luggage.

Bruce couldn't possibly understand and anyway it would be disloyal to talk to him about her own sister. But he did notice something was wrong.

'You've no need to worry, Flea. You'll be all right; you *know* you'll get a good degree.'

She let him believe that she was anxious about Finals, because that was something he could understand. Worrying about work and exams is what normal people do. Worrying about getting your parents divorced and about a sister who lies and does inexplicable things is not.

There are some things, she had come to realize, that can't be shared; they just have to stay locked up inside you.

Nineteen

For a moment, standing on the platform at the Gare du Nord, Felicity didn't recognize her sister. She saw a poised young woman, elegantly dressed, but then the young woman started flapping her arms about and dashed towards her, wondrously transformed into Debbie.

They couldn't stop hugging each other, Felicity still amazed at finding herself abroad, actually in *Paris* with her sister, who was so changed and yet still the same, while Debbie was simply overjoyed that at last she could share her new life here with someone she loved. They stood savouring the moment, then Debbie picked up one of the cases and led the way out of the station.

Felicity watched, lost in admiration, while Debbie worked the ticket machine, knew which bus to take, talked in French so fast that she couldn't follow a word. Content to let Debbie take over, she realized, as she climbed on the bus after her, that it was the first time in years that she had really thought of her as an elder sister.

'I can't wait to show you the flat,' Debbie said once they were settled on the bus and the cases stowed away. 'It's part of an old house. Madame, who owns it, lives downstairs. Her flat is huge and so *elegant*, Flea. But not exactly cosy. I do think the French are awfully good at elegant discomfort.'

They laughed and talked for a while until Debbie said, 'Nearly there. The flat's in the Boulevard St Michel, where lots of students live. They call it the Boul Mich. Come on, better grab the cases, it's the next stop.'

Although it was a warm day, the hall of the flat was cool and dim. Oak-panelled, brown-painted, furnished with a vast oak hallstand, it had an air of ancient gloom.

'I'm on the next floor,' Debbie explained unnecessarily as they began to hump the cases from step to step. 'Whatever have you got in here? Bombs?'

She didn't wait for an answer but unlocked the door at the head of the stairs and opened it wide. It was so different from what she had seen downstairs, that Felicity looked around, amazed. Debbie's flat was so light, so airy.

'It's lovely,' she said, awestruck. 'Isn't it terribly expensive?'

'It's not bad, less than it would be in London, and the firm pays part of the rent. Come and see your room. It's a bit small,' she apologized, opening the door.

'Oh, how pretty!' Felicity exclaimed. 'It

reminds me of that little parlour up at the Thorntons' farm.'

'Madame had the walls painted for me and, though she didn't really like the idea, she did agree in the end to have this magnolia colour. And I made the rest. It took ages sewing the curtains by hand, and then someone at work lent me a machine when I made the bedspread.'

'I'd forgotten you always liked sewing,' Felicity said, remembering the dreadful sun top Debbie had made all those years ago. Everything she touched then seemed to go wrong, and now everything was going right.

'If it isn't bombs in these cases, what is it?' Debbie was asking.

'Books. I'm going to work while you're at the office.'

'But not all day, Flea! Honestly, you mustn't spend all your day working. You're in Paris, for goodness' sake.'

'And I've got Finals at the end of next term,' Felicity told her, pulling books and files out of her case.

'Oh, yes. I'd forgotten. Well, almost forgotten. I knew really. Have you thought about getting a job afterwards?'

'I'm going to teach.'

'Oh.'

'Surprised?'

'I shouldn't be. You'll be good at it.'

'Thanks. Actually, Debbie, I have a plan.'

'Go on. Tell.'

'Daddy keeps talking about moving into a service flat. I think it will be really bad for him, living on his own. I mean, you don't make friends living in the middle of London, apart from friends at work. He needs proper family friends. My plan is that I'll get a job somewhere in the country, not too far from London but somewhere really healthy, and I'll find a little cottage and he and I can share it and you too, of course, when you come home.'

'But how would you find a school in the right place? And then you'd have to find a house. And where would you get the money?'

'It'll work out somehow,' her younger sister told her, airily brushing aside such minor problems.

'But you won't work all day while you're here, will you?' Debbie insisted, reverting to the former topic. 'It's such a *waste*.'

In the end she worked out a routine which consisted of working in the morning, exploring Paris in the afternoon and going out with Debbie in the evening. Debbie wanted her to see everything, took her to the Madeleine, to Sainte Chapelle, to Montmartre and Notre Dame, out to Versailles. Sometimes they just sat outside a restaurant on a mild evening and watched the world go by.

'They're so elegant, the French women,

281

aren't they?' Debbie remarked suddenly one evening as they sat at a little table under a striped awning, drinking coffee. 'But there are two things about them which aren't very elegant. Have you noticed how some of them wear ankle socks? I don't mean in the country, but here in Paris, with those smart skirts and jackets. It seems so odd.'

'What's the other problem?' Felicity asked, smiling.

Debbie lowered her voice.

'Their armpits,' she almost hissed across the table. 'They don't always shave under their arms. I've seen them, on hot days when they're wearing a cool summer dress and look lovely, then they put their arms up in the air – you know how they do gesticulate a lot – and it's like *bushes* under there. Do you think they don't *know*?'

Felicity laughed. There were some things about Debbie which never changed.

'Of course they do,' she assured her. 'It's just that people do things differently in different countries. They like it that way. Shall I ask for the bill?'

When they were out together, Debbie always insisted that Felicity should do the talking, to improve her French. She also made her read all the street names as they walked.

'You should be the one going in for teaching,' Felicity told her, when Debbie had made her repeat *Rue du Roi* three times.

'Oh, no, I'd never be able to keep order. But really, Flea, your French is much better than when you arrived.'

'Oh, it's just practice, I suppose.'

She practised her French so well that she was soon able to have long conversations with Marie-Noelle, Debbie's maid, who came in three times a week.

Marie-Noelle was tiny, her little face dominated by her huge brown eyes. She was clearly devoted to Debbie, talked of her *gentilesse*, which Felicity at first mistook for gentleness and then realized meant kindness. She brought in little offerings of home-made almond biscuits and of flowers from her own garden. She asked about the English royal family, wept over the death of George VI earlier in the year. She was easily moved to tears.

'Mademoiselle Debbie will miss you,' she said, her eyes filling, on Felicity's last day, as she began very slowly to move a duster along the bookcase, shaking her head the while.

'I'm making the supper tonight,' Felicity told her. 'I haven't decided what to cook.'

'I'll teach you how to make a French omelette,' Marie-Noelle told her, instantly dry-eyed and practical. 'And look, I bought very good peas in the market today and I will help you pod them,' she added, abandoning her lugubrious dusting.

'But you bought the peas for yourself.'

Marie-Noelle shrugged; *tant pis*, she could get more on her way home. 'And you have the new potatoes and you must go to the *patisserie*. Mademoiselle Debbie prefers the strawberry *tartines*. And perhaps a nice light wine, not too strong?'

Felicity did as she was told and bought a decorative candle too, although it was still broad daylight when Debbie came home, and they stood drinking each other's health in the pretty little kitchen with the table covered with blue and white American oil-cloth and the matching curtains and the frilled gingham around the sink, which Debbie had made to hide the pipes.

And once again Felicity thought how everything seemed to be going right for Debbie after so many years when everything seemed to go wrong. Even the spots had disappeared and her eyes, always her best feature, were lively, where once they had had a permanently anxious look.

Impulsively she turned and hugged her sister.

'Oh, I'm so *pleased* for you, Debbie,' she said. 'It really suits you being here, doesn't it?'

Debbie looked at her, surprised.

Then she said slowly, 'Yes. You're right. I didn't want to come, you know, I tried not to show it because I didn't want you and

Daddy to worry –' Felicity remembered the awful leave-taking at Victoria Station and said nothing – 'but I really love it here now. I think,' she went on, 'that it wasn't easy for me growing up so close in age to Vicky, yet so different. It was all right for you, you were so much younger, nobody expected you to be as good as she was. It was much easier for you.'

'Oh, no,' Felicity exclaimed. 'There were lots of ways ...'

Her voice trailed off. She'd determinedly not told Debbie about the episode of the so-called stolen clothes, but now knew she just had to. Perhaps the wine had loosened her tongue, perhaps it was the thought of leaving tomorrow, knowing that nobody but Debbie would understand, or even believe her. Whatever the reason, she poured out the whole story of her visit to Vicky.

Debbie was at first horrified, then thoughtful.

'If it had been anyone else,' she said slowly, 'I'd have thought they must have gone temporarily mad. But somehow with Vicky, it seems all part of her character. She needs to put people down, to outshine them by any means she can. And she doesn't care, Flea, what harm she does. You know I've always told you what a lovely time I had that time I went to her college dance? Well, I didn't. It was horrible.'

So, over omelettes and new potatoes, she told her sister about the shaming pink dress, which was supposed to be too tight for Vicky to wear, and about the awful humiliation over Alan. 'I see it now, but I'll never know why she behaved like that,' she concluded.

'Any more than I'll ever know why she made up the tale about the lace-edged petticoat. That's why lies like that get believed, because nobody thinks there'd be any point in making them up.'

'She does it to other people too, Flea.' She hesitated, then went on, 'You won't remember this, but years ago when we were all still at school, she had a friend called Gwen who lent her a rather precious art book—'

'I remember. She lost it and we all had to look for it. She was in a real panic. We thought she'd probably left it on the bus but didn't dare say so.'

'Gwen kept asking for it back and Vicky kept promising that she'd bring it. On the last day of term Gwen asked again and Vicky just looked at her and gave a little laugh and said, "Oh, Gwen, you're *hopeless*. I gave it back to you *ages* ago." And, oh Flea, Vicky was my sister and I felt I had to be loyal to her. So ...' her voice trailed off.

'So you didn't say anything?'

Debbie shook her head.

'No. I should have done,' she said. 'I'm sorry I didn't.'

'Probably nobody would have taken any notice of you, if you had,' Felicity consoled her.

'I think Gwen knew that Vicky was lying, but she couldn't do anything about it, but – oh, I should have spoken up for Gwen.'

Felicity took her hand.

'It's easy to think that now, when Vicky isn't here,' she said. 'But when she's actually with you, she's always so convincing, it's as if she believed her own lies. Even at that Christmas when she said Mummy had insisted on coming, we knew she was lying, but we didn't say anything, did we? It's as if we get tangled up and end up conspiring with her.'

'But,' Debbie said slowly. 'Those were just convenience lies, weren't they? But later, they seemed so pointless. Like why butter you up and say how helpful you'd been and then accuse you of stealing? What did she gain by it?'

'She was angry because we'd criticized her. Younger sisters aren't allowed to do that.'

'But it's not just us, I've seen her treat other girls like that, so sweet to them, as if she needs to enchant them and then destroy them.'

'Girls. Not men?'

Debbie hesitated.

'There's always Ferdy,' she said.

Felicity thought about it.

'He doesn't seem to mind. And I don't think she tells lies about him, just undermines him. She never, ever supports him about anything. And he's such a dear.'

'You're right about his not minding. Once when I was up there, when you were still at school, she was quite awful to him at a dinner party the three of us were at, mocking everything he said, and Ferdy just laughed and said something like, "Isn't it good for us men to have women to cut us down to size? We need wives to stop us getting pompous."'

'But he isn't pompous.'

'No. He wouldn't have said that if he had been.'

They were quiet for a moment, both thinking of their sister, then, 'Flea,' Debbie began, 'there's something I've always – oh, I don't know. It's too awful to say.'

'Go on. Say it.'

'Well, you remember that day, the day Arthur ... ?'

'Yes.'

She remembered it, every detail of it as clearly as if it was happening in front of her eyes: the ledge, the scree, the crumpled body, unforgettable, unforgotten.

'And we sat in Mr Thornton's van and they were in the back and Daddy asked Vicky what had happened?'

'Yes,' she said, smelling again the earthy smell of Mr Thornton and his van.

'And she said she'd got to the end of the ledge and looked round and seen him falling?'

'Yes. I remember the words.'

'Well, she didn't, I mean, couldn't have.'

'How do you know?' Flea asked, startled.

'Because he led the way, didn't he? He was in front.'

'I didn't see.'

'I did. You and Daddy were sitting watching the little red van going down the lane, but I was watching them set off and Arthur was in front,' Debbie went on, speaking very deliberately, as if giving an exact report of what she could see stored in her memory. 'And they couldn't have changed places because they were already on the narrow part and after that you just have to go in single file. I saw them, Flea, and he was in front.'

'But you never said anything.'

'How could I when everything was so terrible?'

Yes, it would have seemed childish, selfish to go on about something so apparently trivial.

'And I sort of believed her, I *had* to, because *she'd* said it. You know how it always was with Vicky?'

'I know. I'm not blaming you, Debbie.'

'But at the same time I could see it quite clearly in my mind, and it didn't match with

what she'd said. So I was all mixed up
somehow.'

'Oh, poor Debbie.'

She reached out and took her hand,
remembering how nervous Debbie had
always been, how overshadowed by Vicky.

'But somehow since I've seen how she's
behaved about the divorce and everything
and what she's capable of doing, I just know
for certain that she was lying and something
happened on the ledge which was different
from what she said. But I don't know what.'

'We'll never know what really happened,
will we?'

Debbie shook her head and they sat for a
while, saying nothing, aware now of the
distant hum of traffic in the street far below.

'Do you think other families have things
like this?'

'No, I think all the families we knew were
normal.'

'How can you be sure?'

'Because the children were sort of
innocent. I mean, when a few of us went to
see *Othello* in Oxford, everyone said they
couldn't understand Iago's wickedness because there was no point in it. They said nobody would behave like that, manipulating
and full of hatred, but smiling all the time.'

'But you knew, didn't you? And I suppose
I did too. At least, I do now that I'm free of
her and can see it all clearly. Oh Flea,' she

added, turning suddenly to face her sister, 'I never want to be in her power like that again.'

She spoke desperately and for a moment the old anxious look reappeared.

'It's all right, Debbie,' Felicity told her gently. 'You never will be.'

'It's easy for you, you were never in her power the way I was. And she could seem so kind and charming. So I felt ungrateful if I didn't do what she wanted.'

'I promise you, Debbie, the moment that sweet, compelling look appears on her face, we'll do a bunk.'

Debbie laughed and, pushing a plate towards her sister, said, 'Have one of these strawberry tarts.'

And so, both knowing, without needing to say so, that they weren't going to spoil this last evening by talking about Vicky, they sat companionably together munching flaky pastry, thick with confectioner's cream and tiny wild strawberries.

Marie-Noelle called in early the next morning to say goodbye, reassuring Felicity that she would take great care of Mademoiselle Debbie, sending her respects to their parents, and once again bewailing the death of their king.

'He was such a good man,' she said, the great brown eyes welling up with tears, 'such a father to his people, so strong to fight with the French in the war and now, alas, he is dead. And to have to rule a protestant nation, that must have been very difficult for him, but I read in my magazine that as he was dying he converted to the true faith, so now he is with our blessed saviour and his sainted mother in paradise.'

All this and much else, Felicity related to her father when she got back to London. He was interested, as always, but it seemed to her that he had an air of resigned sadness. He asked after Debbie, laughed when she told him that, apart from minor problems with ankle socks and armpits, Debbie was gloriously happy. He was delighted for Debbie, but somehow the happiness did not seem to reach inside him. Soon afterwards he told her that he had arranged to leave the flat next month, immediately she went back to college, and move into a service flat.

'It's all newly decorated,' he said with determined cheerfulness. 'There's a service lift, a kind of pulley, up which they send meals. They called it a Lazy Daisy – nice name, isn't it? Always breakfast – and dinner if you want it. There is a nice little spare bedroom for you or Debbie and they could always arrange something if you were both there at the same time. Ideal really.'

He wanted it to seem ideal, but it struck her as being horrible. It was all wrong that he who had lived all his life in proper houses should come to this. She said nothing of her plans to make a home for him, just said she was going to look for a teaching job after she'd taken Finals.

With half her year going in for teaching, the *Times Educational Supplement*, with its lists of job vacancies in schools, was easily the most popular reading matter in the Common Room.

'Not much this week,' somebody said. 'All seem to be wanting men. Girls' schools don't seem to have much on offer. Oh, here's one for Sherborne, oh no, it's the boys' school. There's a head of department wanted at Cheltenham.'

'Not a hope for any of us, well not for another ten years or so.'

'There's one at a school called Northrop Hall. Anybody ever heard of it?'

'Are you sure it's Northrop Hall?' someone said. 'My sister had a baby there in the war. It's a maternity home. Has the *Times Ed Supp* taken to advertising for midwives?'

'Probably that was just for the duration. For mothers from London, you know.'

Felicity, listening, asked for the paper, suddenly sure that getting this job would be the first step towards saving her father. No, the second step; she had no doubt that getting the divorce was the most important of all. She read the advertisement carefully, but had already made up her mind to apply for the job.

It was only after she had done so and been given leave to go for the interview, that she rang to tell her father.

'Northrop Hall?' he repeated. 'Are you sure?'

She laughed; he sounded so stunned.

'It's where the Arndales used to live, isn't it?'

'Yes, that's right,' he said, still sounding bemused.

'And where I learned to play croquet.'

'Yes. Well, good luck for the interview, my darling.'

'Thank you. Oh, there are the pips. Better stop.'

'You can reverse the charge.'

'No, I've got to go and revise.'

Finals were looming; inevitable all along, yet unexpected as death when they actually happened.

The interview was ten days before her first exam.

'Northrop Hall?' the porter said when she asked the way at the station. 'You'd better be taking a taxi. It's not easy to find, especially not from here.'

The road outside the little station was empty, devoid not only of taxis but of any other vehicle, nor was there any sign of a bus stop. *I'll be late for the appointment,* she thought, *won't get the job, spoil everything. Don't panic, go back and ask directions.*

'Did you say you wanted to get to Northrop Hall?'

She turned round. The man smiled. He was tall, fair-haired, friendly looking, she thought.

'I've just been seeing a friend off at the station,' he was saying. 'I can take you up to Northrop. I'm going that way myself. The car's round the corner.'

'Oh, thank you!' She was almost overwhelmed with relief. 'I was getting really scared. You see, I've got an interview at four o'clock.'

He glanced at his watch as they walked together to the car park at the back of the station.

'Bags of time,' he said. 'It's only half past three. My name's Tommy by the way,' he added. 'Tommy Proctor. Christened Thomas, but all my friends call me Tommy.'

'I'm Felicity Crawley,' she said, as they shook hands. 'And I'm not going to tell you what my friends call me, because it's rather childish.'

He laughed and opened the door for her.

'Anyway, it would be a shame not to use a lovely name like Felicity,' he said.

'My father chose it because I smiled a lot when I was born,' she told him as they set off.

'It suits you,' he said, smiling down at her.

It suddenly struck her that if Arthur had lived to grow up he would have looked rather like this Tommy, which made it somehow all right to accept a lift from him, stranger though he was.

'It's really awfully kind of you to give me a lift. I hope it's not out of your way?'

'Not at all. My mother lives at Northrop – in the village, I mean – and I'm going there now. Her cottage is very near the school. In fact, she used to work there.'

'When did the school come here?'

'After the war. It had been requisitioned for a maternity home so that mothers-to-be could get away from the bombing and have their babies safely. And before *that* it was a home for disabled ex-servicemen. And before that it was a private dwelling of a family called Arndale. So it's seen some changes, the hall has.'

She wondered if she should say something about it, something like *I used to visit my cousins here when I was little*, or some phrase like *I myself come of Arndale stock*, which sounded so ridiculous that she almost laughed aloud.

He slowed down as they drove up a long, steep hill.

'Just there on the right,' he told her, 'there's a lane that takes you up to the school, useful if you're walking. It saves you about half a mile on the road, but it's steep and very rough underfoot.'

'I wouldn't mind that. I love walking. I was brought up in the Yorkshire Dales and it's beautiful walking country.'

'You'll find Gloucestershire isn't too bad either,' he said, glancing down at her.

'Oh, yes, I didn't mean – I'm sure it's lovely,' she said, frightened that he would think she was comparing his county unfavourably with her own. 'And very healthy too,' she added, thinking of her plan to remove her father from unhealthy London.

'That's all right,' he told her, wanting to sound reassuring because she seemed so young and vulnerable and was clearly jittery about this interview, which must be for her first job. 'Most of us love best the place where we grew up. You're in plenty of time,' he assured her as he opened the car door for her. 'Good luck with the interview.'

She thanked him and stood waving for a moment as he drove away, then she turned and faced the hall.

She remembered the front façade of the house quite clearly, the steps had seemed steeper then and the windows beyond all counting. She smiled as she remembered how Debbie had remarked, all those years ago, that they must take an awful lot of cleaning. Debbie, the worrier.

The door was opened by a stout woman whom she took to be some kind of domestic, so explained that she had a meeting with the head, whereupon the stout woman said that she *was* the head, Mrs Coulter. Felicity blushed and apologized, furious with herself for making such a bad start, sure now that she wouldn't get the job. As she followed Mrs Coulter into her study, she had no doubt that she had wrecked her chances before the interview had even started.

She had never been interviewed for a job before, so didn't know what to expect, certainly nothing like what followed: a chat over tea and crumpets, talking about anything except the matter in hand. They talked about books, about the theatre and acting, she told Mrs Coulter about going to Paris to see Debbie, so then they talked about languages and so it went on with never a mention of the job she was applying for. Mrs Coulter told her the history of the school building, how it had once been a private house, then a home for disabled soldiers, then a maternity home in the war and now a school, most of whose pupils had come from her previous school, which had been massively damaged in the war.

Listening to her, Felicity again couldn't make up her mind whether to say that her own grandfather had been born here and that she had visited her relations here before

298

the war. It might sound as if she was trying to impress, trying to get the job by the back door. On the other hand, if she didn't say anything and Mrs Coulter found out, it might seem odd, deceitful even, which was worse. She had just made up her mind to come clean about her link with Northrop Hall when Mrs Coulter said, 'You will certainly be hearing from me. I shall send you a telegram in a few days. I do have a few other applicants to interview, but shall only do so out of courtesy.'

She was actually being offered the job! She was panic-stricken and heard herself protesting, 'But I don't even have a degree yet.'

Mrs Coulter only smiled. 'You will certainly have one soon if your tutor's reference is to be believed,' she said.

'And I haven't done a teachers' training course.'

'Good. I am very glad to hear it. You can't teach people to teach. What is the point in all these theories, all this reading of psychology books? The children haven't read them so don't know how they're expected to react. No, it is a matter of personality. You either have it or you don't. You do.'

She stood up and held out her hand.

'Our man Slater will drive you to the station,' she said. 'He is an elderly man of few words, but a very capable and experienced driver. He came with the house, which was fortunate for us. Goodbye, Miss Crawley. I look forward to having you on my staff next term.'

They shook hands and, bemused, Felicity followed her to the door. She was still hardly able to believe any of it when Slater drove her to the station; even on the train she sat staring out of the window, dazed and disbelieving. But slowly it became real and then quite suddenly she felt elated: she had done it! She would live in the boarding school at first, then find a cottage, of which there must surely be plenty in all this countryside. She saw them out of the window; it seemed to her that the route was dotted with them, lovely cottages with roses around their doors, their gardens beautiful in this leafy month.

In one of them she would make a home for him. He could travel to London, but wouldn't have to live there, in that city where her mother had said people died young. And in time, surely, oh surely, in time the divorce would come through and maybe he would remarry or, if he didn't want to, he could just live with her – and with Debbie when she was in England – in this lovely cottage she would soon find.

She rang her father that evening.

'Congratulations!' he said. 'Well done.'

'You'll be able to come and see me. It's not far.'

He laughed.

'It's as well you're not teaching geography,' he said. 'It may not be far from Oxford, but it's quite a long way from London.'

'Oh.'

She sounded crestfallen.

'But that's all right. Of course I'll come and see you, darling.'

'You mean, it's not the sort of place where people live and travel to London each day?'

'No, certainly not. Whatever made you think that? You'll be living in your boarding school.'

'Oh, nothing. I'd better go, there are the pips.'

She didn't allow herself to be depressed for long by this conversation and her own stupidity in not realizing he wouldn't be able to travel each day to Gloucestershire. She told herself that even if he had to be in London during the week, he would be able to live in the cottage at weekends; it would be his *real* home, his base. There was a world of a difference between living in a service flat all the time and merely having it as a convenient pied à terre while your real home was in the country. She was sure of that.

Now she had to try to see what could be done about the other, even more important, problem. When Finals were over, when the long vac started, she would go up to Netherby and convince her mother that she should agree to the divorce. Since Vicky had refused to help and Debbie wasn't here, it was up to her to do it, she resolved with all the force of her new-found confidence.

Twenty

'Gentlemen, please stop writing.'

Every time she heard that order, Felicity glared at the examiner: at least ten per cent of the undergraduates sitting there in their subfusc were girls.

'What would happen if I went on writing, since I'm not a gentleman?' she demanded of Bruce. But he only laughed and warned her not to.

'Anyway,' he said. 'Things are getting better all the time. You know how boys' schools had to employ women during the war when male teachers were called up?'

'Yes.'

'Well, in my prep school we had to call the women teachers *sir*.'

'You didn't!'

'Yes, we did. And we weren't the only school to do that either. And, you know, it didn't seem too odd, because we grew up

302

thinking that anyone in authority must be a man, so, since these women were now in charge, they had to be given a kind of honorary manhood. In my house we even had a woman who was known as the Junior Housemaster.'

'And you say things are getting better!'

'Well, that was wartime. All the young masters had been called up, so schools were being run by old men with old-fashioned ideas. But things *are* much better for women at universities now, Flea. Not very long ago they weren't allowed here anyway, and when they were accepted their numbers had to be limited and there were all kinds of restrictions on them. They weren't even allowed to use the university libraries. So they had to create their own.'

'Ah, so that's why our college library is so much better than yours?'

'Yes, so you see, some good came out of it in the end.'

'For all the wrong reasons.'

'Granted. And have you heard about the misogynous professor before the war who came in to give a lecture, looked around the hall, saw there were only women there, said, "Ah, nobody here, I see," and walked out? That wouldn't happen nowadays, would it? And one day they'll drop this gentlemen nonsense. So there's no need to risk your degree by staging a protest, Flea.'

'That doesn't make it right,' she told him. 'I'd still like to go on writing and see what happens. And another thing – subfusc is so *unfair*. The men get away with wearing any old dark suit, and just look at us – made to dress up like something to frighten the kids at Halloween.'

Nearly everything she had on was borrowed. The regulations specified that a woman should wear, under her gown, a black skirt and coat, white blouse, black tie, black stockings and black boots. Since she possessed none of these garments, she wore a black skirt lent to her by a fresher, a kind but fat girl, whose skirt was about a foot too wide round the waist and had to be held in place by several safety pins, the gathers being covered by an old black jacket of Debbie's which her father posted to her from London. It was long but somehow contrived to be uncomfortably tight across the shoulders. She did have her own blouse and Bruce lent her a black bow tie. A second year lent her some black shoes which were a size too large, so that when she walked they always seemed to be trying to catch up with her feet, which had gone on ahead. A stall in the market was doing a good trade in selling cheap black stockings. 'I hope all you girls pass them exams,' the kindly stallholder said, handing her the stockings, which were thick and rather hairy, 'We could do with more nurses.'

'It's so hot,' she grumbled to Bruce. 'It's all right for the men, they're wearing the sort of clothes they're used to, but none of us ever dress up like this. *And* they can take off their mortar boards once they're inside, but we have to keep our caps on, and honestly they're much heavier than they look and ever so *itchy.*'

All the same there was something about the pageantry of it all which appealed to her; even the cars gave way to the crowds of black-clad undergraduates surging on foot or bike towards the examination schools. Once inside, the solemnity was impressive: the tension of those hundreds of dark figures crouched over their desks, the formality of the Proctors when they came in to inspect the examiners, the intense silence.

She was almost late on her first morning, having had a struggle with the bow tie, despite repeated lessons from Bruce, and having to go back to retrieve a shoe which fell off as she ran up the steps. Then she couldn't find her way to her desk: the hall opened out into three great wings and she didn't know which aisle to choose, but was finally rescued by an official who led her, silently, to her named desk near the door where she had come in.

Officials patrolled the aisles, watching out for a hand raised to attract attention. They could escort you to the lavatory, she'd been told, but there was rarely any need, most bladders being awed into submission by the solemnity of the occasion. Did the official go in with you, she wondered, or just stand outside. Rumour had it that the door had to be left ajar. What possible cheating could there be, she wondered, in exams like these? Maybe it was suicides they were worried about.

So the days passed until it seemed that she had always got up on a summer morning, climbed into an array of ill-fitting, stuffy black clothes, cycled to the schools, found her familiar desk like a homing pigeon, concentrated for three hours, which sometimes passed with surprising speed, cycled back to college for lunch, then back to the schools for another three hours of mind-stretching application, while, outside, the carefree world went on its way and freshers went punting on the river.

Afterwards she sometimes had tea with Bruce, who told her to relax.

'You can't do any revision for tomorrow, it's pointless, better to come for a walk in the Parks, get an early night.'

'It's all right for you. You're going to get a first anyway.'

'Don't be so silly.'

They squabbled in a desultory manner, then he usually went off for a walk and she went back to college and tried to read anything relevant to next day's papers, which she knew was pointless but still felt compelled to do.

The last day was the hottest of a very hot ten days. The afternoon was stifling as she found her place. They were only a few minutes into the paper when the man in front raised his hand and was led away by an official. Pale and wan he looked when he was led back. She felt sorry for him, told herself not to be distracted and returned to the essay on mediaeval capitalism. A few minutes later his hand went up again, and again he was escorted out and returned. The next time he didn't raise his hand but dashed out without leave or escort. An examiner appeared from nowhere and came and stood by the empty desk, a tall dark figure, nemesis in waiting. The wretched undergraduate crept back. He muttered an explanation, trying to whisper it into the official ear. Whereupon the examiner, in a voice which carried all around the hall, proclaimed, 'Urgency is no excuse.'

'It was so *mean*,' she said to Bruce afterwards. 'Poor chap might have dysentery or enteric fever. Think what might have happened if he'd waited.'

'The escort always arrived promptly.'

'Well, I think *he* was the best judge of timing.'

'Let's not quarrel about it. Now is the time to celebrate.'

The odd thing was that, having spent the last ten days longing for it all to end, it somehow fell very flat. Even taking off all the horrible clothes wasn't as liberating as she'd expected, she realized as she peeled off the black stockings, paler now as quite a lot of inky water had poured out of them every time she washed them. Instead she felt very weary and very anxious about results.

She said as much to Bruce next day after he had tied up the punt in the shade of a weeping willow which overhung the bank.

'Do you know what it says in the University Handbook?' she demanded as he began unpacking the picnic.

'No, but you obviously want to tell me,' he said, taking a bottle of cider and another of beer out of the rucksack and arranging them in a pool of water among the roots of the tree.

'It says, "The strain of the final honour school is considerable. No one who has taken it and been awarded a class may take it again, so his academic record is indelibly stamped upon him by his performance in the final school."'

'Good lord, did you learn that stuff by heart?'

'No, I just remembered it. *Indelibly stamped*, Bruce.'

'So?'

'So if you get a fourth, that's it for the rest of your life.'

'Well, you won't get a fourth and nobody in the outside world bothers with what class of degree you've got anyway.'

'Of course they do.'

Northrop Hall School for Girls would hardly want to have her on their staff if she got a fourth. And if they didn't take her, the whole plan of making a home for her father in the country away from dangerous London would fall through. But she couldn't explain all that to Bruce; he came from a normal home where people didn't want each other dead.

Suddenly her eyes prickled with tears. Schools were over, true, but that no longer seemed like something glorious to celebrate; it just meant that the wonderful three years were over. It was back to reality now and none of this had ever been quite real.

Bruce was watching her.

He came and sat beside her under the willow tree.

'What is it? You're not happy, are you?'

She shrugged.

'I hate it when you're like this,' he said. 'I know you're anxious and you won't tell me why. It's more than exams, isn't it? Look, I'm not sure you're doing the right thing going to Northrop. I'd far rather you stayed up here with me and did research—'

'What, with a fourth-class degree?'

'Oh, do stop talking nonsense. I'm serious. You're burying yourself in a boarding school at the back of beyond, away from all your friends, especially me. Of course, I'll come down at weekends—'

'You can't. It's a boarding school. We work at weekends.'

It was true, in a way. They did have duties most weekends, but any free time must be given entirely to her father. In future Bruce would be a distraction.

'Not all the time, not every minute of every Saturday and Sunday, you don't.'

She didn't reply. He watched her as she lay back against the tree, her eyes closed. She had always puzzled him; from the time he first met her, when they were both freshers, he had never been sure if she was young or old for her years. It had been easy to tell with the men. Those who came straight from school were still sixth-formers, while those who, like himself, had done their National Service, were adults. But what was Felicity Crawley? Sometimes she seemed young, naive, impulsive; at others she seemed to have the cares of a grown woman on her shoulders. Occasionally, she had that wistful look which made her seem both at once, stranded midway between child and woman. It was then that she looked at her most vulnerable, and then, more than ever, that he wanted to shield and protect her.

'If we got married,' he said, 'we could find a cottage somewhere between Northrop and Oxford and—'

'Oh, *no*!'

He drew back horrified at the ferocity of her denial.

'Oh, I'm sorry, I'm sorry, Bruce, really sorry. I didn't mean—'

She couldn't explain, so kissed him instead.

For once, he held her a little away from him, determinedly unmollified.

'I just think that we're all right as we are,' she said. 'We needn't think about marriage.'

'You may be all right as we are,' Bruce said, 'but I'm not.'

There was an edge of anger in his voice that she'd never heard before.

'One minute you're loving and kind and we get as close as can be and yet when I ask you to marry me you react as if I was some sort of fiend, so foul that the very idea of marrying me is abhorrent. If that's how you think of me it might be better if we parted.'

She looked up at him, dumbfounded. Was this really Bruce speaking? Kind, tolerant Bruce? He even looked different, his face stern, his eyes accusing, as he said, 'I can't take any more of this cat-and-mouse game.'

'It's not like that!' she exclaimed.

'Then what is it like?'

She shook her head. She couldn't explain. To go on as they were now was all right because it didn't affect anything in her other world, but marriage would. It would wreck her whole plan of finding this cottage, making a home for her father. It was unthinkable that she should share the cottage with Bruce and not her father. But the thought of being without Bruce, the thought of hurting him, the pain of having him judge her so harshly, that was unbearable too. Or maybe it was just a price she had to pay.

'Bruce,' she said at last, 'I don't want us to part, but if you'd prefer it ...' She couldn't go on to say those final words.

'Of course I wouldn't prefer it, I'd prefer you to be consistent, that's all. One way or the other.'

She shook her head. She'd never thought of it like that, never thought of it from his point of view. She'd been too wrapped up in her own problems, blind to his.

'I'm so sorry,' she said again. 'I really do mean it, Bruce.'

'I don't want apologies, Flea. I want honesty. I wish,' he went on more gently, 'that you could talk about it reasonably, but you can't, can you? We've got on so well for nearly three years. Sometimes I've thought you loved me. All right, not as much as I loved you, which was all the time, but sometimes you did, a little. And you do now, don't you? Be honest with me.'

She didn't reply. How could she, when she didn't know herself? Sometimes she thought she did, but then this barrier came down, as if to say, this way is not for you. She didn't do it consciously, it just seemed as if there was a road she couldn't go down, open and beckoning though it seemed. Besides, it might be lovely at first, but then it could turn out to be the wrong road and end in misery for everybody, like her parents' marriage.

Bruce, watching her, saw it all in her face, the doubt, the hurt, the anxiety, and he knew it was not the face of one who played heartless games with men.

'I'm sorry,' he said. 'I know it's not a game. It goes deeper than that, doesn't it? One day perhaps you'll be able to tell me all about it.'

'Perhaps. But Bruce, I'm truly sorry.'

She lifted her face towards his. And this time he didn't hold her away from him.

So, apologizing, tentative, each fearful of causing more hurt to the other, they lay close together under the willow tree, gazing into each other's eyes, treasuring the peace all the more for the storm that had preceded it. They didn't speak, aware that nothing had been resolved but that reconciliation was a fragile thing that the wrong words might destroy. Better not to argue, better just to comfort each other, live for the moment, postpone decision, pretend that everything was exactly as it always had been.

A midday stillness hung over them, as they lay unmoving under the motionless branches of the willow tree. The only movement was the slow rocking of the punt as the water lapped gently against it.

'Your beer's escaping,' she said suddenly, and ran down the bank and grabbed a bottle as it bobbed out of the pool and began to sink in the river.

It broke the spell. They rescued the bottles and sat on the parched grass under the tree, spreading bottles of beer and cider, bread rolls and cake around them.

'Do you know what?' he asked, opening the cider and handing it to her. 'All that stuff you were quoting just now from the Handbook about "his academic record being indelibly stamped upon him by his performance in schools"?'

'Yes?'

'Well, I've just realized that it said *him* all the way through. So it's like the *gentlemen please stop writing* order, and doesn't apply to you. Nothing is going to be stamped indelibly upon *you*. Well, not exam results anyway, other things maybe.'

Oh, yes, she thought, some things *are* indelibly stamped on us. What happens in our childhood, *that* is indelibly stamped on us.

The thought stayed with her as they ate and drank and even afterwards when she was lying in his arms, sleepy with sun and cider. She thought of next week too, when she would be going down for the last time, and it seemed hardly any time at all since she had sat on the train coming up for her interview. She had been coming from Netherby then. Next week she would be going back there for an interview with her mother, which she dreaded, and still hadn't worked out what she would say.

'A penny for them?' Bruce asked. 'You're looking anxious again,' and she realized he had been watching her, wondered if he had guessed what was on her mind.

'I was thinking,' she improvised, 'that I'm glad I'm not a gentleman.'

He laughed.

'Me too,' he said, kissing her.

A ladybird landed on her arm, crawled around in a puzzled kind of way.

'It's only recently emerged,' Bruce said. 'Look at its wing cases, they're just getting their colour.'

He knew a lot about nature study. It was one of the things she liked about him, because it reminded her of Arthur.

They watched as the ladybird stretched out first one pair of wings and then the other, folded them and then began to walk purposefully on its tiny legs, moving rapidly like a well-wound mechanical toy. Bruce put a blade of grass in its path; it climbed over it without stopping and flew away into the low branches of the weeping willow.

Twenty-One

'And how much are you going to be paid for this job?' Sebastian asked.

'I've no idea,' Felicity told him.

'Didn't you ask, at the interview?'

'No, I couldn't possibly have asked.' She was shocked. 'We were having tea,' she added.

He smiled.

'It's quite usual, darling, for people to find out what they'll be paid before they accept a job,' he told her gently. 'But never mind,' he added, thinking that it was better that she was like this than like the money-obsessed Celia and her miserly old aunt and uncle.

They were sitting in his service flat having breakfast, which had been delivered to them by the Lazy Daisy on trays beautifully laid with cloths and napkins, highly polished silver and a cooked breakfast under a domed lid.

'You see how well I'm looked after,' he said, removing the lid with a flourish.

She knew he was trying to convince her that he was very happy about moving here. And, of course, it was very tidy and civilized and quite grand compared with their old flat, but it felt like a place to be passing through, a place where you didn't really belong, like a hotel. Yes, that was it, a hotel, not a proper home. Soulless. Not that it really mattered, she kept telling herself, because although he didn't know it, this place, with its elegant anonymity, was just a pied à terre in her scheme of things for his future.

'The post's late,' she remarked later on, as they sat over the remains of breakfast, drinking coffee.

'They put the letters in the rack in the hall if they miss the breakfast tray. More coffee?'

'No thanks. I'll go down and look for the post.'

She returned with a bundle of letters.

'Give me the boring ones,' he said. 'And you read the one from Debbie.'

So they sat quietly together; when he had finished his letters, she was still reading Debbie's.

'So what does Debbie have to say?' he asked, pushing his letters to one side.

'There's a lot about Algy.'

'What's that?'

'It's not a "what". It's a man. Called Algy.

317

He's come to work in Paris for two years and has taken her to a concert and out to Versailles. His mother is staying with him at the moment and Debbie's been invited to meet her.'

'And?'

'The rest is silence.'

'She doesn't say anything about how things are between them?'

'Not a word.'

'You were smiling.'

'It's his name. I kept thinking of that silly rhyme you used to recite to me when I was little.'

'The bear met Algy, The bear was bulgy, The bulge was Algy,' her father recited. She spluttered into her coffee.

'I'm not going to think of it,' she said. It was disloyal to laugh at the name of any friend of Debbie's. 'She sounds quite serious about her Algy. She seems—'

'Smitten?'

'Well, he does keep creeping into every paragraph. "There was a party for a girl who's leaving. Algy was there too." And "I went to see the film *Brief Encounter*. Algy had told me it was very good. And it was. They had an intermission – what we'd call an interval – and someone played the piano. Algy said they used to do that in England, and still do in France at some of the cinemas." And so on.'

318

She handed him the letter.

'What are your plans for today?' he asked, as he took it.

'Sort myself out ready for going to Netherby. I suppose ...' she began hesitantly and stopped. 'I mean, I don't expect you've heard anything more about the divorce?'

'No. I did make another attempt to negotiate but it was no good. It's hopeless until there's a change in the law. Oh, Felicity,' he said, looking wretched and shaking his head, 'I do hate, really *hate*, to think of any of you children being involved in all this mess, even having to know anything about it.'

'But we're involved already, we're bound to be,' she told him. 'We're your children. And we've known for ages that you're better apart.'

'You know, Flea, that children are supposed always to want their parents to stay together?'

She shrugged.

'Other children, other parents,' she said. She could have added that she thought she could get on with either parent, so long as she didn't have to be on the battleground which they created whenever they met. And that Debbie felt the same.

'We just wish that she'd agree to the divorce,' she said instead. 'And we can't see why she doesn't.'

'She has her reasons, religious and

319

financial,' he said with an edge of bitterness in his voice. 'But you just put it all out of your mind, darling, and enjoy being back in Netherby. The forecast's good. You might manage to climb Sawborough at last.'

She smiled. For years they had teased her, reminding her that she'd always said she wanted to climb it but never had. She let them think it was idleness or cowardice and never told them the real reason, which was that Arthur had often said he would take her up there when she was bigger, so the idea of going up there without him had somehow seemed disloyal. It was ridiculous, of course; Arthur would have wanted her to get up there now that she was years older than he was. Yes, time to put away such childish ideas.

But Sawborough would have to wait; her priority on this visit was to persuade her mother to agree to the divorce. That was her mission, but she knew better than to upset her father by saying so.

'Yes, I might just do that,' she said. 'It's time I did.'

The bus was full; it wheezed and puffed as it dragged itself up the long hill out of Pendlebury like some overladen beast of burden. At the top it stopped to draw breath, hissing as steam rose from the engine, before starting on the long descent.

''E used to freewheel down 'ere, George did,' the woman sitting next to Felicity remarked, nodding towards the driver, 'to save petrol, like. But it were dangerous and they stopped 'im – is wife were right suited because she never did like 'im doing it, 'er cousin, Maggie Preston, told us.'

Felicity smiled. She'd forgotten how everybody knew everybody up here and, if they didn't, they always knew somebody who did.

All the same, she was glad when the woman was dropped off at her farm gate; she wanted to concentrate on what she was going to say to her mother, though she knew that it was easier to plan what to say than actually to say it to somebody as hostile and unapproachable as Celia. It always puzzled her that a woman so full of good works could be so uncharitable, so unloving. How could someone so pious ignore the warning that without love all their observances are as nothing?

Her father had once explained to her that her mother had been brought up by a cold-hearted aunt and that allowance must be made for the fact that people brought up like that sometimes find it hard to show affection. Oh, he was always so tolerant, never spoke harshly of her to his children. Her mother, by contrast, never said a kind word about him.

She remembered with shame the speeches she had prepared in the past and had failed to deliver. But she was older now, she told herself, she was grown-up, with a job waiting for her at Northrop Hall. She could talk to her mother as an equal. Well, more or less. Besides, she'd promised Debbie. *Don't back down*, she told herself as the bus turned off the main road, taking the sharp bend into the narrow road that wound its way into the village.

Soon she saw it, their house, looking so peaceful from here as it nestled among its surrounding hills, yet so full of tensions and disagreements. Like those great boulders on Southerby, which looked so smooth from a distance but were full of cracks and fissures when you had a closer look.

She always rang the doorbell when she arrived, although the door was never locked, locking doors not being something people ever did in Netherby. She supposed she did it because she didn't feel the house was her home, that she was a visitor viewed with some suspicion. Yet Netherby did feel like home, the very air, fresh even on hot days, seemed to smell and taste of home. She took a deep breath of it; it was not like the air anywhere else.

From the moment her mother came to the door, she felt something was different. Her mother seemed subdued, more hesitant, and her eyes didn't probe her daughter seeking something to disapprove of. Puzzled, she followed her into the kitchen, where high tea was laid on the big wooden table.

They didn't talk much as they ate the ham and salad. She would wait until afterwards, no point in spoiling the meal. So she made a few polite enquiries about people in the village and her mother made comments about how she had picked the lettuce and raspberries that afternoon, so everything was fresh, not like the stuff they sold in Pendlebury.

The big round clock on the wall ticked loudly; it had a curious, hollow tick. When she was little she had never liked the cold, unfriendly sound it made, unrelenting as the stone flags on the floor. Little had changed in the kitchen; the old range was still there, unused now, except as an extra place to put things. It was once the only warm and welcoming thing in the kitchen in the days when Sarah used to blacklead it and polish all the brass knobs and hinges. She had a vivid memory of Sarah sitting on her haunches, rubbing away with the boat-shaped brush, the knuckles of her fingers ingrained with soot and blackleading powder, her plump forearms pink from the effort and the heat of the fire. But most of all she remembered the big round face, smiling up at her, warm and comforting. She would have liked to talk about Sarah, but instinct told her not to, not to cause trouble before she'd even begun.

Now is the time to start, she thought as, the table cleared and the dishes washed, they sat down again at the table, cups of tea in front of them. But before she could begin, her mother spoke, almost as if she too had been preparing her words.

'I have something I must talk to you about,' she said.

'Yes?'

'It's about Victoria.'

'Is she ill?'

'No.'

Everything seemed very quiet, the silence broken only by the malign ticking of the clock.

'She's in trouble, Felicity,' she said at last. 'I don't understand it.'

'What sort of trouble? What's happened?'

Her mother hesitated, then took a deep breath and said, 'Evidently when she was away at work she got in with the wrong kind of people. I think they led her astray.'

The thought of her eldest sister being led by anyone was ludicrous, but maybe it was easier for her mother to believe it.

'Go on,' she said.

'They used to go out in the evening, drink rather heavily and smoke, and there is something they call substances, which I don't understand at all, but apparently they're illegal.'

Puzzled, because none of this sounded too bad, Felicity asked, 'What kind of *substances*?'

'I don't know. I just know it's against the law and the police are involved.'

'You mean they'll take her to court?'

'It depends. But it's worse than that. She's been abusing her trust at work. Taking things from the laboratories. There was a doctor in this group she went out with, an older man. She became friendly with him.'

Her voice trailed off, leaving Felicity wondering what precisely her mother meant by *friendly*. Oh, poor Ferdy.

Silence again except for the cold and unremitting tick of the clock.

'They found he had been writing prescriptions for drugs for non-existent patients,' her mother went on. 'It only came out because a local chemist thought something suspicious was going on and reported it.'

'But that's nothing to do with Vicky—'

'They shared the drugs he obtained, as they shared hers. It's called an addiction. The company have said that they'll prosecute Victoria unless she gets treatment. The doctor will be crossed off, though there is a possibility that he won't be prosecuted so long as he agrees never to practise again, never to write another prescription and he—'

She was reeling all this off like a lesson she'd learned.

'But the point is,' Felicity interrupted, 'what about Vicky. And Giles, who's looking after him now you've left?'

'That nurse stayed on. She's all right. But, oh Felicity, the lies your sister's told, not just to me, but to Ferdy too.'

'How has he taken all this?'

'He's forgiven her. He says he'll still love her whatever she's done,' she said, smiling for the first time, then she went on more forcibly, 'but really he should have been firmer with her from the start. He shouldn't have let her go off like that. He shouldn't have *believed* her.'

That was too much to take.

'*You* always believed her. You believed her when she said I was a thief.'

'Yes.'

For a moment she thought her mother was going to apologize, wondered if for the first time in her life she would hear her say she was sorry. She didn't, but she did say very slowly, 'I was mistaken. She looked so upset and I thought her tears were real. Yes, I was mistaken,' which was probably the nearest she could get to an apology.

'But I had to come away,' her mother went on, sounding suddenly old and weary. 'I couldn't stand it any more. I mean, think of

326

the scandal if it got out! Ferdy's family are so respected up there, the whole neighbourhood knows his father the JP. And you know Ferdy was invited to be one too. Of course, he won't now.'

'Do Ferdy's parents know about it?'

'No, oh no. Only Ferdy. And, of course, Victoria's employers. You, of course, will say nothing, not even to Debbie. There's no need for her to know. The fewer people who know, the better for everyone. I mean, if it got out ...' her voice failed, she was almost in tears. 'I sometimes wonder if she knew all along that she was pregnant and made a fool of all of us with her white wedding dress and everything. She even said she'd swear on the Bible. Oh, I don't know, I don't feel sure about anything any more.'

Felicity said nothing. Compassion had not been an emotion that her mother had ever excited in her, but now for the first time she felt sorry for her. Her mother was out of her depth, she was struggling. The wrongs she had inflicted were not in the same league as Vicky's.

'Ferdy took her to this place for treatment,' her mother was saying. 'She agreed to go, just quietly packed her case and let him drive her there as if she was going on holiday. She had a nice room all to herself, he said. And then, you won't believe this, the nurse went to help her unpack and she found these drugs hidden in her stockings, in her slippers, hidden in everything.'

'But what are they?'

'Oh, I don't know, I don't know. All I know is that she told them that her mother was mentally sick and must have put them there when she packed her case for her. She said I'd insisted on packing for her. *And they believed her.* She got into a taxi and went home.'

'But she can't get away with it ...'

'No. This time Ferdy was firm. She's to go back. And there'll be letters from the manager of her company. It was all done too secretly last time, as if she was going in voluntarily, which really she wasn't. But, oh, how could they have believed such a story?'

'As you know, she's very convincing,' Felicity said drily.

She could have said more, but refrained out of pity. Besides, she didn't want to alienate her mother before she had even started talking to her about the divorce, which, awful though all this was, was still the main object of her journey.

'But where in the world did they think I could have got such things? What do I know about drugs and substances? To be falsely accused by your own daughter! What could be more dreadful?'

She could have said that being falsely accused by your own mother wasn't too pleasant either, but again refrained.

'But, Felicity,' her mother was saying. 'I'm terrified it will all get out. Just before I left, Ferdy said, "It'll all blow over so long as the papers don't get hold of it."'

'What papers?'

'Oh, you know, these wretched cheap and nasty common papers that go in for scandals. He said they'd make such a story out of it.'

She got up suddenly and began to pace about the room, her voice getting more and more passionate and tearful. 'I couldn't face a scandal,' she said. 'I could never hold up my head in the village again. I'd have to leave the Mothers' Union and Women's Institute and the Parish Council. I think I might leave Netherby altogether and go and live elsewhere, somewhere I wasn't known.'

Felicity listened to her, astonished; she'd forgotten about her mother's horror of even a minor scandal. She sounded far more distraught now when she talked of a scandal than she had done when she was talking about Vicky.

'Look,' she reassured her gently, 'it would all be forgotten in a few weeks. There'd soon be something much more interesting for the scandal sheets to get their teeth into.'

Suddenly her mother rounded on her.

'It's all your father's fault,' she said. 'He spoiled her from the start.'

All Felicity's sympathy for her mother evaporated. In two little sentences it was destroyed.

'But, of course,' her mother went on, reverting to the scandal, 'as Ferdy said, who would tell the papers, who would know about it and do such a thing?'

'I would,' Felicity said quietly.

Her mother looked at her, puzzled, thinking she'd misheard.

'What did you say?'

'I said *I* would write to the papers and give them the story.'

'But you wouldn't, would you? Why on earth should you?'

'I wouldn't if you promised to give Daddy a divorce.'

'You couldn't be so wicked!'

'Yes, I could.'

She spoke with certainty, but all the same kept her fingers crossed under the table. 'I wouldn't hesitate. It would just be a question of choosing the newspaper with the biggest circulation.'

Her mother looked at her through narrowed eyes.

'It wouldn't do your reputation any good either, Miss. Scandal would harm you as much as any of us.'

'No, it wouldn't. I'm not responsible for anything Vicky's done. And we don't even have the same surname.'

There was a long silence, only the hollow ticking of the clock.

'I'll think about it,' her mother said and abruptly left the room.

Felicity sat, unmoving, still surprised at what she'd done.

Her mother came back. She was carrying her blue Basildon Bond writing paper, her fountain pen and a bottle of Swan's ink.

'What do you want me to put?' she asked, impassively.

'I want you to promise that you'll act on the evidence he provides to give you grounds for divorce. You'll accept the terms he offered before, that guarantees that you'll be no worse off as his ex-wife than as his widow if he dies before you. If you don't keep your side of the bargain, I am free to go to the press.'

'You know that collusion to divorce is illegal?'

'Yes, and I know that what you did before in taking his money and not giving him the divorce was immoral as well.'

Felicity watched as her mother wrote the letter in her small neat hand. She felt neither triumph nor pity, just that she had done that which she ought to have done.

'You can post it,' her mother said, after she had addressed the envelope and stamped it.

'I'll go now.'

'It won't go until tomorrow morning.'

'That's all right. I want a walk. I need some fresh air.'

It was a warm evening; cows grazed placidly in the field next to the garden as they had always done, and the only sound was the occasional bleating of sheep in the field beyond. Nothing changed in this calm outside world, whatever was happening within doors, she thought as she walked slowly down the garden and out into the road. Here she hesitated and then chose to go down the lane to where the beck went under the packhorse bridge.

She stood on the bank listening to the gentle rippling of the beck and remembering. There under the tree, Vicky used to sit wearing her big sun hat, over there Debbie had lain scorching her back, and before that Arthur used to sit on the bridge with his bamboo cane and piece of string while her younger self squatted down there on the island watching the caddis worms drag themselves along with their burden of sticks and pebbles while the dragonflies flew over her head, their colours flashing green and blue in the sunshine, and Sarah spread the picnic out on the grass.

It looked idyllic, this vignette of the past. How different the reality had been! What the beautiful and gifted Vicky had become was inexplicable, Sarah had disappeared in an

332

ambulance the day war broke out and Arthur had gone she knew not where, and although her father said that he lived on in their hearts as long as they remembered him, nothing could ever really bring him back.

Don't dwell on the unalterable past, Felicity Crawley, she told herself, but think of the future, for soon her father would be free and surely her mother, once it was all settled and they didn't meet and argue any more, would be less bitter. And she would try to be charitable about her, as her father was. And Debbie, how delighted Debbie was going to be.

It struck her suddenly as she stood there that the great burden of anxiety about her parents, which she had carried for as long as she could remember, dragging it along with her as the caddis worm dragged its burden of sticks and stones, had been lifted. She was no longer set apart from the others, from those children from normal homes, she was free at last to think about herself, as they all did, and of her own future at Northrop Hall, and she could think about Bruce too, she realized. She would go now and post that precious letter in the box outside Mrs Bushell's shop. And tomorrow she would climb Sawborough.

Before she turned back she allowed herself one last look at the beck, on whose far bank bullrushes and kingcups still grew, dragon-flies still darted over the stream and, as for the caddis worms, hadn't Arthur told her that in their season they would miraculously turn into insects with net-veined wings, which would fly with the dragonflies over the water?